MW00897822

The Missing

A Horror Novel by
Olin Lester

A Mecklenburg Story
Book I

Cover photo by Ian Espinosa

Three girls are sitting on a swing. Holding each other, smiling off
into the sunset while the ocean's gentle breeze blows through their
brown and blonde locks.
They drive me, they define me, love me, they make me, me. My girls
are my why and my life. This story is for them—

WHERE CHARACTERS SUFFER

Escape

creep creep the darkness grows
creep creep through the veins it flows
Darker and deeper with each hearts flutter
Deeper and darker it wants no other
creep creep as the light begins to dim
creep creep as the devil seems to win
extinguishing life one false notion at a time
suffocating hope until there is none to find
creep creep as the heartbeat slows
creep creep as the blood don't flow
starved for life as vital organs shut down
drowning in regret, a sea of disappointment abounds
creep creep as the idea of life seems to flicker
creep creep as the mind cries to reconsider
but it's too late—too far to take it all back
it's too far—too late as it all fades to black

By John Day

Chapter 1: Mecklenburg

The sun was bright and warm on the face of Joe Hodges. He was rowing a small boat, coming to a stop in the center of Darby's pond. Joe was fifty-five years old, skinny, and frail with a stone face—a blank, lifeless face. He was sitting in the boat, stealing time, while local kids were playing baseball on the far shoreline.
The crack of a bat echoed across the pond as number twelve hit a dinger thirty feet over the center-field fence. The outfielder ran back, and turning around he watched the ball land in the water. The young player, wearing number ten on this beautiful summer day, looked up from the splash of the ball and noticed a man in a boat.

The man stood up, effortlessly balancing that boat while holding a cinder block with a rough brown rope tied to it. It was the kind of rope you would find in an old barn while exploring as a child.

Sweat dripped from the man's brow as he threw the block into the pond, while simultaneously looking over at the young outfielder. They made eye contact. That's when the boy realized the other end of the rope was tied around the man's neck.

The man vanished into the dirty water, leaving his boat vacant, rocking in the ripples.

Nothing good ever happens after midnight. Those are words to live by. Those are words that have been proven time and time again. But those words are cheap and thin, once you have arrived in the town of Mecklenburg. It could be high noon or dinner time; the air in the city is a perpetual "midnight."

Not all towns are the same. You don't realize this while growing up, but once you hit a magical adult age, you start to see it for yourself. Some towns are bigger than others. Some have more people, and all have a history. Some have secrets, but the city of Mecklenburg is a brutally uncommon place. So much so that no other town can compare.

The secrets are what separate this town from the rest. The unknown, the evil, the uneasiness that makes the hair on your arms stand up, the things that people do in this town, and worst of all, it's the things people don't do in this town.

The secrets are tangibly evil, visceral! The darkness is in a twisted way, which binds the people of this town together.

In Mecklenburg, people often went missing. But so did animals and peculiar things. Lots of people, animals, and things, over centuries, went missing. I mean, every town has crime and problems, but this town was different. This town attracted trouble, like an avalanche casting down a mountain.

Mecklenburg was a small metal ore mining town with a population of thirty-five thousand. Most of the town's people worked for the Duke Mining Company or the Harbor House Psychiatric Hospital.

The strangest thing about Mecklenburg wasn't just the town, but more the people of the city—the strange obtuse people of the city.

The town had a way of either bringing out the extraordinary in people, or the darkest part of the human condition from deep inside. There was no in-between. People are either born with a soul of brightness or a soul consumed with an unmeasurable black. Mecklenburg brought out the best of what you were born with: good versus evil and right versus wrong.

Chapter 2: Walter and Heidi Pauls

At forty years old, after having served his country, today was a big day for Walter Pauls. Walter had worked his way through college after the war. He double-majored in mining and mineral engineering as well as geology. And was about to get the best opportunity of his life.

For the past ten years, Walter worked for Duke Mining Corporation in Blacksburg, Virginia. He worked long days, leaving blood, sweat, and tears out in the field for this company. It was finally about to pay off.

Walter was nothing special to look at but wasn't ugly either. He was average, standing five foot nine, 150 pounds soaking wet, with premature greying for a man his age (his hair war nearly white), and wore glasses. But Walter had a good soul and had an exceptionally high IQ. He was a mineral engineer by trade and somehow landed a bombshell of a wife, Heidi, and had beautiful preteen twin daughters, Becca and Amy.

One warm June afternoon in 2018, Walter opened an email from Duke's corporate headquarters.

---Walter Pauls,

Your name has come up for the newly created position of Junior Vice President of mining operations at the Duke Mining facility in Mecklenburg, Colorado. In addition, this has created an opening for the senior VP of operations position. Walter, you are being highly considered for one of the openings. Our CEO Brad Harvey will be in town tomorrow, to speak with you about the opening(s).

To accept the meeting request, just click the link below.

Have a great day
Shirley Winters- Human resources---

Walter's eyes grew big. This could be an excellent opportunity. Walter eagerly accepted the meeting.

With a smile on his face and butterflies in his belly, Walter took off for the rest of the day and headed home.

Walter walked inside, noticed Heidi was at the kitchen sink, and immediately picked her up in a soft and affectionate bear hug.

"Well, I guess you had a good day," said Heidi as she smiled.

"It's was good. And tomorrow could be even better. I was checking my email before leaving work, and I noticed a meeting request from corporate," said Walter.

"Okay, obviously there is more to it. What's the meeting about? I mean, you don't get meeting requests. What gives? Spit it out!" said Heidi.

With a devilish smile, over the next few minutes, Walter explained what he knew.

"Holy shit, Walt. This could be big. I mean, this could mean having to move, uproot, change the girls' schools; everything would change," said Heidi.

"Let's not get too far ahead of ourselves. They just want to talk with me about it. I doubt they'll offer me a position that quick. I have been with Duke for a long time, and I'd love to progress, but let's just see what tomorrow brings, okay?" Walter said with a twinkle in his eye.

"Okay, babe," Heidi said, smiling as she embraced Walter, gently kissing his mouth.

Heidi Pauls was a beautiful woman, overly sexual, almost as tall as Walter, a muscular 120 pounds, and a stunning redhead with emerald green eyes. Her beauty was natural and rare. She never went to college; she wasn't an intellectual like Walter, but he loved her nonetheless, even though she had a checkered past.

Heidi birthed two children for Walter, worked from time to time, but never had a career of her own. She loved Walter in her own way. However, she genuinely loved her daughters, giving them more of herself than she ever would give Walter.

Chapter 3: June 5, 2018

Walter woke up at his typical 5:00 a.m., downed his morning coffee and a protein shake, took his morning constitution, and laced up his running shoes. Walter loved to run; it was his addiction, his mental medication, and how he started his day six times a week.

"Take me down to paradise city, where the grass is green, and the girls are pretty," played in his ears as Walter ran. Guns N'Roses is what got his legs moving this morning.

Paradise city? he thought, striding out, foot after foot. His heart rate was rising, but not too high. Walter was in his zone, in that run pace that he could hold forever while letting his mind wander.

This was his time, his thinking time.

Blacksburg had been a great town, but what if Mecklenburg was paradise city? An out-of-state move would be hard and challenging, but damn, it could be the best move of our lives, thought Walter as he clicked off the miles.

Six miles later, he was back home and in the shower. Walter's mind continued to think, race, and plot. He couldn't wait to get to work. He had a short drive-in, and the meeting was at 9:00 a.m. He would have plenty of time to do a little bit of prep beforehand and even research the town of Mecklenburg on the web.

Duke Mining Corporation Blacksburg was an average-sized operation, but the Mecklenburg operation was more considerable and different. Blacksburg mined coal and Mecklenburg mined metal ore. Quite a difference, but Walter knew he could handle it.

Walter pulled his truck up to the main gate, said hi to his favorite guard, swiped his badge, and drove inside. He continued to think and smile, hoping everything would work out. They normally did.

The office was starting to wake up; it was 8:00 a.m. as Walter walked inside. Almost immediately, he ran into his boss, Tom Porter. As luck would have it, his boss was standing with none other than Senior VP of Mining Operations Mecklenburg, Brad Harvey.

"Walter, we were just talking about you. You're early as usual. This is Brad Harvey," introduced Tom.

Walter shook his hand firmly, and Mr. Harvey said, "Great to meet you, Walter. I hope you don't mind I am early. It's just what I do. The military in me makes me early for everything."

"Not at all, Mr. Harvey. The military instilled that in me as well. My old first sergeant used to say, 'If you're not at least thirty minutes early, you're late,'" Walter chuckled.

Laughing, Mr. Harvey agreed.

"Walter, if you're not busy, do you mind if we go ahead and knock out that meeting now?" asked Tom, while nodding.

"Absolutely, sir. No problem. I'll follow you guys," he replied.

So much for prep time, thought Walter as he followed Tom and Mr. Harvey down the hall.

"Can we get three coffees? How do you take yours, Mr. Harvey?" asked Tom.

"Black, sir," replied Mr. Harvey.

"Perfect. Three black coffees, please," Tom told his secretary as the three men entered Tom's office.

"Have a seat, guys. Mr. Harvey, would you like to start?" Tom asked. They sat around a small table inside Tom's large office.

"Tom, Walter, please call me Brad. This will be pretty informal. Walter, you come highly recommended. I took the liberty of making some inquiries about you. You spent four years in the Army, then worked your way through college, top of your engineering class, while double majoring. That's pretty impressive," Brad said.

"I don't mind at all, and thank you, sir," replied Walter.

"Please, call me Brad," he said.

Walter smiled. "Okay, Brad."

"Walter, I want to tell you upfront that you're my first pick for this job. This position is unique. We gave it a title of junior vice president over operations, but really, it's more than that. We have a problem with the mine in Mecklenburg, and we need your help. Now before I go any further, I need you to sign this confidentiality agreement," Brad explained as he pulled two multiple-page forms out of his briefcase. He slid one over to Tom and slid the other one across the table to Walter.

Walter knew this was highly unusual, but also intriguing. In ten years, he had never been asked to sign anything like this. Additionally, he hadn't heard any rumors or political moves about the Mecklenburg operation, leaving him clueless about the problem.

Both Tom and Walter both signed their forms and pushed them back across the table to Brad.

Tom's secretary knocked on the door and entered his office with the three black coffees.

"Thanks for the coffee, ma'am. I really enjoy a good cup," Brad said.

"You're welcome, sir. Will there be anything else?" asked the secretary.

"No, thank you, and don't let anyone disturb us, please," replied Tom. The secretary nodded and left his office, closing the door behind her.

Brad pulled out his laptop and opened up a video for them to watch. "Guy's last week, we found something. Well, not 'we.' I didn't find anything, but the men. They found something in the mine. Something we can't explain. I've never seen anything like it before. I know both of you have worked on some of the hardest projects Duke has encountered in the last decade. Still, more so Walter, I am really hoping your background can serve us on this one," He said.

Brad pushed play, and they all watched the three-minute video. Their eyes grew big.

"What is that?" mumbled Walter as he stood up, leaning closer, and pointing to image on the screen.

"We don't know," shrugged Brad.

Brad continued to talk with Walter and Tom. The offer was for both of them to move to Mecklenburg with Walter as the new junior vice president of operations and Tom as an adviser to the president of operations. They both would get a thirty-percent raise, moving costs, and all their expected benefits.

"Guys, again, I have to remind you that you *cannot*, under penalty of law, tell anyone about any of this. I need an answer within twenty-four hours. Once you have spoken with your families, we will chat about the next steps," explained Brad.

Both Tom and Walter agreed to take the time and talk to their families but keep the details to themselves. They all stood up, shook hands, and Brad walked out. Tom and Walter sat, bewildered, void of all noise.

Brad Harvey walked out of the Blacksburg building, got into his rental car, took out his cellphone, and began to dial.

"Hello? Yes, sir. The meeting is done. I'm not sure what Mr. Pauls and Mr. Porter will decide. How many are you missing? okay, did you say three? I'll be back as soon as I can, sir. No sir, I won't leave without at least Mr. Pauls," Brad explained as he drove back to his hotel.

Brad knew the situation was dire, but he had done all he could do on his end.

Chapter 4: Decisions

As Walter drove home, he gamed what he was going to tell Heidi. He seriously thought about being honest but discounted that quickly. Not because of the confidentiality agreement, but because Walter knew she would worry. He knew if she found out, the drama would scare the girls.

Walter pulled into the driveway, wiped the stone look off his face, and tried to appear excited as he walked inside.

"Heidi, are you here?" he called out.

"Why are you home? Why aren't you at work, babe?" she yelled down the stairs.

"Well, come on down, and I'll tell you," he said jovially.

Heidi walked downstairs. "I just finished some laundry. How'd the meeting go? Did you—"

She was cut off by the smile on his face. "You got a job offer, didn't you?" asked Heidi.

"I did. It's for my boss Tom and me to oversee a pretty big project. The only catch is, it's in Colorado."

"Where in Colorado? How much? When would you start? We would have to move, and the girls would be..."
She stopped, took a breath, and asked, "You look happy, Walt. But also scared. Are you okay?"

"I am honey, but it's a fleeting offer. What I mean is Duke Mining wants an answer by tomorrow. The project is pretty important. Metal ore mining can be more difficult than coal mining, but I won't bore you with the specifics," replied Walter.

Walter and Heidi spent the next hour chatting about the pros and cons. They both knew the money was going to be a game-changer in their family's quality of life. Still, Heidi, while scared of change, was supportive and they both agreed the best decision for the family was to take the job.

After speaking with the twins, Walter took out his cellphone and dialed Tom.

"Tom, hi, yeah, we talked. The twins aren't the happiest, but I had to promise they could pick their own rooms at our next house and buy them new cellphones. But Heidi was excited," said Walter.

"My wife was easy. She will stay here initially and meet up with us once the job gets going. I didn't give her any real details. I'm a little scared myself. Do you think we can figure out what's going on there?" asked Tom.

"I hope so, sir, but I do know one thing: I'll be saying a prayer tonight!"

Walter hung up and began to ponder what was happening. His next step was to call Brad Harvey.

Both Tom and Walter accepted the offer but also required some yet-to-be-disclosed conditions. In response, Brad asked for all of them to take the company jet to Denver, then they would be driven to the Mecklenburg mine. Again, Tom and Walter agreed to do so.

Walter tapped the end-call button on his cell. His face was blank as he looked up and said, "Nine o'clock tomorrow, Tom and I will fly out to Denver. Apparently, the company jet has been on standby since Mr. Harvey flew in late last night. They want Tom and me to join Mr. Harvey on his return flight."

"Say what? Tomorrow? That's fast. Shit. Are you okay with this?"

"Heidi, it's okay. I'll get there and see what we need for the project. I've also told them we would need a house and a list of quality schools in the area. They agreed to set those things in motion once I flew in. They really want Tom and me and seem willing to do what it takes to get us there as soon as possible," Walter explained.

Heidi was not happy. This was moving too quickly, but she had zero control over it. Heidi would do the best she could while balancing the twins' needs, her needs, and making Walt happy. In the back of her mind, she knew the big picture was the best for the family. It would be hard at first, but the payout in the long run was worth it. Or was it?

"Okay. Well, shit. The girls and I will join you as soon as we can. But with school and the house here, I'm not sure how quick that will be," explained Heidi.

Duke Mining Corporation spared no expense. This was painstakingly obvious as Walter bordered a custom Gulfstream G550. A briefcase in one hand, an old overflowing green Army duffle on his back, and a heavy gym bag in his other hand, Walter made his way to his leather seat just outside of the cockpit.

The flight was eventless. Smooth sailing, even though the only three passengers aboard were thinking about what was found in the mine. Aside from that, they enjoyed the luxurious flight.

Walter, Tom, and Brad got into the waiting company Suburban and began the hour drive up the mountain.

"Gentlemen, I have instructions to take you straight to mining operations. You can leave your bags with me. I will keep them safe and have also taken the liberty of booking two suites at The Mecklenburg Regency. Walter and Tom, the corporation will cover these suites as long as you need them. They are awfully nice, and the best this small town has to offer," the driver said.

"Thank you, sir; we appreciate it," said Tom as Walter echoed the response.

The driver continued to drive up rural Route 3. The incline was steep, and the Suburban's engine whined as Walter looked out his window, thinking about his girls. The views were breathtaking with hair-raising drops as they looked down.

Tom looked up out his window and noticed a large black bird flying above them, gliding on the winds in the same direction as they were driving. He smiled, wondering if this bird was a bald eagle. But then the bird turned slightly, revealing its full blackness and began cawing. This perplexed Tom. He didn't think crows got that big or were in this part of the country. He wondered, *what the fuck is that?*

Chapter 5: Welcome

"Welcome to Mecklenburg. Home of the unique, population approximately thirty-five thousand," Walter read out loud as they passed the city sign.

The sign was like most you would see along any road before entering any town. Except this one was chard from a fire, and a dead mule deer was cut in half lying under it, and smelled of old rotted meat.

Walter stared at this deer as they drove past. He found it not only odd but creepy as hell. He rolled the window back up, turned around toward the road, and began to take notice of the town.

The Suburban continued on Route 3 right through the heart of the town, passing buildings and people like white noise.

The road was older, cracked asphalt with traffic lines twenty years faded. Overall, the town appeared aged, used, dark even. Little to no streetlights were seen, but it was still daylight.

"What the fuck," yelled Terry as he felt the slice of the blade and hot blood flow down his jawline.

Bobby was in the process of shaving a customer when he noticed a black Suburban drive by, distracting him.

Bobby was a strange bird, fat and sloppy. He had owned and operated Bob's Barbershop for nearly twenty years. He had seen and experienced so much during his time in Mecklenburg.

"God damnit Terry, you must have moved," Bobby replied while staring at the black Suburban like a kid staring at a clown. He was "caught up in the show."

Tom looked out of the rear passenger window as they passed Bob's Barbershop. "That's the best place to get your hair cut in town," said the driver.

"I'll stop by later this week; I could use a trim," said Tom, and then noticed a man holding his face with blood flowing from it as he argued with the barber.

The mine was outside of town, but operations were between town itself and the entrance to one of the principal mines. The driver continued through the void, the mindless black spot of Mecklenburg.

The church bells seemed to ring quite often. More than the normal on-the-hour-every-hour of a typical Baptist Sunday.

The other odd thing Walter pointed out was what he saw in the center of town: an area with several tall wooden chard poles sticking out of what looked like a giant burn pit. Strangely, next to this pit was two sets of actual medieval stocks. Both were thick wooden blocks. At a glance, it appeared one of the bindings was about the height of a man with placements for wrists and a head. But the other binding was low to the ground, with only positions large enough to wrap around a person's ankles.

"What the fuck," Tom mouthed as he looked at what Walter had pointed out.

As the Suburban drove north of town, it came to the end of Route 3. The traffic light was red. The road to the left was Harbor House Road, which led out to the psychiatric hospital, and the road to the right was Duke Mining Road.

They turned right and headed the last couple miles out to operations. The mine entrance was just a few miles farther, at the end where the road turned to gravel.

The driver parked, and all three men got out. Duke Mining Mecklenburg operations were more considerable than either Walter or Tom had expected. The building itself was quite lovely from the outside, newer looking with pleasing architecture, six stories tall with plenty of parking underneath as it appeared to be on giant stilts. So far, this was the nicest building they've seen in this town.

"Walter, Tom, welcome to Duke Mining Operations Mecklenburg. We have been anxiously awaiting your arrival. I hope your flight and drive up Route 3 was good. I'm Allison Walker, President of Mining Operations here. Please call me Alli," she said.

"Nice to meet you. We have been treated well," replied Tom.

Before Walter could talk, Alli instructed the driver to take the luggage to their rooms at the Regency.

"Gentlemen, please follow me," Alli said as she walked down the hall to the bank of elevators.

Alli was a tall drink of water—blonde hair, athletically thin with a natural beauty that made guys look twice, even if that second look would get them in trouble.

They got off the elevator on the ground floor and walked outside to an awaiting grey Suburban.

"Walter, Tom, let me again remind you of the confidentiality agreement you signed. We are headed to the mine right now. We need you to get a look in person. Attached to the back of your headrest, you will find a black bag. This bag will contain a hard hat, respirator, and flashlight.

"Guys, as you know, we operate a metal ore mine, mainly nickel, lead, and zinc. But a few years ago, we discovered the fourth largest deposit of copper on earth, right here in Mecklenburg," she said.

"I assume since what you found was underground, you are not open-pit mining. You guys have chosen to dig under the copper?" asked Walter.

"Yes. Our test holes showed the copper was more than a mile down. It would be faster and more cost-effective to go underground."

"Walter, that's our entrance up ahead. The tunnel is nearly a mile and a half long, with a grade of 13 percent. At the bottom is where it's at. We have had armed security 24/7 since the discovery," Alli replied.

The Suburban's automatic headlights turned on as they entered the blackness. The tunnel was dimly lit, casket tight, damp, and the farther they went, the hotter it felt. Ten minutes later, they arrived at the bottom. The wait was over.

Chapter 6: The Mine

Walter stepped from the Suburban, dawned his spotless white Duke Mining hardhat, and took a deep breath. Tom was right behind him as Alli led them into a side room full of people with a table, desk, and numerous computer monitors lining the far wall.

Armed guards were outside of the room and stepped aside as they approached. Once they walked into the room, the guards swung back in front of the doors.

Silence fell as they entered.

"Gentlemen, this is Walter Pauls and Tom Porter. They will be taking over this project. Please give them anything they need, and I mean anything!" explained Alli.

The room sighed, and greetings were exchanged.

"Walter, Tom, please sit down. I'll show you a video—" said a man from the back of the room, as Walter interrupted.

"We've seen the video, we just don't understand—" Walter said, interrupted by the same man.

The man emerged from the corner of the room. It was Stewart McHenry, a bear of a man in his mid-fifties. Everyone called him Stew. He was the head mining foreman and brother of one of the missing miners.

"No, you haven't seen this video, sir. This is what they couldn't show you. Brad could *not* take the chance of you refusing the job. Please, guys. Sit down. I'll explain as we go," said Stew.

"As you guys know, we are nearly seven thousand feet below the surface. We run crews 24/7. Our goal is to dig out under the copper, drill up, blow the rock, and have it fall down for us to, in turn, scoop it all up, and haul it all out. We have been fantastically successful thus far, with zero accidents, averaging sixty-eight thousand tons per day. That is, until two weeks ago," explained Stew as he pushed play on a video.

Quiet fell over the room. The video began.

Walter and Tom watched the monitors. They noticed men working a newer model Sandvik crawler road-header machine. The teeth on the device were as big as an average-sized man. They spun like a circular saw in the shape of a ball. This was accomplished using a boom a safe distance away from the operator.

As the cutter spun, the teeth broke through into what first looked to be a gas pocket or natural void in the earth. But then it all stopped, and the haze and smoke cleared out through the ventilation.

The operator of the Sandvik crawler backed it up, revealing what appeared to be a cavern or tunnel. The men were standing silent and motionless.

"Guys, at this point, you'll notice the men stopping and backing up a bit. The three men up front, next to the crawler, pay attention to them," explained Stew.

The video continued, and three men were chatting with each other, then they all walked forward of the crawler. The three men peered into the cavern, looked at each other briefly, and climbed inside.

"Those three men, one of which is my brother Jordon, never came out of that cavern. That tunnel. Whatever the fuck that thing is, they went inside and haven't been seen since," Stew explained with grief in his voice.

Stew looked at the men, tears dribbling down his cheek, and said, "I'm gonna now play the last video. This is where we are hoping you guys can help us. I pray you guys can help us!"

Stew pushed play. The video was from a handheld camera attached to a pole being extended into the tunnel.

"Guys, we have no clue what you are looking at now."

Both Walter and Tom were up close, watching the most detailed monitor in that room. The video showed an unnatural circular area. The geometry of that room was exact, and nothing mother nature created. It was more like the inside of an underground rock dome. It was emitting a natural light that could not be explained. This light lit the room like a warm sunny day in Florida. The floor was flat but the walls and ceiling were circular in nature. The roof itself looked to be fifty feet tall at the least. And in the center of this dome-like room was a rock that looked to be hovering in midair.

The video panned around, showing the dome clear and complete, with no signs of the three missing men.

"It's not a magic trick; that rock or whatever the fuck it is, is just there. Defying gravity, void of the laws of physics, that rock is just in the air, like it was placed in that spot by God himself. There's one way in and one way out. Our guys went inside, but never came out," Stew said.

Chapter 7: Heidi, the Girls, and the Witch

After Walt was gone, Heidi poured herself a cup of coffee. She had taken it black for the past few years and preferred a slightly bitter blend. She sipped the blackness and savored the warmth as it trickled down inside of her.

The girls were still asleep and wouldn't be up for a little bit. *I wonder what Mecklenburg is going to be like*, Heidi thought as she flipped open her MacBook.

Heidi began to research houses for sale and general information about their new town. She wouldn't move to Mecklenburg until the girls' school was done for the year, but it didn't hurt to do a little research.

"Ah, there's a cute house," she whispered to herself as she opened the link.

The house was on Foxtail Lane, close to the north side of town, a few miles from the mine and an equal distance to the necessities in life. The house was two-stories with a full basement. The pictures were gorgeous, and the price was well within their budget.

"Hmmm," she mumbled as her mind raced, and she saved that house for future reference.

Heidi continued to look at the housing market, schools, and local businesses. She then typed "the history of Mecklenburg Colorado" into Google.

Heidi browsed the results but was drawn to an old newspaper article titled, "June 1772, Witch Trials." She clicked the link and began to read as her coffee continued to warm her.

Witch Trials
June 1772

One warm summer night, a town-crier was on board a beautiful white stallion, trotting through the outskirts of town. An assembly had been called in the recently established town of Mecklenburg, Colorado. He rode slowly, repeating, "A witch has been caught, a town assembly has been called, come witness the justice."

He repeated this for a few hours and disappeared. The night sky was red, and the wind felt like a warm whisper as it passed. The town folks were brought outside of their homes by the "crier." Still, that brilliant night sky kept them out gossiping about the following day's trial.

Just after sunrise, people began to make their way to the gallows in the public square, just outside the constable's office, in the center of town. Hundreds of people surrounded the area awaiting the trial.

A used firepit was directly next to the gallows, with four tall, thick pieces of oak pointing toward the sky; the pit was large enough that it could hold several witches who faced justice.

Friends, family, and neighbors all stood around, chatting, waiting for the trial to begin.

Two hours after sunrise, a horn bellowed through the morning fog, silencing the crowd as the beat of a drum began to echo.

"Make way, make way. Move yourselves," a man yelled as he led a column of officials and suspects. The crowd began to part down the middle, and the line stopped near the pit with officials circling the suspects.

All of the officials were similar in height and weight, wearing brown robes and black hoods to conceal their eyes. They looked like faceless monks.

One official made the short walk up onto the gallows platform, pulled out a piece of paper and began to read.

"The town of Mecklenburg has found evidence suitable enough to warrant a town trial for the charges of witchcraft, a. k. a., the devil's magic. Sarah Black, Martha Black, Abigail Black, and William Black, you have all been accused of behaving strangely, outside of the possibilities of mankind. A witness has come forward and under oath, detailed stories of levitation and mind manipulations. How do you plead?"

As the formal charges were read aloud, the officials escorted the suspects into the pit, quickly tying them to the oak poles in the center.

"Not guilty. I stand for all of my family and beg for mercy! We have been falsely accused!" William yelled.

The crowd booed and began chanting, "Liar! Burn the witches! Burn them to hell!"

William Black was an older husky man, tall with leather hands. He had worked all his life, manually. A farmer by trade, he grew tobacco half the year and summer corn the other half. His wife Abigail was ten years younger, small, almost sickly skinny, and also helped around the farm. Their twin daughters Martha and Sarah were young teenagers; both had red hair and emerald green eyes. The twins were copies of each other, impossible to tell apart.

"Leave my family alone. I won't tell you again!" screamed Abigail as she struggled with the rope binding her hands behind one of the oak poles in the pit.

"Doctor, can you come upon the platform?" asked the reading official.

Doctor Henry Lynch began to make his way through the crowd. As he moved, the crowd chanted and created space for him to pass. He made his way up onto the platform.

Doctor Lynch was older than most people in Mecklenburg. He had skinny tree-limb legs, but was so fat around the waist, he was a peculiar sight. He wore glasses, but spoke with such intelligence, if you closed your eyes, you would have thought the excellent doctor was in his forties.

The reading official took out another piece of paper, handed it to the doctor, and asked, "Doctor, is this your sworn statement? And may I remind you that you are still under oath."

Doctor Lynch looked at the paper and during the next couple of minutes, silently read over it. "Yes, sir. That is the statement I gave the officials," replied the doctor.

The reading official took the paperback and began to read:

"I, Doctor Henry Lynch, give willingly and to the best of my recollection this statement of facts. On the night of the full moon, a week ago, I was called to the Bradley farm for a sick child. Billy Bradley was strapped with the fever. It was terrible, and I had to work hard to get it down. I was lucky I had some acetylsalicylic acid paste, freshly made a few days prior from willow leaves.

"Over an hour or so, I was able to get the boy's fever down, so I left to head home. The moon was full and wicked. It was getting late when I saw it.

"As I was walking home, on the old farm road, I noticed a person. It was a female, and she had her back to me. I saw her speed began to slow and finally stop. *Strange*, I thought. So, I called out to her, asked if she was okay.

"The female, she turned toward me, was Abagail Black and then—"

The reading official was cut off mid-sentence when the crowd began to scream. The screaming was blood-chilling and painful. Most people began to run.

"She's flying!" someone yelled.

The reading official turned toward the fire pit.

"Oh, dear God, please save us, deliver us from this evil." A man dropped to his knees praying aloud.

Abagail was mad! Indeed, she was a witch and a dreadfully-powerful one. While still tied to the oak pole, she was now levitating above the crown. "Let my family go!" she screamed. "Let them go, or I will burn this town! I will kill you all," she said with hate in her voice.

Abigail's husband and daughters were still tied to their poles inside the pit. They all struggled and were yelling, but her daughters were crying, "Momma, help us! Please, Momma, help!"

Wood had already been stacked in the firepit and primed with whale oil for an accelerated and incredibly hot fire.

As Abagail began to free herself from the bindings, three officials lit their torches. They began to run toward the pit and her family.

"No!" shrieked Abagail, as she floated down toward the running officials.

The first official held his torch high, but as he began to swing it toward the pit, Abagail was able to land directly on his head, stopping his momentum and killing him instantly.

The second official was scared to death, leaving a trail of urine as he ran. Abagail didn't have to deal with him, as this official tripped, dropping the lit torch on himself, and he began to burn.

Abagail turned her attention toward the third official. She grabbed him, and out of the corner of her eye, she noticed the official that was on fire was now screaming as he rolled around inside the pit. His entire body was ablaze. A bright yellow and orange hue was burning him alive, but it had also ignited the pit. Her family all began to scream as they burned.

The sound of burning flesh was not overshadowed by the wood popping as it helped fuel the fire. The flesh hissed, sizzled, bubbled over, and wept on itself. It was haunting, almost as haunting as the smell.

The twins walked into the kitchen, interrupting Heidi's reading. Heidi had been deeply enthralled in the article and almost didn't notice them.

"Are you guys hungry?" Heidi asked as the twins sat at the kitchen table.

Chapter 8: The Missing

What the fuck was that? repeated in Walter's head. His heart rate rose considerably with his morning run pace. Three miles in, his music was flowing, and his mind was racing.

The beat was solid and fast. An eclectic guitar was screaming as Marilyn Manson sang.

"The beautiful people, the beautiful people. It's all relative to the size of your steeple. You can't see the forest for the trees. You can't smell your own shit on your knees."

The forest for the trees? Walter thought.

Walter came to an abrupt stop, like hitting a brick wall. He stopped in front of Harbor House Psychiatric Hospital's east gate, breathing hard and in awe of the size of the rock walls and the tower centered by the entrance.

The wind stopped. Not a sound was present. Walter could only hear his lungs enormously expanding and deflating while he breathed. The noise broke moments later when he heard a metal clanging approaching slowly from behind.

Walter's attention was on the wall when he saw her for the first time. He turned his head to the left as he noticed a little girl pass him just off of his shoulder. She was in a ruby-red dress that fell just over her white knee-high socks. She was strolling, dragging a dog leash, which had a dog collar and tag attached, but no dog. Just a lifeless leash clanging as it skipped off the ground. The girl's face was obscured by her long brown hair but she whispered unintelligibly as she walked.

"Little girl. Little girl, are you all right?" Walter asked.

No response. The little girl kept walking, whispering, dragging. The lack of response was eerie, making time feel slow and dead.

Walter turned and ran. Nothing made sense to him.

"Walt, hey, hon. I'm so glad you called," answered Heidi. "How are things going so far?"

"Babe, I miss you. Tom and I got set up with really nice suites and have hit the ground running with work. The mining operation here is so much bigger than Blacksburg's," said Walter.

"That's nice. How do you like Colorado? Is the town nice?" Heidi asked.

"I haven't had a lot of free time, but took a long run through town this morning and out to the hospital." Walter's eyes widened, his mind briefly thought of the little girl in the ruby-red dress. He quickly dismissed that encounter and continued to talk with his wife.

"It was an interesting run. Hey, the company has offered to fly you down and set you up with a real estate agent. You can get your mom to watch the girls and then bunk up with me when you get here. Would you like to do that?" Walter asked.

"Hmmm, the girls have a few more weeks left of school, but I think mom could handle them for a week. I'll see what I can do, and I'll get back with you on that. Say, Walt, I've stumbled across an old newspaper article about witch trials way back when, right there in Mecklenburg. Crazy stuff. I'll email it to you," said Heidi.

"Witch trials? That's old school Salem! It should be a good read. Let me know about the visit. I got to head to the mine. I love you." Walter smiled.

"I love you. Have a great day," Heidi said as she hung up the phone.

Tom headed out of the hotel intending to acquire a morning coffee from the nearby Starbucks and planned to meet up with Walter in the hotel lobby after.

He walked toward Main Street, one block over from the hotel. He could see Starbucks's green sign as soon as he rounded the corner. The smell of fresh coffee was in the air resulting in a feeling of calm and warmth inside of him.

Tom opened the main door to "coffee heaven" and held it for an older lady. She walked inside, stopped, and stared at him briefly, then went about her business. *Strange. Why did she look at me that way?* Tom thought.

He dismissed her look and walked inside. To the right, he noticed the community board and stopped dead in his tracks. Community boards are in every coffee shop in every town, used to post community events that usually pertain to non-profits and sometimes work advertisements. But not this one. Not in Mecklenburg.

Tom read the board, counting the flyers as he went. Fifteen different missing persons flyers. Kids and adults, all missing. Some of the posters were weathered, aged. Some of them had phone numbers you could tear off, like a flyer for singing lessons, just take the number and call later.

Two flyers stood out over the others. A missing ten-year-old girl and her dog. This flyer was one of the oldest ones, paper faded with age. The little girl went missing three years earlier, last seen before church, wearing a ruby red dress and walking her dog, a black lab named Shelby. The other flyer was of an older woman in a wheelchair. The flyer explained "Betty" was ninety years old and had dementia, but could roll herself around, and was last seen near the train tracks off of Harbor House Road. The hair on Tom's arm stood on end, based on the age of the flier, he realized that Betty was more than likely dead.

That community board was as eerie as standing in a cemetery at night with a light breeze looking for a loved one's headstone.

Tom sipped his coffee as he and Walter rode out to the mine. His coffee didn't sit right this morning. It was still hot and tasted like any other americano, but that Starbucks was strange. Anne, Betty, Billy, John-Michael, and Noel were some of the names of the missing from the community board that kept swimming laps in Tom's head.

As the black Suburban reached the end of Route 3 and the intersection of Harbor House Road and Duke Mining Road, Walter said, "I ran down that way this morning, Tom," pointing to the left. "The hospital walls are so tall and old. I was standing at one of the entrances, had taken out my earphones, and was in awe of the vintage look. That tower. Then a little girl walked past me, wearing a red dress," Walter said.

"What did you say?" Tom asked as he choked on a mouth full of warm coffee.

"The hospital..."

"No, the girl," said Tom.

"A little girl in a red dress, with white knee-highs and brown hair, walked past me. She was dragging a leash and dog collar behind her, but no dog. Strange. Very strange!" Walter said.

Tom's eyes widened, and his ears perked up. "Was the dress ruby red?" asked Tom.

"I'd say so. It was brilliantly beautiful and looked like a polished ruby," Walter answered.

"She looked out of place. I tried to talk with her, but she kept walking and whispering. Creeped me out. Why do you ask?"

Tom sat quietly, thinking. Was he crazy? Is this the same girl whom he just saw on that old faded flyer?

"Driver, take a left. Let's drive by that hospital. Please," Tom said with a slight crack in his voice.

Walter was at the east entrance to Harbor House Psychiatric Hospital for the second time this morning.

The Suburban pulled up near the gate, parked, and all three men got out.

"Tom, what's got you spooked?" Walter asked.

"The girl you saw. The one you just described. I think I saw a picture of her and her dog on a missing person flyer at Starbucks. I know it sounds too coincidental, but my heart is telling me it's her. This tower has to have cameras, video, something," Tom explained as his heart rate rose with beads of sweat trickling off of his forehead.

Tom was in a mental state Walter had rarely seen before. But he knew when Tom was like this, he should pay attention and go with it.

A guard walked up to the gate and met the three men. Walter explained to the man what had happened on his run, and politely asked if they could view that morning's surveillance tapes.

The guard was reluctant and rude, but eventually agreed to contact his superiors. The three-man walked back to their Suburban and took a seat as they waited for an answer.

A while passed, and about the time Walter opened his mouth with a suggestion to leave, the gate opened, and a tall older man in a white doctor's coat walked toward them. Walter and Tom got out of the Suburban.

The three men began to shake hands as the doctor began to speak.

"Gentlemen, my name is Doctor Charles Nunez. I am the chief physician of Harbor House. I've been briefed on why you are here. Am I correct in that you are looking for a missing girl and believe she may have been seen this morning and maybe on our security cameras?" Doctor Nunez asked.

"That's correct, sir. My name is Walter Pauls, and this is my colleague, Tom Porter. We both work for Duke Mining."

As Walter ran the story down for Doctor Nunez, Tom stepped a few feet away, noticing the top floor windows, visible above the perimeter walls and larger than expected. Tall, but not exceptionally wide, almost the size of an average man. Strange.

Chapter 9: Harbor House

"Gentlemen, please come inside. I'll take you to our security room and give you a small tour after if you like. But I must warn you: stay with me the entire time, don't talk with any patients, and if anything happens, whatever you do, stay off of the fifth floor," Doctor Nunez said with a smile and a jovial wink.

"I'll stay with the car," said the driver.

Walter laughed as he and Tom followed the peculiar doctor through the gate.

The Harbor House Psychiatric Hospital was located not far outside of Mecklenburg. It was close to the mine, just off of Route 3. Harbor House was a dark and dreary seventy-year-old, stone-built, five-story building that could accommodate five hundred live-in patients. The basement of the place was primarily used for maintenance, yet had a guarded wing marked "medical" and never talked about.

Harbor House also had a prisoner wing on the fifth floor. This wing was used to house some of the most notorious criminals deemed "legally insane" by the courts. But the real prized gem of Harbor House was the sex offenders wing, also on the fifth floor. This wing housed the most depraved mentally ill predators.

The sex offenders' treatment program at Harbor House was award-winning and known throughout the mental health community as "the last hope before hell." Because of this, the program treated the exceedingly worst sex offenders in the country.

Harbor House had a stellar reputation in the psychiatric medical world, another reputation among town folks, and a third reputation among patients.

Outwardly the facility was made of stone walls topped off with concertina wire and a secondary electrified industrial chain-link fence nearly fifteen-feet high. Guard towers along the perimeter made the facility look more like a prison, but were well worth it.

It was 9:00 a.m. when the gates slammed behind Walter and Tom. They followed Doctor Nunez as a loudspeaker began to play a steady tone, ultimately announcing, "Visitors on the yard. Visitors, code blue."

There was a yellow line on the ground, dead center of the asphalt drive.

"Stay on the yellow side of this line, away from the rooms, at all times. Every floor will have the same markings. This will keep you out of reach of any patient," Doctor Nunez explained.

Tom stared up toward the building as he followed the small group. He was amazed at how tall and dark this facility was. It reminded him of an old Scottish castle. He thought the only thing missing was a king and a moat.

That's when he saw it. Something caught his eye, floating, hovering parallel with the roofline. It was white with the sun shining through it. A balloon with a white ribbon streamer trailing beneath it. *How out of place*, he thought. *How odd.*

"Walter, do you see that balloon?" Tom asked as he pointed toward the roof while looking back himself.

The balloon was gone. Walter shook his head and looked back at Tom.

"Are you okay, Tom?"

The doctor interrupted, "Guys, I'm sorry. That was probably from a patient. We have a criminal patient here, Ronald. At times he has the mind of a child. While he is not the only patient with diminished mental faculties, he is, however, assigned to the fifth floor for reasons I can't explain to you, but he has a... how do I explain? Let's say he has a fixation or more like enslavement for balloons. We tolerate this because nothing else keeps him calm."

The men continued to walk on the far side of the yellow line, going through multiple different security checkpoints. One at a time, they were searched, a thumbprint taken, and a visitor badge assigned.

"Gentlemen, as we are buzzed through this last door, we will be inside the facility. Again, stay with me and on the far side of the yellow line," reminded the doctor.

As the buzzer began to tone, the thick metal door opened, and the noise became almost deafening. There was laughter, screams, crying, yelling, and all in different languages. It was quite an assault on the senses, and maddening.

Doctor Nunez guided them down that first long corridor and into a room on the yellow side of the line. The door was marked "IT."

The room was quite spacious for a surveillance and media room. Mounted all along the walls were large plasma television monitors, each one showing a different area of the facility. Desks were everywhere. Almost like a call center, men and women were at each desk wearing headsets and intently watching the monitors.

"Tom, look at the center monitor," said Walter as he lifted his hand up and pointed. Tom brought Walter's attention to a naked man violently masturbating in front of the camera.

"You don't see that every day," uttered Walter.

Doctor Nunez motioned Walter and Tom over to the corner desk. "Gentlemen, this is Amy. She will be able to help you with the video from this morning. Amy, this is Tom and Walter; can you pull up the security footage from the east gate, under the tower?"

"Nice to meet you, Amy. We are looking for a young girl that's missing. I believe I saw her this morning around 6:30 or 6:45," said Walter, as he took note of how stunning Amy was.

"No problem, guys. I'll pull up the time frame," said Amy as she began to work her computer mouse, pulling up multiple screens.

A few moments later, Amy was able to locate the footage.

"Here we go. I think this is what you're looking for," Amy said as she pushed play.

The video was without noise, in color, and showed an exceptional high-definition view, as if the gate itself was looking out onto the gravel entrance. Clearly, the video showed Walter running along Harbor House Road and stopped in front of the east gate tower. It was clear as day. From a distance, Walter ran toward the gate, slowly becoming bigger as he came to a stop.

Then she appeared. Out of nowhere, as if a portal opened up and she crawled out. She was all of a sudden walking past Walter. The girl looked young, maybe as young as twelve. But her dress was black and her skin pasty. She indeed walked right past Walter, dragging the collar without a dog. The video showed her walk a good way, and as soon as Walter turned and began to run back, the girl turned to the far side of the road and vanished into the woods.

Amy, Tom, Walter, and Doctor Nunez stood in silence—an awkward mute without even a breath drawn to silence and eyes glued to the monitor.

A few moments later, Amy played the video again, and then again. Nothing changed; it was just as creepy as the first time they watched it.

"That's the girl from the flyer," stammered Tom.

Silence engulfed the room for the second time.

Nothing more was said. Amy copied the file onto a thumb drive and handed it to Tom.

Doctor Nunez walked the men back out to the east gate, stopped, and said, "Tom, Walter, nice to meet you. Good luck with the mine. If you need anything else regarding—well, let's just say, I'll see you again. Good day." The good doctor walked back inside, perplexed at what he saw on that video, but not surprised. His Harbor House experiences had eliminated the word "surprised" from his personal dictionary.

Chapter 10: 7,000 Feet Deep

At seven thousand feet down, Walter and Tom stepped out of their Suburban and into the mine once again. The guards greeted them kindly as they walked into the show. It was their second time deep inside the mine. Although they were confident in their abilities, the future was blank, yet as dark as the fresh asphalt leading out of this town.

"Stew, has anything changed since yesterday?" asked Tom.

Stew, five foot ten, two hundred pounds of "I'll deadlift your car," complete with goatee and the cleanest high and tight you'll ever see, looked at Tom and snidely stated, "Nothing. My brother is still gone. So are the other two, and I don't know what the flying fuck this hovering rock thing is."

Walter stood there for a second, carefully selecting his next words. He knew everyone was counting on him. He knew the burden of this "thing" lay on Tom and his shoulders alone.

"Stew, look at me. I promise you, I'll cut throats till my breath is gone to find your men. We will get the answers!" Walter said.

The dismay on Stew's face began to fade. He looked at Walter and began to believe he meant what he said. Stew took a seat and let his breath out. "Please. You are the best at what you do. None of us know what's happening. Help us."

"Then let's get started," said Tom as he began to unpack a large black duffle bag.

Tom and Walter began to pullout "level C" full-body hazmat suits equipped with SCBA respirators. They took turns helping each other dawn the equipment. Thirty minutes later, they were ready. Each man had a sixty-minute air tank, suit, and a 120-foot rope attached to them.

"Stew, hit record on your cameras as Tom and I go inside. Keep your men out here. But have them keep a hold of the ropes attached to us. If anything goes wrong, *do not* come in; just pull us out," Walter said.

"I gotcha," replied Stew as he instructed four of his men to "stay" the ropes, two men on each.

Walter and Tom stood in the opening to the "dome room" like paratroopers standing in the open door of a perfectly good airplane. It was surreal. They were about to "jump" into the abyss, the void, the unknown. In that room lied answers, but also reeked of death. The tension was thick in the air as Walter looked at Tom and said, "Follow me."

The crawler had been pulled back but was now used to hold poles and cameras. Stew had gone back to the monitor room and was now watching the two men.

Walter took a deep breath, briefly closed his eyes, and stepped inside. Tom followed. The men instantly felt a temperature change and their ears popped. After a few feet, Tom turned around and looked back at the entrance. The room was vibrant with a brilliant view inside, but the outside was blurry as if underwater. The sight reminded him of being a child and opening his eyes while swimming in the deep end of the pool. This made zero sense. But really, nothing did.

The room had a natural light that could not be sourced. The ceilings were tall, too tall, made of stone, and appeared geometrically precise, circular, as if a template was used to create it.

The men outside the room slowly let the rope out, giving Walter and Tom just a few feet of slack.

Tom and Walter split and began to walk around the walls, away from the hovering stone. The stone itself was as big as a man; at least six feet tall by three feet wide; brown, black, and tan but had a slight blue glow in the center. Both of the men were carrying handheld readers. Tom had a Geiger counter attached to his belt, a micro-core soil sampler in his left hand, and a fresh stone swab-sampler in his right hand. Walter also had a small Geiger counter, a handheld thermal imager hanging across his chest, and a video camera on a short pole in his right hand.

Both men continued to move.

A mine gets hotter the farther down you go, simply because you're closer to the center of the earth, but this room was cool, almost cold, like standing in front of an open refrigerator on a hot summer day. It felt nice; even through the suits, the room felt nice, almost inviting. Calm.

The stone was in the center of the room and the center of attention. Both Walter and Tom surveyed the area around it. They gathered soil samples and stone swabs of the walls and returned to the men outside of the room using a third rope attached to a five-gallon bucket. They verified there were no doors inside the room, so no way for the three missing men to get out. The walls surrounding the hovering stone appeared solid and natural.

"Let's back out, Tom. I don't want to sample that stone yet. It's not natural. I think we have enough to start," Walter said as he turned backed toward the entrance.

"Sounds good, buddy."

Tom turned and began to walk back with Walter, who was a few feet in front of him when Tom's Geiger counter began to blare an unholy sound and his rope became taut. His waist started to hurt as he turned to look at the rope behind him. His jaw dropped as he was pulled off his feet and sped headfirst straight toward the stone.

When Tom turned to walk back, the slack in his rope began to pass under the hovering stone. A moment later, a brilliant Carolina-blue light swallowed Tom, severing the rope. Tom was gone. Vanished.

Stew, watching from the monitoring room, stood up and began to vomit on the desk. His temperature shot up, creating an instant river of sweat running down his back as he clutched his chest and collapsed, face first, never to move again.

Chapter 11: Ronald Black

Summer 1993

The shadows from the streetlight on Lunsford Drive danced in the wind. One resembled a darkened shadow-man moving in the breeze. It was well past midnight, and as everyone knows, nothing good happens after midnight.

The crunching sound of the key entering the deadbolt was a unique sound Vicky King was used to hearing as she entered her house. But the howl she heard behind her, was not. Vicky abruptly turned and noticed only the dancing shadows. She nearly fainted. Vicky had worked much later than usual, and she was a bit jumpy.

What Vicky failed to notice, was the tall man watching her from just a few feet inside the woods, across from her house, standing with a stone face, holding a white balloon. Watching.

The white balloon caught in the night breeze, moving out of the woods, floating level with the street. The wind pushed the balloon in a slow circular dance across Lunsford before it turned skyward, lifting into the moonlight until out of sight.

Ronald watched that balloon fade into the night, absent of emotion. He stood silent, as motionless as a stone monument. Calm enough, crickets were chirping all around him.

The crickets fell silent as Ronald took his first step toward the road. He walked out with the purpose of violence but was in no rush. Step after step, Ronald's bare feet slapped the pavement with a meaty sound. His feet carried a six-foot-two, two-hundred-pound muscular framed man. They were leathery, rough, dirty, bleeding, and cracked.

Ronald walked in the darkness of the night, stopping in Vicky's backyard. He knew she lived alone. He knew her blinds in the back were always open, that her lights inside of the home at night would allow him a perfect view while hiding Ronald in plain sight. He loved watching, but Ronald wasn't the only Watcher in town.

Vicky made her way upstairs for her usual routine of changing, taking her nightly shower, and crawling into bed. Ronald watched.

As the minutes ticked by, Ronald stood in the shadows of the night, silently thinking. Watching. At 2:00 a.m., Ronald walked around a child's swing set, moving toward the utility shed behind him.

The door opened with a slow metallic squeal. Ronald stepped inside, looking around. A push mower stood on the floor with hand tools lining the walls around it. Ronald reached out to his immediate right, pulling a stubby two-and-a-half-pound, ball peen hammer off the wall and smiled. It felt light and natural in his hand, eighteen inches of wood and steel.

Ronald made his way to Vicky's back door, hammer in hand. He bent down on the porch and retrieved the hidden house key from the planter.

Vicky was a heavy sleeper, continually moving most nights, but the movement was more pronounced tonight. Maybe it was because Ronald stood over her while she dreamed. Maybe she could unconsciously sense the evil that watched her.

Vicky's face was smiling at first, as she dreamed of children laughing and playing in a field of sunflowers. The sun was bright and warm on her face, and those flowers were forever long, yellow, and smelled of complete happiness. The children were her own, running and playing into the yellow setting.

After a few minutes, Vicky's face changed from a beautiful smile to concern, then ultimately fear. Those sunflowers had begun to wilt. They began to slump and fall over. Vicky's children ran toward her and away from an unknown blackness consuming the dream. They were yelling and pleading with Vicky, but she couldn't understand what was happening.

Then she woke up.

Her eyes opened, and a different fear set in as she noticed Ronald lurking over top of her. And with one swing of that hammer, Ronald stopped her dreams forever.

"Charlie-232, copy a stop?" requested Officer Tucker to dispatch as he turned on his overhead blue lights, pulling over a black BMW.

"Go ahead, Charlie-232," replied dispatch.

"North Carolina tag, CYT-1278, a black four-door BMW. We will be stopped on Lunsford, about the 2300 block, near The Plaza."

Officer Greg Tucker, a tall country boy, stepped from his patrol car, flashlight in hand, and walked up to the driver's door. The driver rolled his window down, pleasantries were exchanged, and Officer Tucker took the man's state license. He glanced at it and walked back to his patrol car. He ran the man for warrants and looked up his driving history. The only thing unusual was the tall dirty man in nicely pressed overalls standing on the porch of the house to the officer's left.

The hair on the back of Officer Tucker's neck stood on end. He picked up his car radio and, with a high-pitched voice, told dispatch to start him backup. Officer Tucker opened his car door, even before he could put his radio mic down. He stepped out and squared off to the man on the porch, while also shining his light at him.

As soon as the officer's light turned on, Ronald began to step off the porch.

Officer Tucker was looking at Ronald Black for the first time. He had worked that area for years, and knew the house wasn't his, and that the man didn't belong in the neighborhood. Tucker was in awe of Ronald's build. But more so, his jaw dropped when he put together the open door behind the massive man. Blood dripped from Ronald's face and a hammer was clinched in his right hand.

Ronald was now running at Officer Tucker while raising that bloody hammer above his head. Officer Tucker had a split second to react. That's how things happened for officers—at the snap of a finger. The only thing to stop Ronald's violence was with violence itself. Violence begets violence.

Officer Tucker drew his pistol. He raised that newly issued Glock-19 and took aim. Ronald was no more than ten feet or so from Tucker.

"Officer are you about done—" said the driver of the BMW, with an entitled smirk as he stepped out of his car. The man looked back at Officer Tucker and then saw the muzzle flash. The man instantly pissed himself and fell to the ground.

Ronald took the first couple of rounds but didn't stop. He kept moving toward the officer. Tucker quickly shot again and again and again. The madman finally fell. Ronald's last step was near the curb, and he pushed forward as he fell, landing on top of the officer.

Officer Tucker was on his back with 220 pounds of Ronald on top of him, and Ronald wasn't dead. He was bleeding heavily but still breathing. Tucker continued to fight Ronald. He was trying to get out from under him but then noticed Ronald must have dropped that hammer, and nothing was in either of his hands.

"Shots fired! *Shots fired*, headquarters!" Officer Tucker screamed into his radio.

Tucker knew other officers were coming; he only needed to survive a few more minutes.

"Headquarters, I'm about to pull up. Close the channel!" requested Officer Miller.

Miller pulled up and saw Tucker in the middle of the road with a big man on top of him. The tires on Miller's patrol car came to a screeching halt, slinging his K-9 partner Jack against his kennel in the back seat. The patrol car's brakes were sizzling and could be smelled as Miller jumped out.

Miller was quickly closing the distance to the suspect and noticed Tucker's hands were holding on to the suspect's forearms for all he was worth. The suspect continued to fight, then Miller hit him with as much force as he could. He tackled the suspect, driving him off of Officer Tucker.

All three men were now separated. Both officers were rising to their feet as Ronald was on his knees and refusing to give up. Officer Miller hit a small black box on his chest and yelled, "Here, Jack, *here*!"

The rear driver's side door popped open, as if on springs. The box Miller hit was an actual remote that opened the kennel inside of the car for K-9 Jack to get out.

Officer Miller had called for his dog Jack. Jack was a ninety-pound muscular Shepard. That dog loved to work, but more importantly, Jack loved Miller more than life itself.

K-9 Jack jumped from the vehicle. He had been watching the fight from his rear window, and even before the door was opened, Jack knew the officers feverously needed his help.

Jack made eye contact with Ronald and took off at a sprint. He was fearless. After a few feet, Jack launched into the air, mouth open wide, and grabbed Ronald by his right arm. Jack held on tight, like a pair of vise-grips. Nothing was going to stop him.

Ronald had been shot and was getting weak from the blood loss. He tried to fight off K-9 Jack, but the dog was trained too well. The suspect beat Jack and bashed him on the ground, but Jack wouldn't let go. Ronald fell to his knees for the last time, and when he did, Officer Tucker took his two-foot Maglite and cracked a final blow to Ronald's jaw. Like flipping a light switch, Ronald's "lights" went out. He was barely alive, unconscious in a pool of blood.

As the chaos concluded, Ronald was placed in cuffs and taken to the hospital. In a separate ambulance, Officer Miller and Tucker were taken to the hospital for their injuries as well. But K-9 Jack seemed to get the worst of it. He was in Tucker's lap, barely breathing, as the medic worked the scene. Another officer scooped Jack up and took him to the closest emergency vet, running blue lights and his siren.

As the next few weeks passed, homicide detectives discover Vicky's body. Still, they also located human remains at Ronald's residence and inside of his car.

ZANE
Worf

Ronald Black, May 2018

Ronald Black, Patient 0227, simply known as "Ronald," was one of Harbor House's most violently insane guests. His story was so unique, the only answer a Mecklenburg judge could order was to send him to Harbor House for the remainder of his natural life. That was twenty years ago.

July 1, 2018
Doctor Phillip Wyzenski, annual evaluation about Patient 0227, Ronald Black:
I, Doctor Phillip Wyzenski, swear before the court that the following report is true and accurate to the best of my professional knowledge.
I have been working with Patient 0227, Ronald Black, henceforth known as Patient 0227 for this annual evaluation. Patient 0227 has been a resident at Harbor House for the past twenty-five years. I have been treating Patient 0227 ever since his last doctor was killed ten years ago.
For this report, we were able to conduct multiple MRIs, one CT scan, and numerous EEGs of Patient 0227, but only while the patient was sedated.
During this time, doctors were constantly evaluating Patient 0227 for a conscious mental status, appearance, and demeanor. They gauged his thoughts, mood swings, delusions, and hallucinations. Finally, they reevaluated for potential violence, whether the patient was homicidal or suicidal.
Patient 0227 had been diagnosed with [at times] catatonic schizophrenia, bipolar disorder, paranoid schizophrenia, and dissociation disorder [dissociative identity disorder].

The patient is of above-average size. He stands six-foot-two, two-hundred-twenty pounds, muscular, and physically appears unkept [facial hair, body hair, never groomed, teeth yellow/brown and hardly ever brushed]. His clothing [hospital scrubs] is always clean and worn appropriately.

The patient's different mental disorders appear when appropriate. For example, the patient suffers from a dissociative identity disorder, causing the patient to have at least three [that we have found] separate personalities. The patient's first personality is Ronald. Ronald fits the mold for someone who is six-foot-two and two-hundred-twenty pounds of muscle.

Ronald is the violent, bipolar, schizophrenic side of Patient 0227 and manifests himself when he is upset and or homicidal. This is the personality that is the patient's criminal side and is the personality responsible for all the violence the patient has inflicted on his victims.

The patient's second personality is Sam. Sam is, mentally, a young emotional female that has an infinity for not only balloons but white latex balloons with long white streamers that hang down as the balloon floats. While Sam mentally is younger, this personality manifests itself before Ronald does. It's almost a "tell" of what's to come. Sam appears, and eventually, later, Ronald comes out.

The third personality has no name. He's quiet and lives in this mental state most of the time. This personality has a catatonic schizophrenia. This personality we refer to as Black. When Black is present, my colleagues and I feel that Patient 0227 is thinking, plotting. This personality, while almost a mute, is the analytical one of the three.

During this past year, Patient 0227 has shown signs and symptoms of all the above mental disorders initially diagnosed. While he shows little improvement in all areas, we have learned that a "white latex balloon with a white streamer" tends to bring out the personality of "Sam." This could be seen as a therapeutic tool for soothing or calming the patient.

Criminally, it is still my opinion that the patient's mental faculties are without a doubt insane, and the best facility for this patient is still Harbor House. If Patient 0227 were to be transferred to a conventional prison, other inmates would be at risk of injury and death from actions taken by the patient. Simply put, the patient will victimize anyone if given a chance, and society is safer with this patient confined within Harbor House.

In my ten years of treating Patient 0227, I can say unequivocally that he is a rare case that has taught us a lot. Still, moreover, he is the most violent patient I have ever treated.

Chapter 12: 911, What's Your Emergency?

"911, do you need police, fire, or medic?" an operator asked as she began to work up an emergency call sheet.

"I... I... I'm not totally sure. All of them? There has been an accident in the mine. Our staff paramedics are doing CPR on Stew, and we are missing another guy," answered one of the workers who had been holding Tom's safety rope when disappeared. "Please send them all and... and... um... we will meet your medics at the top of the mine shaft."

The 911 operator dispatched fire, medic, and police. The notes explained to all of the emergency workers that guards from the main gate would be waiting to escort them to the precise area. The Duke Mining property was so spacious, this was standard procedure during an emergency. It would cut down on response times and gain faster aid to injured workers.

It took medics ten minutes to arrive, but for the workers involved, seemed like an hour. The guards quickly escorted them to the top of the mine, where Duke Mining paramedics were working on Stew.

As the medical personnel began to transfer care, the mining paramedics shook their heads, as if Stew were a lost cause. CPR was continued as the ambulance drove off, running lights and sirens toward the hospital.

Walter was still in his bio suit. He took his helmet off as he sat at the top of the shaft and watched the ambulance scream into the distance. He leaned over, placing his face into his palms and slowly began to breathe deeply.

As he sat on that picnic table, he was in awe of what had occurred.

"Where the hell did Tom go?" Walter softly spoke to himself. "He just vanished. What the hell is that thing?"

Walter slowed his heart rate down and let his mind go. He had stepped into something above his head, something his mind could not comprehend, something not of this world. He closed his eyes and slowly let his mind take him away.

Walter's eyes opened. He was back in his hotel room and his body felt as if a truck hit him the night before. Yawning, Walter slowly pulled himself out of bed, walked to the bathroom, and turned the shower on. He looked in the mirror and realized he must have been dreaming. It must have been a dream.

"One hell of a dream," stammered Walter as a solid knock came from his door.

"I'm good. I don't need room service," said Walter. All he wanted was to stand in that hot shower and scrub the stress off of him.

"Mecklenburg Police," was the answer from the other side of the door. "Sir, can you talk?"

Even before the words fully registered with Walter, he knew he had not been dreaming. Reality sat in. Tom was gone, and Stew more than likely had not survived his heart attack.

Walter opened the door. "Yeah, how can I help you? What's going on, sir?"

"Are you Walter Pauls?" asked the stocky, severe, and sharp-looking officer.

"I am."

"Sir, my name is McKinney. I am with the Mecklenburg Police Department. I'm sure you're aware of why I may be here. May I come in?"

Walter stepped back from the door and allowed McKinney inside.

"Let me make a cup of coffee. I just woke up," Walter said.

"Stew passed last night, sir. I'm sorry about that. His heart gave out. From what I understand, he fought hard, but the doctors couldn't bring him back. Again, I'm sorry."

"Thank you," replied Walter, but before he could speak anymore, McKinney continued.

"Walter, I'm here because your friend Tom Porter is missing."

Walter and Officer McKinney spoke for the next hour about what brought Walter to Mecklenburg. They also talked about the mine and what happened seven thousand feet below ground.

McKinney listened carefully, taking notes and asking questions.

When he was finished, McKinney thanked him for his time, got up, and left. Walter took his cup of coffee into the bathroom and stepped into the shower. He held that warm cup of hotel coffee under his nose, sipping as the hot water soothed his weary muscles as it ran down his back.

Walter stood in the shower for the next hour, barely moving, soaking up the hot water and thinking. He had been in this town just a few days, but it felt like a lifetime. His head hurt, his back ached, and his hope was fading. But worst of all, he had lost his friend Tom.

Walter had not only promised Stew that he would find his brother and men, but he had also lost Tom. Where the hell did Tom go? He touched that rock and then vanished.

Walter knew his day would be cold. He dried himself off, poured another cup of coffee, and picked up his phone. He knew this call to Tom's wife was going to be hard.

Chapter 13: Officer McKinney

McKinney left Walter's hotel and headed for the police station. It was off of Route 3, near Bob's Barbershop. He was driving an unmarked Ford Explorer, a typical car for a homicide detective that also worked missing persons.

McKinney had fifteen years of law enforcement down in Denver but moved up to Mecklenburg for a change of pace, better schools, and opportunities for his family. He was burned out from the job, city life, and had high hopes of a low-key life in Mecklenburg.

McKinney pulled into the local Starbucks, near The Hotel Mecklenburg. He pulled out a couple of fresh flyers and walked inside. He had started using the community boards a few years ago to post flyers of missing people.

McKinney pushed a fresh red thumbtack into the four corners of the flyer and stepped back.

"Tall Pike, please," McKinney said as he ordered his coffee.

"Busy today?" replied the barista.

"It's turning out to be that way." He paused briefly, handed a new flyer to the lady, also taking his money. "That's Tom Porter, he went missing from the Duke mine earlier today."

"I'll hang it up on the board."

"No need, I already did. Just pass that one around or leave it at the register, if you don't mind. I have a bad feeling about this one. Reminds me of poor old Betty."

McKinney left with his warm coffee, dropping the transmission into drive, and sipped his black gold. His mind began to wonder. He had had bad days for a while.

McKinney started to drive, and his brain drifted off. He couldn't stop thinking about how his wife fucked him over. His mind kept replaying it over and over. That day. That mind-melting day back in Denver where she fucked that guy...

The day McKinney caught her:

McKinney pulled up to his house and parked his 2010 blue Dodge Ram. He sat with the engine off, keys in his hand, with his forehead resting on the steering wheel. It was 11:00 a.m. and he had just quit his job and was about to walk inside and explain this to his overbearing bitch of a wife. To top the day off, a strange pickup was parked in his driveway, and it wasn't the first time.

McKinney took a deep breath. "Why?" he whined. He opened up his driver's door and stepped out into the bullshit. *Why does she hate me? Why can't she love me?* he thought.

As McKinney walked under the carport and past the living room windows, he could hear her. She moaned as the owner of that strange pickup truck was inside of her. He paused and turned toward the last window. The blinds were cracked.

Not only could he hear his wife fucking another man, but now he could see it. She had her way with him in McKinney's recliner— the same recliner in which he read all of his books. The same damn chair where he drank his beer. She was boning the guy, in *his* fucking chair.

McKinney's head dropped again as he turned and walked to the front door. He sat on the front steps crying and waited for her to finish.

A short time later, the moaning stopped. Then, a tall, good-looking man walked out the side door of the house and, with a big smile on his face, got into that strange pickup truck and left.

McKinney, feeling dejected, stood up and went inside through the front door.

He had been married going on ten years and had two beautiful kids with Becky, his cheating ass wife.

Becky was a beautiful skinny girl, with curves only dedication and hard work can get you. She had natural breasts, red hair, and emerald green eyes, which McKinney would always get lost in.

Ever since her sister was murdered, Becky had become a time thieving, life-draining bitch that cheated on McKinney every chance she got. She acted as if her wedding vows didn't mean anything.

"Becky, who was that guy?" McKinney asked. Amused, Becky smiled and looked away, ignoring the question.

She knew how to handle McKinney. She had been doing so for years. "Honestly, McKinney, don't ask stupid questions. The better question is, why the fuck are you home at 11:00 a.m.?" she quipped as she walked past him, lighting up a Camel.

"I quit my job. I couldn't take one more day working for that department. I just couldn't."

Dumbfounded, Becky stood and stared at McKinney. She had a look of hate in those emerald eyes. "McKinney, what am I going to do now? What are we going to do? The kids are at school. You're an asshole. How'd this happen to us?" Becky bitched as she took drag after drag of her cigarette.

McKinney sighed. "I don't know, my love, but I'll find something. I always do. I'm a smart guy. I have been a cop for most of my adult life. I am good at it. I just can't do it in Denver anymore."

"Smart, you say? You quit your damn job, asshole. How smart is that? I knew I should have never married you. My mom was right. You're a loser," Becky screamed as she smacked him in the face.

McKinney walked off, thinking, *I hate you.*

Even though McKinney was mad, he knew this was par for the course with Becky. She was a selfish, self-centered, self-obsessed, self-seeking, narcissistic, sex-addicted whore. If it weren't for the kids and the pure fact that even though she was mentally abusive and he genuinely loved her, he would leave. But not on this day. This was the day that would lead him to Mecklenburg.

Back at the office, McKinney shook the bad memories from his mind and began to type his reports.

He had a friendly little office with views of Route 3 and a good look into the businesses across the way. The walls were adorned with more commendations, accolades, city awards, and pictures than any other office in the building.

McKinney was a one-name kind of guy. He was known only as McKinney, and his reputation was like a Rembrandt painting. It spoke more than words could adequately describe and was worth millions for how many lives he had saved. He was a short and stocky guy, with a mind as sharp as Paul Bunyan's ax.

McKinney was not someone whose bad side was worth it. He was extremely good at his job, and like most cops, had a feeble judgment of women.

Chapter 14: Escape

The river was crystal clear, shallow, and the current was slow-flowing this time of year. The local Fish and Game had recently stocked the area with browns and rainbows. It was trout season again, and Doctor Charles Nunez, Harbor House's chief physician, never missed an opening day. He even had an inside source with Fish and Game, Todd, his lifelong best friend.

With a smile from ear to ear, the good doctor was knee-deep in that river. He tied on a fresh fly and began to flip his rod back and forth, casting the fishing line to dance across the top of the beautiful water.

Back and forth, the doctor cast his line, then one hit, and a nice size rainbow was on the line. He pulled back hard, but not hard enough to rip the hook from the fragile trout's mouth. With a big bend in his rod, the doctor began to reel in the line.

The trout swam back and forth, up and downstream, trying to get away. But the doctor was no rookie. He patiently battled this fish and reeled him to just beneath his knees. The trout was exhausted and gave up.

The doctor held the rod straight up and reached into the water to pick up the fish. He grabbed and held it hard enough to keep control, but gentle enough to keep it from dying. He began to bring that fish to the surface as the water rolled off his hand, revealing a black iPhone.

Strange, he thought as it began to vibrate and ring. The doctor looked down at the phone, then up at the sky.

The sky turned black, and the doctor looked at his hand again. This time he realized he was still holding his black cellphone but was now laying in his bed with most of his body under the covers.

His mind was coming to. He had been dreaming, and now his phone brought him back to reality. The doctor placed it up to his ear. "Hello?"

"Doctor Nunez, I'm sorry to wake you, sir, but..."

The doctor knew Harbor House wouldn't call in the middle of the night unless something truly awful had happened.

"No, no, it's all right. I'm awake now. What happened?"

"Sir, Patient 0227 has escaped. Ronald Black is gone."

Doctor Nunez lay in silence as his nightmares were coming true. The worst-case scenario was unfolding. The town's most prolific home-grown serial killer was missing and on the loose. Instantly, the doctor knew innocent people were going to die—lots of them.

"Make the calls. Begin escape protocols. I'll be right there!" said the doctor as he ended the call.

Doctor Nunez arrived at Harbor House within fifteen minutes of the phone call. He was waved through security as the external sirens were blasting. A few minutes later, he was inside.

"Sir, we don't know where Patient 0227 is. He was last seen at 9:00 p.m., and by 2:00 a.m., we realized he was missing. Security looked back on the video of the hallway and have no one entering or exiting his room. The only thing on video was around midnight his door cracked open, and a white balloon floated into the hallway. A few moments later, the balloon bumped into a sprinkler head and burst, but that's it," explained the night guard.

The doctor pulled out his radio and contacted the video room. They had the video pulled and ready for him to view. The doctor stood in place for a few moments, thinking.

The doctor watched the video. The balloon was creepy. Even though he knew a single white balloon had been used over the years for medicinal purposes to calm Ronald, it was never any less weird.

That mental switch, when Ronald grabbed the balloon, was quick and evident. That single white latex balloon would bring out the calming female personality of Sam, Ronald's second diagnosed personality.

"Where is Doctor Wyzenski?" asked Doctor Nunez.

"Sir, we have no clue. He is the on-call psychiatrist and hasn't returned a call," replied a guard.

Strange, thought Doctor Nunez as he scratched his back. He did this as a nervous tic to relieve stress.

As the doctor thought, he began to walk out of the video room. "Let's go to his room. I want to see Ronald Black's room."

Ronald's room was on the fifth floor at the end of the east wing of the facility. His room was small and simplistic: ten by ten, with a bed, TV on the wall, and a standard stainless-steel "prison style" toilet. There were no windows and a metal fortified door that electronically locked from either the master control room or any guard.

The fifth floor was highly guarded and reserved for the most dangerous of the criminally insane patients at Harbor House. The walls were a dingy off-white concrete block, and the fluorescent lights above them began to hum and stutter. As Doctor Nunez and the convey of people made their way down the fifth floor.

The lack of noise was deafening.

They walked. The footsteps fell one after the other, echoing through the stale hallway, passing occupied rooms. The closer they got to Ronald's room, the worse the lighting.

At the end of the hallway, the light in front of Ronald's room blew out with small orange shards of electricity flickering in the air.

"You'll never find him. He's an angel; he took flight into the wind. About to do God's work, he is... the red rain will come. You can't stop it, peasants," rang out from the room before Ronald's.

Doctor Nunez stopped and turned his head to the room. "Open his door."

A guard waved a key fob over the door sensor, causing a metallic pop and the door unlocked. He looked in the small window center of the door. The patient was deep in the room.

The door opened.

"Where is Ronald Black?" asked Doctor Nunez as he squared his body off in the door.

The patient was standing against the far wall, soaked to the bone and dripping liquid all over the floor. His head was down and arms out, resembling a limp crucifix.

He said nothing.

"If you know something, now is the time to say it!" said Nunez.

"There will be a reckoning. Judgment will come. Judgment will come for us all! In the end, they will win. This town, it... *it* will win!" screamed the patient as the thumb on his left hand scratched the head of the single wooden match he held.

The patient stood still and silent as fire flashed over the liquid covering his body. The patient's discipline was absolute as he burned alive. He never flinched, nor uttered a sound, but stood, burning for all to see.

After the fire was put out, Doctor Nunez and the others entered Ronald's room.

"Plain Jane. That's the term that comes to mind, boys. No books. Nothing on the walls. Nothing," said Nunez.

"Where the fuck did he go?" asked a guard.

Doctor Nunez stood in Ronald's room completely silent.

He knew only one thing: the devil was loose in Mecklenburg.

Chapter 15: Breaking News

McKinney was sitting at his desk, typing away. His job, while highly important and mostly satisfying, was ninety percent paperwork and ten percent hold-on-for-the-ride-and-try-not-to-die-today kind of fun.

McKinney picked up his work phone. "Detective McKinney, how can I help you?"

"McKinney, there's been an escape at Harbor House. Officers are working the scene right now. I need you to head up the investigation on this thing," replied his captain.

McKinney's face was ten shades of pissed off. He was not the only detective in this town, but was so good at his job, command rode him like the best horse at the Kentucky Derby.

He hated command. Cases were piled on him every damn day. But McKinney also brought it on himself. Not because he was so eloquently good at his job, but because he didn't know how to say no to the assholes in charge, which would have worked wonders.

Every weird, gruesome, raw, or "messed up" case was assigned to McKinney, and it was beginning to take its toll on him.

"Sir, I'm busy working a new case from the Duke mine. You said that was a priority, so I've been—"

"Stop and listen carefully, McKinney. I don't care what I told you the other day; today I'm telling you different. Ronald Black has escaped. Do you hear me? Does that name ring a bell? He's fucking out, McKinney. He's out, and if we can't find him quick, blood will flow in the streets!"

McKinney sat silently with his phone pressed firmly in his ear. He hated command, and his captain was a giant asshole, but for once, they're making the right call. He remembered the stories of Ronald Black—the bodies found, the bodies still missing, the families destroyed.

"Captain, I understand, sir. I'll head out to Harbor House now," McKinney replied as he hung up.

For once, my asshole captain was right: blood will flow in the streets, thought McKinney as he grabbed his notepad and headed for the door.

BREAKING NEWS… BREAKING NEWS… BREAKING NEWS… 99.7 FM, The Road, interrupted their morning playlist: "People of Mecklenburg, we have urgent breaking news. Police are on the scene of an incident at Harbor House Psychiatric Hospital. We are being told that a patient has escaped. Stand by. Wait, just a moment. [Dead air silence for the next few seconds]. We are getting word now that Ronald Black, a mentally ill patient from Harbor House, has escaped. Again, Ronald Black has escaped. He was to be institutionalized for life at Harbor House. He is described as a white male, six-foot-two, two-hundred-twenty-pounds, and muscular. He has dirty brown and grey hair and should be wearing white hospital attire."

[whispering off the mic] "This can't be right?"

"We are being told to remind everyone not to approach this man, but to call 911 immediately. Ronald Black is extremely dangerous, and if you don't remember, in the early nineties, Ronald Black was responsible for the disappearance and death of countless people here in Mecklenburg," explained the morning DJ, with tears in his eyes, as he recalled his mother is still missing from that same period.

McKinney turned off the car's radio leaving only the thunder, lightning, and heavy rain for his mind to consume. He was driving alone with his thoughts until he heard the bellowing whine of the sirens from the top of the control towers at Harbor House.

The closer McKinney got to the place, the more patrol cars, police officers, and blue lights he saw.

A few miles later, he pulled up to the north gate. McKinney presented his badge and was quickly waved through. People were running around inside the gates with purpose.

He parked and was met by a man holding an open umbrella.

As they walked toward the facility, he realized the magnitude of the situation. Dark smoke was creeping out of a window on the fifth floor and firemen were moving about. People were going to die that night; he could feel it in his bones.

"Thank you so much for coming, detective. My name is Doctor Nunez, I'm the chief physician here at Harbor House. I'm in charge of most of the things around here."

McKinney shook the doctor's hand. "Nice to meet you. I'm told the famous Ronald Black is missing?"

"He is indeed. If you are familiar with any of the cases involving our patient, Mr. Black, then you know we have a terrible problem on our hands."

McKinney walked into Ronald's room and straight to the small window near the bed. Lighting flashed, briefly illuminating the woods outside of the gate. He stared mindlessly into the darkness.

McKinney had seen horrors in that forest he'd rather forget. The atrocities of man lived inside the mist that spread through the trees.

The black abyss of that national forest covered thousands of acres. The rain was coming down hard and had cooled the night air to the point of freezing.

The storm was so loud, no one could hear Ronald Black moving through the dark of the forest.

Ronald walked with a purpose of survival, a purpose of escape, a purpose of hate.

McKinney continued to chat with the doctor and security as well. He quickly got to work, and the case was open.

Chapter 16: The Parallel World

The dust whipped up on the old dirt road the city refused to pave or maintain. The same road Tom Porter just woke up on. Naked.

Tom's eyes fluttered as he came to. His head hurt, and his legs were black and blue. He rolled up to his butt, sitting, dazed, hurting like hell.

"Where the fuck am I?" Tom asked himself. "Where the fuck are my clothes?"

Tom leaned over, and a retched bile began to flow from his guts. The vomit was ghastly, acidic, and full of blood. He sat thinking, hurting.

The dirt road went on for miles. No cars, no bicycles, no people, no sound. Just a dirt road lined with trees and vacant farms.

Tom could see for what appeared to be miles in each direction. He stood up, stretched his back, and began to walk. His feet hurt, just like the rest of his body.

Naked.

Tom walked and noticed something else. He was hairless. From the top of his head to his feet, his hair was gone. *Strange*, he thought. Much like the fact that he was walking past farms, and no one was out working the fields—no one.

Tom walked for nearly an hour. He was starving but had a thirst that would take days to quench. Finally, the road turned to asphalt. He kept walking.

As the road began to bend, Tom could see a familiar building in the distance. One he saw just before heading to the mine for the first time. It was the hospital. In the distance, he could see Harbor House.

As Tom walked up to the east gate, he felt strange. A chill overtook him, and if he had any hair on the back of his neck, it would have been standing tall.

The rusted gate was wide open with no one in sight. Papers were blowing with the wind across the entrance. No sounds were heard. No voices, no patients screaming, no one running, no guards, no nurses. The security cameras weren't even moving.

The windows of Harbor House were old and dirty. Some were broken or missing.

"What the fuck! What the fuck is going on!" screamed Tom. "Is anyone here? Can anyone hear me? *Fuck*!"

Tom heard a metal door slam from within the hospital. He turned his head and immediately started running toward that sound.

"Hello? Is anyone there?" Tom yelled as he ran inside.

No answer. Just blackness.

Tom began to slow his pace and walk. He was inside and following the yellow line in the center of the hall. The electricity was out, and the only light was coming from outside through the shattered windows.

Footsteps fell. Tom could hear loud footsteps progress into running. Then another metal door slammed a short distance ahead of him.

"Hello?" Tom's voice cracked with fear as he couldn't see.

"Please, I need help," Tom uttered.

Tom found the door and opened it. The hinges screamed for oil as he pulled the handle toward him. He looked inside and stopped.

Stairs lead down into a void.

Tom stepped into the darkness and began to walk down.

"Is anyone—" Tom stopped when he heard breathing below him, a raspy wet sound.

"For behold, the Lord will come in fire and his chariots like the whirlwind," the voice spoke. "His anger. His fury. With flames of fire. For the Lord will give his judgment by fire, by sword, on all flesh, and those slain will be many! Isaiah 66:15."

Tom froze with fear. His mind reverted back in time. The voice reminded Tom of a sinkhole he watched open as a child. It was dark and deep, with no ending in sight. Like a hole straight to hell.

"You have been chosen. Welcome to the world of the unknown. This is not heaven nor hell, but a place of nowhere. A place of torment and judgment. A place the rock put you. A place between the world of the living and a world of the dead!"

Tom stood in the darkness, a few feet away from the voice. His body lost all control as fear swept through his veins.

"This universe only exists in the Lord's eyes and in ours. Nothing lives here that isn't put here by him!" explained the voice.

Tom turned and ran from the terror in the stairwell and the horror of his fear. One foot after the other. Tom ran and ran and ran. Tom ran for his life!

After a few minutes, Tom found himself still in the hospital. Alone again, he bent over, chest heaving. Tom tried to catch his breath. He closed his eyes and began to count to himself and slow his rapid oxygen intake.

"Holy fuck," Tom whispered.

Tom was still naked and needed clothing. He hoped he could find something, anything, to put on. Tom looked around and noticed sunlight shining onto a door marked "Storage." *Maybe in there*, he thought.

Tom tried the door, but it was locked. He looked around and noticed a fire ax concealed behind a glass door inside the wall next to him.

Tom picked up a nearby chair and used it to break the glass. He reached inside and pulled out the wood-handled ax. Smiling, he held the ax and looked at the storage door.

A few swings of the ax and he was inside the storage room. Jackpot. Scrubs and hospital sandals were stacked on the shelf.

"It must be my lucky fucking day. I woke up naked in a fucked-up world, had a crazy man preach the apocalypse to me, and now I've found green scrubs and sandals. Wait—saline! At least I can drink it," Tom spoke to himself.

Tom took a few minutes to suck down the salty liquids. His throat was so dry, the liquid felt like shards of glass flowing into his mouth and down to his stomach. The pain was tremendous, but Tom knew if he didn't drink it, dehydration would kill him.

Tom made a makeshift backpack out of other scrubs, filled it with saline, took his ax, and made his way toward the exit. He didn't know where he was headed, but Tom knew he had to get away from there.

Tom was alone and in a parallel world.

Not a soul was around as Tom walked down Route 3 into the center of town.

Step after step, Tom walked.

It was high noon, but the light in the sky was beginning to dissipate as he heard a *swoosh* sound from above. He turned and looked up to see blackness in the distance headed toward him, in the sky like fast-moving storm clouds.

"Crows," Tom said to himself, confused. "Fuck me!"

Tom took off running as the murder of crows got closer. Tom ran down Route 3 and began to cut behind businesses. He ran as fast as he could wearing those damn hospital sandals. Although it still beat running barefoot.

The rolling blackness of the crows shut out the light of the sky, turning day into night in the snap of a finger. Tom kept running.

The sound was louder and louder. The crows were incessantly cawing, thousands of them! They were so loud, Tom's mind cracked. He began to laugh and cry and pissed himself as he ran. Madness set in.

Tom kept running, jumped a fence, and was close to The Hotel Mecklenburg. That was his target. His refuge. Tom picked up his pace and ran for his life toward the front doors. Strangely, a tattered American flag was flying high out front, whipping in the air like any ordinary day.

Tom tried the front door. It was locked. Panic set in.

The crows were getting closer and closer. They were now above the hotel, causing a total blackout. Tom ran. The crows began to dive at him.

Tom ran around the corner of the hotel toward the loading dock. The birds kamikaze dove at him as he ran. All around him, birds were hitting the sidewalk, leaving piles of bloody feathers and bones, killing themselves trying to hit Tom.

Tom jumped up on the loading dock, hiding under the metal overhang. The birds wouldn't stop. He could hear them diving into the roof, killing themselves. It made the birds sound like shotgun shells cooking off in a fire.

Tom pinned himself against the brick wall of the building and began to hunker down. Like a beat dog, Tom laid in the fetal position.

"God, make it stop! Fucking make them stop!" he screamed. Tom closed his eyes while tears began to stream down his face. The metal sounds were deafening and horribly maddening. He was losing his mind.

As Tom cried, a pair of large dirty hands grabbed his ankles, pulling him under the loading dock's metal roll-up door.

"*No!*" Tom screamed, terrified; his breath left his lungs, and his bowels blew into his pants. He was frozen, and his lungs wouldn't work.

Tom was inside now.

"Just breathe. Breathe and listen. I'm not going to hurt you. Do you understand me?" the man asked.

"Please... don't kill me..." Tom squeaked. With tears in his eyes, shook his head. "Who are you? What the fuck is going on?"

Tom turned over and sat up, squirting feces through his scrubs. He had a flashlight in his face and couldn't see anything else. He could tell a man was kneeled next to him, so Tom reached up and gently grabbed the man's arm. "Am I going fucking crazy?" Tom stammered as he continued to cry.

The man shifted the light off of Tom and pointed it directly at the ceiling, illuminating the room. Tom could see multiple people standing around him now.

"My name is Jordon McHenry. Those other guys you see are Andrew and Juan. We have been here for... well, it feels like we have been here for a real long time."

"You've been in the hotel for a long time?" Tom questioned.

"No, this place. This new world," Juan answered from the corner of the room.

"We will do our best to explain things; just give us some time. But first, who are you, and why are you here?" asked Jordon.

"My name is Tom Porter, and I have no fucking clue where I am."

"Are you alone? Are you with anyone? And by anyone, I mean any group?" Juan asked sternly.

"Calm down, Juan," said Jordon. "We will find out if he's one of us or one of THEM."

Over the next few minutes, Jordon, Juan, and Andrew spoke with Tom. They realized Tom had been awake for just a few hours and that he genuinely didn't know much.

"Let's get some food in you, and then I'll explain as much as I know, Tom. Is that fair enough?"

"Yes, please, I'm starving."

Jordon made sure the loading dock door was shut and handed a flashlight to Tom. "Come with us, Tom. We will go to the kitchen and grab some food," he said.

The four men walked through the halls and cut through an old, dusty banquet room. The hotel looked a hundred years old with zero upkeep.

Tom walked, sniffling and shaking the hot mess he had made in his pants, down his leg and onto the floor.

"You fucking stink, Tom," said Juan as he followed. "I'll find you some new clothes." Then he ran off.

The three men continued to make their way to the kitchen as Juan looked for clothing.

Once in the kitchen, Tom noticed several people were eating. When they saw him, a silence fell in the room, and all attention was averted to Tom.

"Hello," Tom said.

Before Tom could say anything else, Jordon interrupted, "Guys, this is Tom Porter. He's just in from the real world. He will be staying with us for a while."

Tom was curious and confused. He wondered what Jordon meant by "in from the real world."

"Tom, grab a plate and help yourself. We will all go ahead and eat. Once Juan gets back with some unstained clothes—damn, you smell like shit—I'll help you shower and then I'll take you to the numen," Jordon explained.

"I really need a shower," Tom said as he piled cafeteria-style food on his plate with his head hung low.

"Well, we don't have running water. Sucks, but basically we have an old shower in the locker room; I'll get on a stool and slowly pour water over you. It's primal but does the trick."

Tom didn't answer; he was too busy stuffing his face.

Juan came back with some clean clothes he thought would fit Tom. A pair of jeans, a black t-shirt, and a zip-up hoodie with the number 227 printed on the front.

Once Tom stuffed his belly and Jordon helped him shower, Juan gave him the clothing.

As Tom got dressed, Juan noticed a tattoo on the inside of Tom's left arm. It read "BC3." Tom realized Juan was staring at him and said, "Don't worry yourself with the meaning."

Juan nodded and looked over at Jordon, who gave him a look back, and Juan left them alone.

Jordon started to speak, stopped, and carefully chose his words. "Tom, we all use this hotel as kind of a base. A headquarters, if you will. There are about thirty people who live here for now. It's only temporary. Well, we hope it's only temporary. But, well, shit. Instead of me stepping all over my words and getting you confused, I'll take you to our numen. The guy in charge. His name is Luke James. He is like our elder. He is the wisest one here and will be able to answer all your questions."

Tom finished his meal, drank his third cup of water, and turned to Jordon. "I'm ready when you are, sir."

Jordon got up from the table and led Tom out of the cafeteria. They walked through hallways and corridors, passing a few people. Every one of them had the same look of surprise on their face.

After a few minutes, they arrived at what looked to be an office door with no number or name on it, but it did not look like a standard guest room door.

Jordon knocked and waited.

"Please come in. I've been waiting for you guys," said a voice from inside.

The men entered the room.

The room looked like an average apartment, but unlike the other parts of the hotel, it was remarkably clean and appeared new. It was all open, a bed deep in the corner, a kitchen as you entered, and a sitting room between the areas.

"Sir, this is Tom Porter. He is fresh. About five to seven hours old," Jordon explained. "He's been fed and bathed and seems much like one of us."

"Thank you for taking care of him, Jordon," Luke said softly with a smile.

"Tom, My name is Luke James, I'm the one in charge around here. I am sure your head hurts with confusion and have a lot of questions. Before you word-vomit on me, have a seat and let me explain a few things first. And, in the process, most of your questions may get answered."

Tom agreed and opened his ears and his mind as he sat back in a fantastically out-of-place leather sofa.

"Tom, you found the rock. Didn't you?"

"We did," said Tom.

"It's not the only one, but more importantly, you touched it, and that is why you are here," Luke explained.

"Come again, sir?"

"Just listen. I'll answer your questions while you listen. You touched the rock, and it brought you here, Tom. You are in a world that exists only to the people that are here with you. To the people you see. It's a world the same as where you came from but different. It runs parallel with the world you came from. To the best of our knowledge, this world runs concurrently with the real world.

"Life, as you know it, is over for now. It's on pause, yet time does not stand still. Every bit of hair on your body is missing. That is a byproduct of being transported here. It will grow back.

"Let me ask you this, Tom. Where was the rock that you touched?"

Tom sat stone-faced for a minute. His mind was trying to wrap itself around what he was hearing. "In the mine. We found—I mean, we were investigating the disappearance of three miners. The rock was deep in the mine. In a circular room, the miners stumbled across it. It was seven thousand feet below the fucking earth."

Luke got up and walked to his kitchen. He opened up a bottle of water and took a swig.

"As you can see, Tom, you are not the first one to enter this parallel world, nor will you be the last. If you look around, you will notice Jordon, Juan, and Andrew are here at this hotel. They are the miners you were looking for. But you four are the only ones I know of that came here by way of that particular rock."

Luke handed his water to Tom. "What we know is there are many rocks, Tom. Not just the one you touched. So, the bad news is, we don't know exactly how many rocks are out there. But the good news—the good news, Tom, is that if a rock got us to this world, there must be a rock in this parallel world that will get us home." Luke took back the water. "Do you understand? Are you picking up what I'm putting down?"

"Strangely enough, I think I do. You believe there is a way to get back home?" Tom said with a glimmer of hope in his eye.

"I do. But then there are problems. Jordon tells me you ran into one of the problems at the abandoned Harbor House Hospital?"

"You must mean the crazy fuck in the stairwell preaching at me."

"I do, and here's what we know. Over an unknown period, about seventy-five to one hundred people have been brought to this parallel world. Maybe more. We really can't say for sure. This is hard for a lot of people to accept and ultimately has broken many people mentally. Their minds fail, like dropping a glass bottle on concrete. The mind shatters.

"Not everyone brought here is the same. We are all different, and all come from unique walks of life. *But*, there is a divide among the people here. Not at this hotel, but in this town."

Luke stopped briefly and finished the water.

"The people inside this hotel are all of a like mind. We all are searching for the rock that will send us home. But there is another group of people in this town: THEM. You met one at Harbor House. We call them, 'THEM' or 'THEY.' That's the best name we could come up with. They are much like small violent gangs. Some of them are organized, and some not so much. It's impossible to lump them all into one group. Since food here is rather scarce, some of them have also become cannibals. But not all of them are the same. You see, THEY believe God put them here, and in part, they're not totally wrong, but they also think this is the new world, and no one should be allowed to leave."

Tom sat in pain. His body hurt, but his mind had melted all over the floor. "Can I stay here?" he asked.

"Tom, you are free to come and go as you please, but I must warn you: it's not safe to travel alone, especially at night. THEY wait in the shadows, and THEY will kill you."

Tom nodded and said, "Is there someone I can bunk up with? And is there anything else I should know?"

Jordon approached Luke and spoke quietly to him. Luke agreed with what Jordon had said.

"We do have someone you can bunk with, Tom. Her name is Charlotte. She will take care of you, and you will take care of her. We look out for one another here. Don't ever forget that," said Luke as he pointed his finger at him.

Tom nodded in agreement. "Thank you."

"Jordon will get you everything you need, but one last thing we need to show you, Tom." Luke gestured to Juan and Jordon.

"Tom, please follow me," Jordon said as he walked out of the room.

Tom was so thankful for the shelter, security, food, clothing, and the company, he would have agreed to anything. With a smile, he turned and followed Jordon.

As Jordon walked, he exhaled and said, "Everything Luke said is the honest truth. Some of it may sound far-fetched, but remember, you woke up naked and bald on a dirt road today. So, is it really that hard to believe?"

The men walked through hallways and back toward the center of the hotel. They came to a door that was locked with multiple deadbolts and a sign that read, "No one enters!"

Jordon opened the door and turned on a flashlight. Only he and Tom entered.

The men walked down flights of stairs until they reached a door at the bottom.

Jordon turned his flashlight to the ceiling and looked at Tom. "This is where we hold THEM," and he opened the door.

As the air entered the stairway from the doors opening, so did the screams. The basement, or at least at the point they were entering, was airtight. So tight, the sound never left the rooms, nor did daylight ever enter.

Jordon and Tom stepped through the door. The hallway was black, and only Jordon's flashlight gave them sight.

Tom heard a grown woman moaning. They walked toward the sound. Screams were coming from farther down the hallway.

"Stay close, and don't touch anything, Tom," said Jordon. But Tom was already attached to Jordon's hip. He couldn't get any closer.

Jordon stopped in front of a door and could hear the moaning. He opened the door and the smell of fresh feces hit him first, then he noticed in front of them was an older woman. She stood inside of a large steel cage.

The woman became silent and stared into the light that Jordon shined. She was older, in her seventies, smelled of old death, and was bone skinny. She had long flowing grey hair. Her face was abnormally wrinkled, skin white as paper, but her eyes…

"Her eyes are fucking gone. Where are her eyes?" asked Tom.

"I can see you, boy! And I smell the shit in your bowels," the old woman taunted as she reached through the cage at the men. "I'm not the candy man, limp dick, but I'll eat your heart."

She was drooling. She was hungry; oh, so hungry.

"This is what we wanted to show you, Tom. So, you can see firsthand the evil that haunts this world we are in," Jordon explained as he shut the door closing off the old women to all hope.

"How many are THEY?" Tom asked with big eyes.

"We have three here, but only because they broke in one night killing some of our people. They ate them. Parts of them, at least. We killed a couple and ultimately captured what we have here in the hotel's basement."

Jordon turned to Tom. "These people, if you can call them people, are obviously abnormal. We don't know if the cannibals came from our world or if they have always been here. Either way, we avoid them at all costs."

The men left the basement and headed for the fifth floor.

"You'll get along well with Charlotte. She's been here for a few months. She's easy on the eyes and was a cop in the real world," said Jordon as they reached her room.

Jordon knocked on the door.

"Give me a minute," a female voice answered.

Jordon laughed to himself and stood there. A long uncomfortable minute passed, and the door finally opened.

"What's up?" Charlotte asked.

Tom's eyes quivered as his heart smiled. Charlotte was stunning. She stood just a few inches taller than Tom and weighed an athletic 135 pounds. Her eyes were easy to get lost in and reminded him of a blue bird's wing.

"This is Tom, he's fresh in from the real world. He's a geologist miner or something like that. Luke thought you could use a roommate," Jordon explained.

"I have a roommate, but thanks anyway."

"Yeah, you don't. You know Cindy is either dead or found her way out of this place," Jordon said seriously. "No one has seen her in a couple of weeks."

Charlotte dropped her head, stepped aside, lifted her hand up, and said, "Welcome to the room."

Tom stood still. He wasn't listening to the words being spoken as much as he was paying attention to the curves of Charlotte's arm as she waved him inside.

"Thanks," Tom said as he entered the room.

Charlotte Kane was a unique woman. She was five-foot-six, muscular, and sexy. She had a fire in her voice and an air of confidence that would intimidate most other women, while also raising the pheromone levels in men. She was smart, strong, deadly accurate with a firearm, and everyone in the hotel loved her.

Charlotte was a cop in the real world and worked with a task force of officers that chased down only the most violent of criminals. She was used to environments that worked against her.

Tom awoke with a chill. He sat up and looked over at his new roommate. Charlotte was tossing in her sleep with a steady set of moans. It was sometime past 2:00 a.m. Tom had the sweats and briefly remembered being back in the mine with Walter, screaming as Tom stared at the rock.

That's all Tom remembered. His head hurt, and his never-ending nightmare of this parallel world was continuing. He calmed himself. In the real world, he had never been this mentally weak, this mentally broken. He had always been a strong man. But not here. Not now.

Charlotte rolled over and woke up. "Tom, are you okay?"

"Nightmare... I've never been this scared before. I've always been strong."

Charlotte walked over to Tom's bed and slapped the spit out of his mouth.

"What the fuck?" he screamed.

"You feel that? That's pain. That's life. That pain is telling you you're still alive when so many others are not. That pain will keep you alive. If you remember it," said Charlotte as she slapped the other side of his face, blistering her hand.

"That's to even it out. If you don't man up, you will die. It's as simple as that," Charlotte said as she handed him a bottle of water.

"Take a drink and listen up. You must have a family you want to get back to?"

"My wife," he answered.

"The only way home is to survive. The only way to survive is to understand one simple fact, and as soon as you come to terms with this one fact, you can man up and go on living. The simple fact is, you're already dead. We all are. When and where are yet to be determined."

Charlotte had been sleeping in a pair of boy shorts and a sports bra. She stood up, pulled on a pair of jeans and a shirt.

"Tom, you're in a different world, one that we believe runs parallel with our real world. You are missing and presumed fucking dead in that world. So as soon as you understand this is your one chance to live, your mind will fix itself. Until then, you will just be an oxygen thief."

Tom stared at her for a minute. A switch flipped in his head. He knew she was right.

"Get dressed, Tom. I've got to show you something. Maybe it will help you understand," explained Charlotte.

Tom quickly dressed and followed Charlotte. Charlotte had a pair of binoculars in hand and led him down to the third floor to a roof access door.

"Follow me, but be quiet when we get outside," Charlotte whispered.

Tom nodded and followed her onto the roof.

Charlotte lifted the binoculars to her eyes and began to scan the areas below. A few minutes later, she said, "There they are."

She handed the binos to Tom and directed him to look out under a streetlight, across Route 3, about eight hundred yards in the distance.

"Do you see that, Tom?" she asked.

Tom scanned the area, and at first, couldn't see, but once Charlotte adjusted the focus dial for him, he saw it plain as day. Someone was lying partially in the grass, partly on the road and under the only and halfway working streetlight.

"I see her. Is she dead?" Tom asked.

"That girl is dead, and what's feeding on her is not from our world. It hides in the woods and preys on the weak. It preys on those that can't protect themselves. Do you understand?" Charlotte walked away, leaving him alone on the roof. Tom continued to watch through the binoculars. Moments later, the roof access door opened again. This time, Charlotte had a rifle.

"Lay next to me, Tom," Charlotte whispered as she positioned herself on her stomach, chest up with her rifle pulled into her shoulder. Tom dropped to a knee and then laid next to her.

Charlotte clicked the elevation and then the windage knobs on top of her scope, dialing in the distance to the perceived target eating the female in the road. The rifle was a.308, and at eight hundred yards, the round she was using would put an end to the feast downrange.

Charlotte left the front of the rifle to rest on its bipods and shifted the butt over to Tom. "Here, put this part in your shoulder."

Tom had fired plenty of guns in his time, so this wasn't foreign to him.

"Call the wind," he said.

Shocked that Tom knew this term, she answered, "Full value, left to right, seven to ten."

Tom held off for the wind, let his breath out, and pulled the trigger. The shot echoed down the road a moment after the round impacted its target. The feast was over. The female was still dead, but her body stopped moving.

As that round left the barrel, Tom's mind switched over. He was no longer mentally feeble. He was the strong-willed Tom Porter of his old world. He finally realized to live, he must first die and be reborn. He hoped his mind would stay this way.

Charlotte looked at Tom and instantly saw he was a different man. He was indeed resurrected.

"That's the Tom I wanna know. That's the Tom that will get home and help us all get home. That's the Tom that can live in my room," Charlotte said, laughing as she kissed his cheek.

"Thank you," he said from the depths of his soul. She had saved him, and he would not forget it.

"Let's get off the roof and report our kill to the night guards," said Charlotte.

Chapter 17: THEM/THEY and SOLO Kent

The town was dirty. It looked abandoned. There were coffee cups in the street, clothing, trash, and old, dirty, rain-soaked rolls of toilet paper. But strangely there were no cars. Anywhere.

A gate was creaking in the distance as the storm rolled in. The rain came first. Then the wind, and finally, the lighting. But that didn't stop Kent Prather. He had been in this parallel world for what seemed like a year. He was used to the weather and used to life as he knew it now. Kent was a survivor and had survived so long because he trusted almost no one. He moved around a lot while continually looking for a way home.

Kent wasn't one of THEM, nor was he a SEEKER like the people at The Hotel Mecklenburg. Kent was a SOLO. Kent believed in God but wasn't a religious zealot like THEM. He had little to no friends, just a busy time of searching for the exit from this world.

Kent walked out of the singlewide he was hiding in, pulled on his green hoodie, and started north down 28th Street away from town.

It was a hair past midnight when Kent turned off Route 3, near the little league park. He slipped into the woods, moving branch after branch.

Kent made his way through the thousand acres of moss-covered oaks, maples, and tall pines. He had been in this forest hundreds of times and knew firsthand how easy it was to get lost.

Kent pulled out his map, orientated a small compass attached to his watchband, and began to walk a grip square that he had not searched before.

Kent had used this map most of the year in an attempt to find a specific lost cabin that he believed contained a way home—a door, passage an exit—from this misery he called life now.

Chief Sanders was a scowl of a man, oversized in stature, and a heart absent from his body. He was hollow, lacking any morals, and had the mind of a layperson that believed he was an astronaut. Dumb, he was. Dumb as dirt. Yet, he invoked fear by the savage acts he committed upon men.

Sanders believed himself to be a giant, when in actuality, he was a pawn in the system. Cannon fodder. No one was safe from his self-loathing. He was dead inside, free of life where the soulless and decomposed of this parallel world called home at the abyss of Sanders' emptiness.

Talking with Sanders was as fun and as informative as watching paint dry. He was a dick, and in this parallel world, THEY had him as a hunter, as a leader, as one of their leaders. He hunted men who looked for a way back to the real world. Sanders believed God had put him here to stop anyone from going home again. Strangely, he was good at his job.

The rain was substantial, never letting up, causing the Black River to overflow its banks just past midnight.

The water seeped into town, eating the road inches at a time. It rained a lot in this new world but always eventually stopped.

Thunder rolled through town, waking Chief Sanders from a dead sleep. He rubbed his eyes and crawled away from the two-dollar whore he fell asleep beside. He truly loved whores.

Chief grabbed a pack of smokes, torched one up as he did every day of his waking life. He inhaled. "Bitch, get up," he said as he kicked the girl in the back.

The female didn't budge. She was Chief's regular. Most of THEM believed the whore was his girlfriend, but in truth, he bartered with her for sexual favors. She would pleasure him, and he would let her stay at his trailer, give her food, and sometimes loan her out to others.

"I *said, get up!*" Chief screamed as he looked out the window toward Route 3.

Chief peered out into the night, slowly dragging on his Marlboro red. The flash of lightning came just after the thunder rolled. It gave way to a person walking in the rain out on the road. The lightning flashed again, and the man was gone.

Chief took a long slow drag on that old stale Marlboro, then it hit him. That man disappeared into the woods. Chief thought the man must have a small camp inside the tree line, and a camp meant supplies. Supplies meant survival. Or, maybe that man was a SEEKER, looking for the way home.

The storm continued all night and into the following morning.

Just before 10:00 a.m., the rain stopped, yet the daylight continued to hide behind an endless sky of clouds. The Black River was still pushing water through the low-lying parts of town but seemed to stop its march up Route 3.

Chief Sanders left his dirty, white, mold-encrusted singlewide on flat tires. He paused on the street for a moment and surveyed his surroundings. Nothing was stirring, nothing out of place, so he walked to where he last saw the man from last night's storm.

Chief ducked behind the old auto parts store just off Route 3, near Birmingham Road. He noticed a thin trail leading into the thick mosey oaks. Chief crouched down and saw the hint of boot prints. Even after all that rain, the boot prints were still there.

"Must be the guy," he grunted.

Chief knew the man was using this trail and hoped it was not a one-time thing. He was banking on it, leading to the man's camp, where they could rob him blind. Chief turned and began to walk away. He wanted to get some guys to go pay the man a visit. After all, he was a hunter of men.

Kent walked all night. He was sopping wet, freezing but determined.

He had crossed off three grid-squares during that time. Three thousand meters. It was a massive process of elimination. But, looking for a rock that would take him back to the real world wasn't going to be an easy task.

Kent took a break and began to plan his next move when suddenly he heard an explosion far behind him. He had set a tripwire on the trail with a homemade device, just in case THEY were close. Kent heard a man screaming not to let him die, and then the voice slowly faded to nothing. He smiled, knowing he had caused casualties.

Kent picked up and started moving again. This time, as fast and far away as he could get.

Chief was in his "hole" where he spent most of his days. His hole consisted of a manager's office, tucked inside an old run-down Costco. He was in charge—for now—of the ragtag group of THEM, that called the trailer park near Darby's pond home and used the east side Costco to "work."

The group of men had worked over a long period to secure the Costco, only using the one rear door to enter and exit. They had pilfered all the edibles and saved anything handy with which they could barter. The building was a fortress with almost no windows and secured entry and exits.

Electricity was rare in this world, but Chief Sanders had developed a hodge-podge solar-powered generator. Depending on the amount of sun that day, this setup would give them a few hours of electricity at night. Electricity meant hot water, warm food (when food was available), higher morale, and, most of all, made Chief Sanders a god to the men in this area.

As truly dumb as Chief Sanders was, he was a genius at the oddest things, during the strangest times.

Ding, ding, ding. Ding, ding, ding.

A bell slowly rang out, echoing through Costco's aisles, signifying all in the building to come to the meeting area. An announcement was forthcoming.

Like filthy rats on a sinking ship, THEY began to make their way to the meeting spot.

"My men, today is the day. I can feel it in my bones. This afternoon, I sent a hunting party out, for I spotted a SEEKER last night. I spotted a man looking to defile God. I spotted a man looking to defile us. He was looking for the way out. For the rock, for the exit to this world," said Chief Sanders.

"We have to stop him," the crowd of nearly forty-five men and women chanted.

"AND we will," yelled Chief. "We will hunt down every single man, woman, or child. We will convert them. We will make them see the light. We will show them that this is God's new world, and he doesn't want anyone to leave, or we will kill every last one of them!"

The crowd continued to cheer and yell.

"Sir, Chief Sanders, sir!" a voice from the back yelled.

Silence spread through the crowd like wildfire through a dry forest. Everyone turned around to see who dared interrupt Chief.

A young boy, no older than fifteen, was panting and running toward him from the back.

"They're dead, he killed them," the boy said as he entered the crowd, pushing his way to the front, looking up at Chief Sanders.

"Speak up, boy," Chief said as he stepped down from his makeshift pulpit.

The boy was frail, ghostly, half the size of Chief, soaked with sweat, eyes grey from fear, and shaking like a leaf.

"Chief, the men you sent, I followed them out a short distance into the woods. I—I heard a loud boom and then screaming. They're all dead, sir. All three of them. They're all—"

The boy's speech was cut short. Chief Sanders grabbed all eighty pounds of the malnourished kid by his throat.

"Look at this failure closely, men!" Chief said as he held the boy off the ground like a ragdoll.

"Let us not forget what God tells us in the book of Deuteronomy." The boy's feet dangled, kicking and arms flailing. "The SEEKERS will turn your children away from following and will serve other gods. And the Lord's anger will burn you down, immediately destroying *you*!" Moments later, the boy's windpipe snapped; his eyes turned crimson with blood, and his head drooped as the life left his body. "You will not fail me! You will not fail *God*!"

Chief threw the boy's body down like trash at a homeless camp. He ascended his pulpit again, looking out onto the men.

"Let that boy's death be an example of what will happen to all of us if we fail our God. God has chosen us to fight for him. He has chosen us to start this new world. Tonight, we rest. Tonight, we fill our bellies. Tonight, we prepare. For tomorrow, we hunt!"

Chief Sanders turned and walked back to his hole. The men stood cheering as if King Arthur himself had given the order for war.

The front door of the Shell station pushed open, striking a silver bell at the top. Kent was startled awake. He had been sleeping below the main floor of the store. In the storage area, with a basement door that led out to the wash way, creek, and city sewer system.

Kent held still, slowed his breathing to near nothing, and listened. His escape route would be through the basement door and head right for the city's sewer system. Even though the rain had caused flooding, he knew no one would pursue him into the sewers while the creeks were raging. He may drown, but at least death would be on his terms.

Footsteps fell, one after another. Kent could hear two men speaking. They were talking about starving and needing meat. They were scavengers, animals. He had met men like this in the past. He knew they were not allies. He knew they would eat his heart, with an out-of-date beer, if they were given the chance.

Kent was a brilliant and resourceful man with so many redeeming qualities. He let his mind go and looked around for anything he could use to help him either fight or aid in an escape.

There it was.

Kent slowly reached behind him and grabbed an old dusty bottle of liquor. It was ancient, but he didn't have much time and had to take a chance. The liquid inside was flammable.

Kent quickly tore off a piece of his shirt and stuffed it inside the neck of the bottle, flipping the bottle upside down to saturate the rag and retrieved a zippo from his pocket.

Kent slowed his breathing and listened.

He could hear them getting closer. He was just a few feet from the basement door, and they were only a few feet from the top of the basement stairs.

Kent's lungs ached from lack of oxygen, and his ears were pounding as sweat rolled slowly down his face. The men were still talking. They were just outside the door above the stairs.

Then, it happened.

Someone opened the door.

Kent heard a foot hit the first piece of wood on the stairs.

"Fuck, this better work!" Kent whispered as he struck the zippo, lighting the rag. The fire burned quick!

With one motion, Kent threw the flaming bottle again the concrete wall at the base of the stairs and ran like hell for the door.

The bottle broke, and he could hear the liquid ignite. A gunshot rang out.

Kent could feel the bullet fly past his left ear as he ran through the door. Then he heard the men screaming. It worked. At least one of them was on fire, and the other one was telling the man to stop moving and get on the ground.

Kent ran and had bought himself just enough time to get away.

He ran to the creek and jumped into the raging water. The creek was swollen from the storm and was heading for the giant culvert, into the city's sewer system.

A second shot rang out, but missed Kent by a mile.

Kent was a great swimmer, but he fought for his life. The water was fast, tossing him around like a football on Sunday. He kept swimming and gasping for every breath of air. Kent tumbled and started to choke on the nasty brown death he was trying to swim in. His mind was beginning to fade to black when a large plastic bag hit him in the face. The bag was full, fluffy, and buoyant.

Kent grabbed the bag and, with the last remaining strength in his upper body, climbed on top of it. He started laughing uncontrollably. "Plastic bottles! A fucking bag of plastic bottles!" he said. Kent rode that bag of lifesaving bottles all the way into the sewer and under the city. Just like turning off a light, the ride was over. Kent got off the bag and looked around at a maze of underground piping. All of the main pipes were tall and would allow him to walk comfortably inside. With smaller concrete tubes, he could probably crawl through those that branched off to different side streets.

"God loves me today! He really does!" laughed Kent.

While still exhausted, Kent picked himself up and began to walk north. Kent knew he was under Route 3, and the pipe he was walking in went on for as far as he could see.

The last class at Mecklenburg High School dismissed at 3:15 p.m. every weekday with little exceptions. The school was small with a senior class of 279 students, but also led the state in school rankings, especially in the fields of life sciences and mathematics. The school was situated along Central Avenue, which was one of the main arterial roads leading from one side of Mecklenburg to the other.

Yale Daily News, the oldest college newspaper, once wrote an article: "The Best Schools in the Mountains." The report ranked Mecklenburg High School as the number-one school in the upper Midwest.

The 3:15 bell rang all the way across campus. All at once, the students got up and made their way out. The buzz of almost three hundred teenagers walking the hallway, all with the same purpose: to leave. It made a special kind of music that every teacher loved. The sound of done, finished for the day; the sound of happiness.

"Well f-f-f-uck," mumbled Philip Bilkowski, a janitor at Mecklenburg Highschool. Every day that the final bell rang, he dropped his broom, dawned the appropriate jacket for the weather, and walked out to the main entrance of the school to direct traffic.

Mr. Bilkowski was an average size but a dark-spirited man. He kept to himself, and while he could blend in without effort, he was awkward to speak with, obviously uneducated, yet logically smart. Strangely, he spoke with a stutter when he became nervous or mad.

Mr. Bilkowski hated his job, hated his life, and hated the students. They treated him like shit, and the last thing he wanted to do every day, was direct traffic, so they didn't have to waste their precious time waiting in traffic to leave school.

But, today of all days, none of Philip Bilkowski's responsibilities or hatred mattered.

Not on this day, for when Philip opened his eyes, a realization swept over him: he was naked, hairless, beaten, and laying behind Bob's Barbershop.

Confused and sick, Philip was now in the parallel world.

Philip sat up, wide-eyed, and woke as hell. His body hurt and his eyes felt week as he looked around, without a clue as to where he was. Philip slowly stood up, unbalanced with a little vertigo, and stumbled around the corner of the building.

"Who the fuck are you, boy?" Philip heard from a shadow outcropping next to the shop.

Philip stopped, and before he could answer, something hit the back of his head, forcing his body to the ground. Two men stood over Philip as he lay bleeding into the concrete alleyway.

Philip's vision was creeping in on him, yet his perception of time stopped. All the movement around him seemed to freeze. There was no sound, no motion, except for the little girl in a ruby-red dress walking in the street, dragging a dog collar without a dog.

The girl turned and looked into Philip's eyes and let go of a white latex balloon. She stared at him with her index finger pressed against her lips and then he heard a faint, "*Shhh…*"

Philip's vision gave way to the darkness, and the two men carried him away.

For the second time, Philip awoke naked, hairless, beaten, bruised, bleeding, and in a weird place.

Philip's head was pounding, not just from the beating, but also from the reality of his situation. He had been grabbing his jacket from his office near the boiler room and woke up naked in this world. *Then I woke again in this room…*

Philip's eyes opened quicker this time around. He sat up and found himself in a concrete room with one light bulb above him, a door in front of him, and a plastic five-gallon bucket in the corner behind him.

Philip was pissed off. Most people would be petrified with fear, but not Philip. Philip was pissed.

He walked to the door and tried to open it. Of course, it was locked. With a splitting headache, Philip raised his right hand, made a hard fist, and began to pound non-stop on the door. After a few moments, his hand began to hurt, so he started to kick the door. Philip was winded, and his pace rapidly declined until he came to a complete stop.

A metal latch echoed in the room as the door slowly opened into the hall. The light poured in, revealing a man standing in the doorway, but a shadow was obscuring his face.

"Who are you?" asked the man.

"Who a-a-am I? Who the f-f-fuck are you, dick bag?" stuttered Philip.

There was no verbal response. The shadow instead opened up a firehose, complete and fast, soaking Philip from head to toe. The water pressure pushed Philip off of his feet and back into the rear wall, robbing him of energy and oxygen.

A few moments later, the shadow-man shut off the water and didn't move.

Philip lay on the cold concrete floor, coughing in pain. He put his hand up to shield his face from any future water treatments.

"What do you want f-f-from me?" asked Philip.

The hose opened again, but this time for a shorter period. The water was brutally cold. It felt like thousands of needles were impaling Philip all at once. It was agonizing!

The water stopped again.

The sound of the water running into the drain was simplistic and strangely soothing to Philip. It had a peculiar sound of escape, a sound of freedom. That water was able to leave and, in his mind, gave him hope.

The shadow began to speak again, but Philip couldn't hear him. Philip was lying on the floor, having flashes of the little girl in the ruby-red dress motioning for him to be quiet. To stop talking; to *shhhh*.

The door shut.

The locking of the metal latch made Philip's hopes and dreams fade off like a sunset in hell. He knew he was momentarily trapped, and an escape was on pause. He simply sat on the floor, still naked, still hairless, and still pissed off about it. Confused, Philip sat and waited.

Philip was in a small eight-by-eight room in the back of an old Walmart Supercenter on the far west side of Mecklenburg. He was miles off of Route 3 and miles from his old familiar Mecklenburg High School.

Inside the Walmart was a slew of THEM. The west side's THEM. Most of them lived in Walmart, but some had small hideouts nearby. Walmart had no water, no electricity, awfully little food, and exceedingly poor leadership. But it did provide a large enough area to be somewhat organized. Although THEY were not as organized or equipped as the eastside faction of THEM. The eastside's Costco was leaps and bounds beyond what the westside's Walmart had become. It was plain to see one side was of higher intelligence than the other.

An alarm sounded in the distance. It was an old fashion hand-cranked siren used to warn of impending air raids during World War II. The sound continued as THEY all moved toward the front windows of the Walmart.

The siren was a warning. The warnings were always different. Sometimes it was for approaching weather, and other times the alarm sounded when an attack was imminent. Regardless of why the alarm was sounding, THEY all knew to look outside and get ready for what was coming.

As THEY all were at the front of the store, the glass began to break. Shards of thick commercial-grade glass crashed in, cutting people morosely.

The men and women moved back away from the windows. Massive chunks of ice were falling from the sky. Hail the size of baseballs. They started out a few at a time, then rapidly picked up in pace. Within a few minutes, the sounds of the ice impacting the rooftop echoing through the store were ear-piercing, and the people screaming was worse.

"Get back from the windows!" screamed a girl as she fell to the ground with eight inches of shard in her leg. The blood was pooling out fast and bright; she would bleed to death soon.

THEY pulled back just enough to be out of danger, but still close enough for a ringside view. The few people that were hurt, lying on the ground, were left to fend for themselves. There was no honor in this group of people, none whatsoever.

The storm seemed to last for a couple of hours. The violence of the storm made it appear to last forever. By the time it had finished, night had fallen, and THEY needed to regroup and recover.

During the storm, Philip sat in the concrete box listing to the madness. He laughed. He didn't have any care in the world as to what was happening outside of his makeshift cell. That is, until his door cracked open, letting hope creep back in with the light.

Philip stood up and limped to the door. He paused and listened the best he could while the storm crashed into the roof above him. He couldn't tell if anyone was outside the door or not.

"F-f-fuck it," he stuttered as he pushed the door open.

Philip was alone.

No one on site, the door must have unlocked during the storm. Philip looked left and right down the hall and quickly took off running.

Philip's body hurt like hell, but his adrenaline pushed him as he ran to the back of that shitty ass Walmart, looking for an exit point. He was still naked and had stepped in human feces several times on his way to the exit.

Philip found one of the back doors ajar and paused. The hail was massive and coming down like a summer monsoon in Vietnam.

"A-a-ahhhh hell," Philip said as he looked around for something to hold over himself so he could make a run for it. And like a gift from God, Philip found an old, grey, industrial garbage bin on wheels. It would barely fit out the door, but if he turned it upside down, it would work much like a turtle shell.

Philip did just that; he emptied it out, also finding an old sweatshirt and shorts. He put the clothing on and flipped the garbage bin over himself.

For the next thirty minutes of the storm, Philip slowly moved the bin through the rear parking lot toward the wood line. Once at the woods, Philip took a deep breath, and with a leap of faith, he pushed over the bin and jumped into the woods, hoping the trees would provide cover as he ran.

Philip ran as large oak tree canopies exploded above but shielded him completely.

Philip ran and ran.

He ran until Walmart was miles behind him. He ran until his feet bled, and he was near exhaustion.

Chief Sanders laid on top of his whore. She moaned softly as he thrust himself inside of her. This wasn't love, but simple hedonistic pleasures. She was skinny and hungry, so she allowed him to finish inside of her in exchange for a sandwich.

Chief stood up, got dressed, and walked out of his hole. He always got off just before heading out on the hunt.

Chief grabbed his backpack, rifle, and assembled his men.

"It's time to hunt men. It's time to stop those that seek to exit God's new world. It's time for us to purify what is ours!" said Chief.

"Till death, and after, we will follow you, sir!" came from the small crowd.

Chief looked at the men, smiled, and turned to exit the Costco. The hunting party followed, consisting of ten of Chief's best shooters. As a contingency, the rest of the group stayed behind to run operations and provide security for the remaining faction.

They were headed to the forest to where their men were killed by a SOLO named Kent.

Chapter 18: The Search Begins

Bran took a deep breath as his ears stood tall. Bran's nose was to the wind and ten thousand times better than any human nose could ever be. Bran was a three-year-old Belgian Malinois—one of smartest working dogs. He stood tall, weighed ninety-seven pounds, was strawberry blond, and his human was Charlotte Kane.

"You smell one, boy?" Charlotte whispered as she pulled the scope close, resting her face into the cheek weld.

Charlotte and Bran were situated on a rooftop outcropping, on the lower end, the third story of The Hotel Mecklenburg. Charlotte had been a police sniper in the real world and would often utilize her skillset during guard duty.

Bran's breathing changed, and body posture alerted Charlotte to the presence of a person nearby. She scanned the area in front of the hotel toward Route 3, looking for a target.

"I'm looking boy, just hush your mouth and lay down," she said as the dog whimpered.

"Gotcha," Charlotte exclaimed as she leveled her rifle steady and intently focused her right eye in her fixed ten-powered scope. This was not her typical rifle or scope, but the it was the best she could put together in this parallel world.

Four hundred yards away and thirty feet below, Charlotte was looking at a man crawling out from the earth. He was pulling himself into the road, through a manhole in the center of Route 3.

Charlotte kept the man in view, judging him quickly. She needed to know if he was a SOLO or one of THEM. She wanted to know before she squeezed the trigger.

The man was tall and skinny, wet, and looked tired. She kept him in her scope, as she called down to a small two-man contact team inside the hotel. Their job was to support Charlotte, in case a situation like this happened to unfold.

The man looked normal. Or as normal as it got in this world. He did not appear to be injured or have signs of the "crazy," which caused some people to cannibalize others.

Charlotte held her fire and called down to the contact team.

The man crouched down and began to make his way toward the hotel doors below her position.

"Keep your hands where we can see them," Charlotte announced to the stranger as Bran started to bark.

The man stopped, looked up at Charlotte, and said, "Don't shoot. I mean you no harm. My name is Kent, and I need help. I know the SEEKERS are here, and I may have found a way home."

The toothpick in Charlotte's mouth dropped to the roof. Her mind was on fire with what she thought the man just said. "What did you say—"

Charlotte was interrupted when the contact team opened the doors below her and pulled Kent inside.

Kent was immediately searched and quaintly spoken to. He was offered food and a shower. He took them up on both.

"My name is Kent Prather," he began as the water was poured over him for his first shower in months.

"I have been SOLO in this parallel world for nearly a year, but I swear, it feels like fucking forever. I have seen people, things, and animals, come and go. I stay in the shadows. I avoid everyone." He paused, looking at his arms and legs as he scrubbed with a rag. "I know where everything and everyone is in this town. I've mapped it all. I knew you guys were in this hotel, and I know the people here are nice, and all they want is to find a way home."

More water poured over his head. This time it was cold and took his breath away.

"Damn, that's cold," Kent said as his body was shaking.

"Sorry, it's the best I have right now. But please continue," a voice said.

"There is a faction of THEM on the west side of town inside of the old Walmart. Those guys are slack and not very bright, but still dangerous. There is another faction of THEM on the east side of town in the old Costco. Those guys are well organized and have true leadership. Shit, they have actual electricity too. It's crazy. But those people are perilous."

"More soap?" asked the voice.

"I'm good. I think this last bucket you have coming will finish the job," Kent replied.

The man pored the last bucket slowly over Kent and handed him a towel.

"Thank you so much for the shower. It's been a few months since I've had one," Kent said as he dried himself off.

"You're very welcome. How come it has taken you a year to come find us?" the voice asked.

Kent finished drying off and turned around to where he had heard the man.

"I need to speak with the guy in charge; can you take me to him?" Kent asked.

The man stepped from behind the makeshift shower. "My name is Luke James, sir. I am in charge."

Kent was taken aback that the man in charge was so real and down to earth that he helped him shower the piles of dirt from his body.

"Please continue your story, Kent. Maybe we can help you," he said.

"I've been searching for a year, mostly by myself, for the way home. Again, I've mapped everything and everyone I know. I believe if a rock put us here in this fucked-up world, then there must be a rock that can take us home. Do you agree?"

"We all would agree. We have been searching as well," answered Luke.

"A couple of days ago, I took a trail into a forest that I have been mapping. I knew I was in the area where THEY are known to be. Apparently, three of THEM tried to follow my trail but hit the explosive I left behind. It was my safety valve, in case someone did follow. It killed a couple of THEM."

"I follow; please continue," urged Luke.

"I've killed others too. Yesterday, I was nearly caught but took to the sewers to escape. Those guys were scavengers. But, why am I here? I think I found a way home. And I need your help to get there."

Luke's eyes began to water. His mind instantly thought about holding his wife again and seeing his daughter's smile and hear her yell, "Daddy!" as she ran and jumped into his arms.

"Did you say you found a way home?" asked Luke. "A real way home?"

"Sir, I have searched and searched, and I have it narrowed down to a couple of places. But I can't get close enough on my own to verify. I need a couple of people to help me. It's the only way I can do it."

Luke's face shifted, his eyebrows raised, and a smile formed.

"I'll ready some men; let's develop a plan and get after it first thing either in the morning or as the sun sets, whichever you feel is best…"

The next morning, Luke called a meeting with the elders for the people of the hotel. In an old conference room, they gathered. Most everyone was there, minus the people on security.

"Everyone, this is Kent Prather. He has been SOLO for a long time and came to us yesterday. He needs our help as much as we need his help," explained Luke.

"Kent, the floor is yours," Luke said as he took a seat.

Kent stood up, took a deep breath, smiled, and again began to explain his last year and finally told the group he believed he had found a way home. He had found a way back to the real world.

The air in the room noticeably warmed with anticipation, almost as soon as the words left his mouth.

Hope. Hope was in the air once more. Hope had been missing but was back again. Like an open flood gate, hope filled the group and was there for the taking.

"*How? Where?*" yelled a female in the back.

People began to shift around and whisper.

Kent pulled up his backpack and took out a map. "Everyone, gather around this table, and I'll show you what I've found," said Kent as he unfolded the large map.

The map was of Mecklenburg; it was old and used, with buildings on it that haven't stood in years, but more so, the map was covered with notes and handwritten symbols.

"When I first arrived in this world, I was lost like most of us. But the one thing I had was a drive to get home and a will to survive. I have a little girl, Stacey. I'm all she has, and nothing will stop me from getting back to her. Nothing," Kent explained with a tear trickling down his cheek. "In the real world, I was a retired Army officer and historian. I know the history of this town, this country, of wars and of man. It's what I did for a living, and I was very good at it.

"When I got to this parallel world, my mind was Jell-O. I couldn't understand what I was seeing, nor could I know where I was. Like all of you, I was naked and hairless. My body was beaten down, it felt like a truck hit me. Like I had fallen down a flight of stairs. I was confused, but knew I was still in Mecklenburg. Or, at least, the town looked like Mecklenburg.

"After a few days, it hit me…

"During the summer of 1772, Mecklenburg officials held the last witch trials in the area, and it went horribly wrong. The town had four people, all from the same family. They were tied to poles in the center in the city, ready to burn.

"The legend has it that Abigail Black began to fly above the crowd as she was still tied to her pole. Her eyes were red, and she fought the officials. She was attempting to free the rest of her family when the pit went up in flames. Her husband and daughters burned alive in front of her. The legend says she cursed the town as her family died. She killed several officials that fateful day. Then vanished forever."

The silence in the room was palpable. Kent looked around and knew he had everyone's attention.

"The way home is through the Book of the Black. This book was Abigail Black's journal. She wrote every hex, curse, and spell in it. The theory is, when Abigail put the ink on the paper, the words became a reality, thus, giving birth to her magic.

"Abigail was a mighty witch. She is the reason why Mecklenburg is the way it is today. Abigail is why the town is evil. She is the reason why the town creates and cultivates horror. The blood of her family soured the soil. It soured the town. Abigail saw to it that this town would be ruined for generations to come. That is her curse, that is her legacy.

"I believe this parallel world is in that book, and if it's in that book, then so is the way home," explained Kent. "Historians over the years have mentioned this book, but no one has ever seen it. I believe it's here, in this world."

The room was silent. In the real world, Kent would have been laughed at, but in this world, everyone knew anything was possible and what he was saying was the truth.

"Where is it, the book? Do you have it?" asked Luke.

"That's where I need your help. As you can see on my map, I've searched this town high and low. I have not found the book, but I have narrowed down where it could be."

Luke walked away from the table, looked out into the hallway, took a swig of his now-cold coffee, and said, "Book of the Black, wherever it is, we will find it. WE will find it, and WE will get all of us home!"

Kent continued to speak with the group as he pointed out the first location he needed help finding, "Here. There is a cabin lost in the woods of the national forest. I've searched this forest extensively. I know that the Black's used the river's water, so the cabin is somewhere near the river. But this cabin will also be over two hundred years old, so it may have aged away to obscurity. I've narrowed it down to Doll Island. The island sits in the middle of the river, three miles upstream from the West Avenue wooden bridge, and four miles downstream of the Route 3 bridge. I've searched everywhere but that island. It must be there. I feel it in my bones."

Kent rubbed the stress from his face. "It seems like the closer I get to the book, the more of THEM, I come across."

Kent took a deep breath and continued, "I'll need a small four- or five-man team to help me get on that island, run security for us, and we will find the book."

Charlotte stood up, looked at the map, and placed her right index finger on Doll Island, saying, "If the book is there, we will find it. When we find it, we get everyone home, nothing less. You'll need my dog Bran, and you'll need me."

Kent nodded and began to thank her when Luke said, "Bran is a hell of a dog, Kent; you'll be awfully grateful for his abilities when the time comes. Charlotte, I'll go with you as well." Luke paused for a second, then turned to the group, "I can't force anyone to go, but two more would be helpful."

"Jordon, Juan, and I will go," said Andrew.

"That will work. We will leave just after nightfall. The rest of you keep guard and be safe." Said Luke.

Luke, Charlotte and Bran, Kent, Andrew, Juan, and Jordon all gathered supplies and readied themselves for the journey.

Kent pulled out his map again, orientated it on the table, and pointed to Doll Island. "Here. This is where we are heading, guys. It could take a while to walk there. It's probably a good day's walk. I have a route planned; you'll have to trust me on this."

"Kent, you guide us there, we will provide security and keep Bran on point. His nose has saved us on more than one occasion," said Luke.

The six-man group grabbed their gear and headed for the front doors.

"God speed, gentlemen!" A female screamed in the background as they walked outside into the unknown.

Kent led the group right to the manhole he crawled out from the day before, in front of the hotel on Route 3.

"Down there," Kent said as he moved the heavy cover to the side.

The group took turns, lowering themselves into the sewer. One at a time, and then lastly, Bran was handed down to Charlotte.

The drainage system under the road was rather tall, square, damp with an echo that traveled forever.

"Down here, sound and light will give us away. It travels quick and far. Be mindful of this and act accordingly," Kent whispered.

They all nodded.

Charlotte led the way down the coarse concrete drainage with Bran. Kent was behind her, directing the group as they walked with everyone else in a file.

They moved for nearly an hour without turning. The sewer was dark with ambient light from the storm grates above them. It was damp with a foul stench reminding the group of rotten meat and burned electronics.

Kent stopped the group, confirmed their location on his map, and motioned to Charlotte to make a right into a smaller pipe.

"That one," Kent said as he motioned to a pipe about four feet off the ground on their right. This pipe was smaller and would force them to crawl for an unknown distance in near pitch-black conditions.

"In there?" asked Luke.

"Yeah. It's gonna get tight in there. But this will lead us close to our entry point for the forest. Trust me," Kent said.

Bran's ears stood tall, and he cocked his head intently, staring down the concrete sewer. The group took notice, as Bran began to growl at the blackness in front of him. Then they heard it.

Footsteps. Wet, sloppy, uneven footsteps in the distance, heading toward them.

"Move now," whispered Kent as he grabbed Bran and shoved him into the smaller pipe.

"Charlotte, move. Get going. Everyone get the fuck moving!" Luke said as the pace of the footsteps picked up, gaining ground, getting oh so close.

Charlotte climbed into the pipe and started crawling. Everyone else followed with Juan pulling up the rear. They crawled fast. The pipe was about three feet in diameter—tight, claustrophobic.

The group crawled.

In a blackness that could only be duplicated in the deepest depths of the ocean, they crawled.

The pipe wasn't the worst part of this movement. The worst part was the noise. The noise that traveled through the pipe with no escape. The noise that was created by the group's action. Noise from the steady building of water that drained naturally in the pipe. It flowed under their bellies, between their legs, and into their souls.

The minds couldn't digest this noise, it couldn't comprehend the sounds. Was it in front of them? Or behind them? Were they causing the noise? Or, was someone or something else in the pipe with them? Did the sloppy wet footsteps climb into their pipe? Were they now being chased?

Their minds, each one of them inside that black pipe, were going mad.

Bran whimpered.

The group stopped. No one moved.

This pipe was a cement coffin, already six feet under and void of life.

Charlotte caught her breath, put her cheek against the wet concrete, and slowly calmed herself. She let her mind slow. Let all her thoughts slip away. Then, a smile cracked her face.

Charlotte's mind drifted off to a date night many moons ago. She was sipping a cold Bud Light, getting her legs rubbed in front of a fire. It had been a good day and an even better night.

The noises inside of the pipe had almost evaporated. The only sound left was the water draining inside and started to resemble a small mountain brook. Charlotte smiled more and began to accept she had no control of the situation, but only control over herself and her thoughts.

Juan lay motionless at the end of the group. He strained his ears, listening for anything. Then it happened.

"*Fucking move!*" Juan yelled as a hand grabbed his right ankle.

"You're mine, boy!" someone yelled as the hand pulled Juan close enough for the man to bite into his calf.

Juan screamed in pain. He rolled on his back, kicking the unknown man in his face. The sound of Juan's steel-toed redwings crushing the man's jaw echoed off the piping like fireworks on the Fourth of July.

Everyone moved. They crawled faster and faster. They crawled so hard, blood trails were left behind.

The screams from behind them were unholy.

They crawled for their lives.

The wind blew through the pines on the edge of Carmichael Street. It gently moved the branches in the shadows as a coyote stood on the torso of a giant rabbit, ripping its front legs off, feasting for the first time in days.

The coyotes ate on the edge of the wood line, under the moon, but froze in time, like a broken watch, as Charlotte emerged from the end of a concrete culvert drainage pipe.

Charlotte was eye to eye with the coyote and commanded Bran to attack. Bran's legs pushed off the earth directly for the dirty wild dog. The animal dropped the rabbit's entrails as Bran's jaws clamped around its throat, driving both of them into the woods.

Bran made quick work of the coyote and returned to Charlotte's side.

"Good boy. That's my good man," said Charlotte as she stroked her dog's back.

One at a time, the group surfaced from the sewer. Charlotte and Bran stood guard as they all reconsolidated a few feet into the woods, watching to see if anyone or anything else came from the pipe.

"I don't know what the fuck grabbed me in there, but I don't think it's going to be following us anymore," said Juan.

The group stood still gathering themselves. They were wet, and the air temperature was noticeably colder outside of the sewer. The sky was dark, no moon in sight, with clouds so low, they were beginning to hide the top of the pine trees.

Kent began to shiver. "Do you smell that? In the air."

Jordon took a deep breath and nodded. "I smell snow. It's going to fucking snow. Isn't it? Fuck me."

They all looked at each other as Kent read his map.

"This way," said Kent as he pointed west into the forest.

The group followed him into the thick blackness. The trees were monstrous, and it started to snow.

The wind picked up, blowing slowly across the forest floor as the group walked. Step after step, the snow continued to fall. Minute after minute, the endless black void that was the forest turned shades of grey and then white. The temperature continued to drop.

Bran again was out front, and the group was naturally spread out abreast of each other, three-wide, with the others behind them.

After hours of walking, the woods looked like a never-ending mirror of pine trees, with a few mossy oaks tree sprinkled about.

In the distance, Jordon began to hear an eerie sound. "Kent, Luke, do you guys here that sound?"

The sound was similar to a tree branch rhythmically rubbing across a window seal or even two tree trunks rubbing against each other in the distance. It was an unnatural sound that couldn't be pinpointed but got louder the farther the group walked.

"I hear it," Charlotte said as she took a knee and listened with more purpose than before. "It's just up ahead. In front of us."

Bran's ears were standing tall as he became restless.

Charlotte pulled up behind an oak tree and began scanning the area with her scoped rifle. The visibility was low, and even though she could hear the sound, she couldn't pinpoint the source.

They all decided to pick up and keep moving forward. The farther they moved, the thicker the forest became. The thicker the woods became, the darker and more challenging it was to navigate. Then the trees parted way, opening up to the sounds.

As Charlotte and Bran moved into the open trail created by the trees, they identified the sounds.

Ropes.

The sound was of a row of ropes hanging from tree branches. They were rubbing on the trees as the wind pushed the bodies attached by their necks. People were hanging in the middle of this forest, swinging with the wind. A row of bodies hung in the air with an unhallowed yellow light emitting from the treetops. People were swinging in the wind like human windchimes.

"What the fuck is this? Are you fucking kidding me?" asked Luke while letting his jaw hang open.

The forest was so thick, the group had no choice but to keep moving on the path created by the hanging bodies. One by one, they passed the bodies above them. They walked right under the windchimes of death.

"Keep moving," said Kent as he took the lead. "Follow me and don't stop."

The group put their heads down and followed. As they moved, their feet mixed the fresh snow with the blood falling from the bodies. This turned the trail a horrific shade of crimson, like the floor of a slaughterhouse.

They kept moving.

And it kept snowing.

Chapter 19: Hotel Supplies

Tom Porter woke up in his room, absent of Charlotte. The area was drab, cold, emotionless. He looked around and began to feel lonely again. His mind drifted to his wife Kate, and how pretty her face was. How she would smile. He laughed for a second. Then reality seeped back in. He was still not home.

The hotel was lively with people this morning. Some new folks had come in last night and were getting acquainted, as others were keeping security and running the daily operations.

Tom walked downstairs to the dining room. He grabbed a plate and filled it from the usual morning buffet. The eggs were out, and so were the regular grits.

"Where's the normal stuff?" Tom asked the guy working the area.

"Supplies are low. When this happens, a group of people go out and search for more. Typically, we have groups out looking daily, but this week we are a little short on manpower," the man replied.

Tom grabbed a small box of Fruit Loops and an apple. "Thanks," he said as he walked over to an empty table.

His mind began to toss and turn as he consumed his thankful yet straightforward breakfast. *Supplies*, he thought. *Scavenge for a purpose, for the group.* He thought maybe that could be how he made a difference, or how he contributed to the group. He ate his apple and stood up.

Tom walked back to the man working the buffet. "Sir, thanks for breakfast. My name is Tom."

The man reached out and shook his hand. "I'm Brian; nice to meet you."

"Brian, I'd like to help. Who can I talk to about helping to gather supplies for the group?" Tom asked.

"Well it's my lucky day; you're talking to the guy. I need bodies to go out with me in a couple hours," Brian replied as he displayed more apples. "Get a small bag, with a change of clothes, a pistol, a knife, and I'll pack you a dinner."

"Sounds good. Where should I meet you?" asked Tom.

"Right here. We will meet here in two hours."

Tom nodded and walked back to his room to get ready. His stomach wasn't full, but his heart was. Tom was full of a sense of purpose and meaning.

Tom was able to find spare clothing, a 9mm Glock, and sixty rounds of ammo. He was lucky Charlotte, his absent roommate, had these items inside of a bag in their room. He also found a small three-inch folding knife that fit nicely in his front right pocket.

Two hours later, Tom was sitting back in the dining room, ready to go.

"Tom, glad you could make it," Brian said as he walked in from the kitchen area. "Let's see what you packed."

Tom emptied out his bag, and Brian nodded with content. "Add this and pack it all back up," Brian said as he handed Tom an MRE (meal ready to eat).

A few minutes later, more people came in with packs and took a seat.

"Looks like we are all here. Everyone, this is Tom," said Brian.

Tom waved and smiled.

"We have twelve people now, and as usual, we will assign teams of two for an area of town to search. Tom, you will be with me. Everyone else is an old hand at this. Well, almost everyone. As a reminder, we stay out no longer than twenty-four hours and get as much as we can carry. Then head back. It's that simple. Our priority is food, water, weapons, and medicine. We will also stagger our start from different exits of the hotel, just in case someone is taking note."

Fifteen minutes later, Tom and Brian walked out the front door, north of Route 3, and headed toward the run-down Starbucks.

It was colder outside than it appeared. No clouds in the sky, but neither was the sun.

"Tom, we will focus on a six-block range northwest of the Starbucks and mark the buildings off as we go. I've had some good luck in that area. Shit, back in the real world, I used to sleep with a girl who lived over that way," laughed Brian as the two men walked.

A few blocks later, Tom and Brian arrived at Starbucks. The traditionally brilliant green of the company's sign was dull, faded, and cracking from age.

Brian reached for the side door but stopped his effort as he noticed the door was locked. *Strange*, he thought, as he left it unlocked the last time he was there.

"Let's try the back door," said Tom. Brian nodded, and both men walked around back.

Tom froze as sounds from the dumpster behind the store bounced across the parking lot. He turned and looked at Brian. Brian looked back at Tom, mouthing the words, "What the fuck was that?"

Tom took a deep breath, drew his pistol, and moved directly toward the sound. Brian started to follow him, but his feet were glued to the pavement with fear.

Tom moved behind the dumpster as the noise grew louder. Brian held his breath in anticipation of gunshots, while his mind plotted a route to run back to the hotel.

Silence fell momentarily.

"Fucking trash pandas. Damn, asshole raccoons eating garbage," yelled Tom.

Brian's muscles eased as his lungs pulled in air.

"I about pissed myself, man," Brian said as he turned his attention back to the rear of the store.

"Fuck this world," replied Tom as he walked with Brian.

The rear door was unlocked, and both men walked into the old Starbucks with ease. Their flashlights glistened off the spiderwebs in the corner of the storage room.

"Coffee. We need lots of coffee. Let's pack both bags and take it straight back to the hotel. Then we will head back out."

Tom agreed and started grabbing what was left of the Pike Place roast and Sumatra.

Brian walked to the front counter. "Tom, get in here!" His jaw was open as he stared at the register. Tom hustled in and noticed a man standing in the corner, his head leaned against the wall. His arms were out of view, in toward his body.

"Hello?" Tom said and then noticed the man was standing in a pile of red Jell-O. His mind was battling what his eyes were seeing, then it hit him. The man wasn't standing in Jell-O—it was coagulated blood. A lot of it. So much so, he knew the man had to be dead.

Tom kept his pistol tight to his body, walking over to the man. He put his hand on his shoulder, immediately realizing the man was as hard as concrete. Rigor mortis had long taken over the man's body.

On the cash register was a petrified human hand. It obviously belonged to the man standing in the corner. It was cleanly cut, like a guillotine took it off. Apparently, the man stood in the corner until he bled to death.

"What a fuck show this place is," Brian said as he packed more coffee in his backpack.

Tom put his pistol up and walked away from the dead man. He grabbed his backpack and finished filling it. "I'm ready to go, Brian."

Brian nodded, slung his bag on his back, and started to walk back to the storage room.

Tom walked toward the front door. "I need to get a real coffee mug." He reached out to grab a mug, but as soon as his hand pulled it from the shelf, he let go, and it shattered across the floor. Tom had zero reaction to this. His attention was on the community bulletin board, and the missing person flyers posted.

Tom stepped back and pointed at the flyer in the dead center of the board.

"What is it?" asked Brian.

"That girl. I've seen her before. I've seen this missing person flyer before. Right here, on this same community board, but in the real world. I have fucking seen her before. My work partner, Walter, saw her in the real world, before I woke up in this fucking world! I swear to Christ; Walter saw her in the real world. In that very same ruby red dress. She was dragging a leash and dog collar, with no dog."

Brian walked over to the board and stared at the little girl. "You've seen her here?"

"No. Walter did, in the real world. Before I got here. Before everything," Tom replied as his head started to hurt. "There has to be a way home."

Tom and Brian dropped off their coffee supplies at the hotel and grabbed a quick bite in the dining room. They were mentally tired, but the community established within the hotel needed a lot of supplies. The coffee was a nice treat, but the food was their next priority.

The men finished eating, grabbed their backpacks, and once more headed into the fucking circus town.

Tom and Brian walked northwest of the Starbucks. Their new target was Big Ben's Groceries, a "mom and pop" kind of place about ten blocks from the hotel.

Brian plotted buildings on his map, writing quick notes as they walked. The sky was still a greyish-blue, without any clouds and barren of sunlight.

The men walked and twenty "run of the mill" minutes later, they were in the parking lot of Big Ben's Groceries. A handful of cars were parked in spaces, and shopping carts were sitting around. Weird. Like the business was hopping at one point, and then everyone vanished. But then again, every building they went into was a different scene, telling a different story. And all the cars were the same color: white.

On their way to Big Ben's front door, Tom and Brian glanced into each vehicle they passed. They were all vacant. No one around. Just an overwhelming sense of hollow loneliness. Then the wind picked up, pushing the smell of bloated bodies in the air.

Tom stopped, turning his head north. "Do you hear that? That sound, over there," he said while pointing skyward at a black mass in the distance.

The men were thirty yards from the store when the wind began to gust strong enough to knock them off of their feet.

"Gotta get inside now!" yelled Tom.

"Why is everything in this fucking place so damn difficult?" Brian replied as he made a dash for the door.

The winds continued, and the men bounced off the pillars holding up the overhang to the business. The sky was turning black as Tom and Brian pushed open the sliding front door. Air escaped the inside as the door squeaked, gaping just enough for them to squeeze through it.

Tom, now inside, quickly pushed the door shut as a thick blackness consumed the outside of the store. The blackness arrived by way of the wind, with millions of individual motions inside of it. Then the sound came.

The blackness became thicker as the sound got louder.

"Do you hear that?" Tom asked rhetorically as he stared at the blackness suffocating the storefront windows.

"I know that sound. As a child, in the hot summers on my uncle's farm in PA..." Brian said with a pale face as he backed away.

The blackness consumed the store, just as it consumed their minds.

"*Locusts!*" both men said in unison.

Tom and Brian turned away from the door and walked deeper into the store. The darkness consumed the building as the outside became incrusted with insects.

Chapter 20: Hunting of Men

For two days, Chief Sanders and his hunting party made their way through the woods with no luck at all. The trail had gone cold. The man Chief Sanders was hunting, was a savvy one. A veteran of this parallel world and had honed the art of escape over time.

The sky south of them, toward the Black River, was ominous and full of dark swirling thick clouds, and Chief knew to keep his men away from that kind of unpredictable weather.

"Men make camp here for the night. Tomorrow we continue to move east, away from the weather, toward the mine," Chief ordered. "Get a fire going and break out the bottle."

The sun rose over the horizon, or at least the light shined through it. The sun itself has never been seen in this world, but light in the sky comes and goes every day.

The men woke up one at a time. Stretching and yawning, they began to pack their gear.

"We move out in an hour, men. Get some food in ya and keep a sharp eye out. God's will, be done today," Chief said.

The men did as Chief Sanders ordered. With three men on security at all times, they each ate breakfast, and resupplied the water. Within the hour, the men were ready to move.

Chief Sanders led the expedition, with Ziggler on point. One boot in front of the other, the men made their way east toward the Duke corporate mine. Like a row of ducklings, they followed Chief through the forest. Until they came to the field.

The men stared from the wood line, intent on leaving the forest for the town, but froze with concern and confusion as they gazed upon a field of white balloons. They were all eye-level, latex white balloons with streamers that entered the ground itself. They looked as if they grew out of the earth, in perfect rows. Acres upon acres of white balloons.

"What's the hold-up? Move your asses," Chief said as he walked to the front of the formation. He looked into the field and shook his head. Chief was used to fucked-up mental scenery in this parallel world. He was unfazed. "Get moving. Down the middle toward that big oak tree in the center."

"Yes, sir," replied Ziggler as he led the men out of the woods and into the center of the balloons.

As soon as the men approached the balloons, they heard children laughing. There was no source to the sounds, nor pattern that could be understood. Every so often, for brief moments, children's laughter echoed around the balloons.

At eye level, the balloons were uniformed and caused the men to push the white latex bulbs out of their way as they moved. Sounds of the men walking echoed with a squeal, and the static electricity in the air was tangible.

The closer the men came to that old oak tree, the more the ground softened from brown dirt to a sloppy maroon mud. The closer the men got to the tree, the harder their hearts beat.

The men slowly walked, and the sounds of giggling children followed.

Philip slept the last few nights in the forests. His feet often bled from the escape. He was starving and near hypothermic. But more importantly, Philip was pissed off.

He woke to the smell of death, just as he did most mornings. Death in this world smelled like a bloated deer left on the side of the road (after a kid popped it with a stick, in the heat of the summer).

Philip picked himself up and moved through the woods during the morning light. He was weak and needed food soon, or death would be knocking on his door.

"F-f-f-fuck," he said under his breath. "I got to f-f-find some f-f-f-food."

He struggled but reached the peak of the ridgeline he had been walking since yesterday. On the ridge, he could see into the valley and an open area a few hundred yards below him.

The open area was white, with one tree in the center. On the east side of that area were buildings, and buildings meant civilization, and that meant food.

So, he walked. Philip put one foot in front of the other and headed for the open area. He was mentally and physically exhausted but knew his chances of survival waited for him inside one of those buildings.

Philip limped his way down the ridgeline and noticed something strange about that white of the open area. As he got closer Philip realized the open area was a field of white balloons. A uniformed field of white balloons with one giant oak tree in the center.

Mentally, Philip was finally getting used to the fuck show that this parallel world produced. He stood looking above the balloons and noticed a perverted movement within them. It was moving toward the old oak tree. He didn't know what was causing the stir, but it was headed in his direction.

Philip looked around quickly and altered his route. He had to get away from whatever was inside of that sea of balloons but still get to the buildings. He moved with stealth and as fast as his mangled feet would allow.

Tree after tree Philip passed. One tree at a time got him away from the evil that was headed his way.

Philip walked to the edge of the wood line and could still hear the movement in the distance, but it was no longer gaining on him. He paused, obscured by the trees, and looked for any signs of danger before making his way to the rear of the building fifty feet to his front.

Nothing. The coast was clear. Philip moved quickly, but with a noticeable gimp.

Philip limped over to the building's back door, noticing a thick black layer of something spanning from the roof to the middle of the door. The blackness was moving.

Philip stood at arm's length staring at the black mass moving over the door. His first instinct was to leave and look for another building, but his time was limited. Again, he could hear movement behind him in the woods. Whatever was in that nightmare-infested balloon field had made its way to the woods. What the fuck was it?

Philip's brain was fluttering, and he quickly made the decision to take a chance. He reached toward the door, and the black mass parted like the Red Sea. The door was unlocked and opened outward with little effort. Philip entered the building, and as he shut the door, the blackness consumed the door.

"Was that a door?" asked Brian.

Tom shrugged his shoulders. Both men had taken refuge inside of Big Ben's Groceries and were trapped by the swarm of locusts covering the building.

Tom and Brian were gathering food supplies for the hotel when daylight poured inside from the back of the store. A moment later, the sound of a slamming door echoed through the aisles. The men had searched the store and knew they were alone inside, until now.

Footsteps fell with a dragging sound sprinkled in.

Tom pulled out his pistol. "Follow me," he said while leading Brian slowly toward the sound, yet keeping concealed within a small aisle of holiday cards and old Twinkies. It was positioned in such a way that they could allow the footsteps to pass, setting them perfectly to ambush the visitor from behind.

As step after step, foot drag after foot drag, echoed through the sore, Tom held his position, with Brian turned around guarding their rear. The visitor got closer and closer. Seconds seemed like minutes. Tom was beginning to perspire with salty sweat running down his cheek.

The visitor was about to break past the aisle hiding Tom and Brian. Tom slowed his breathing to a deliberate shallow breath. The visitor was only a few feet away.

Was the visitor one of THEM or a SEEKER or even a SOLO? Could this one be hungry enough for flesh? So many thoughts ran through Tom's head.

The visitor stepped past the aisle, dragging his left foot. He stopped and turned his head toward Tom. And with a sound of porcelain hitting a countertop, Tom put his pistol against the man's front teeth.

"Show me your fucking hands," Tom said with a calmness reminiscent of answering a phone call from a friend.

The man stood as firm as concrete. His breathing completely stopped, and his heart began to race as he raised his hands to his shoulders so Tom could see they were empty.

Brian stepped from behind Tom and stared at the man. "Who are you?" he asked.

Calmly the man replied, "Philip Bilkowski."

"Philip, put your hands on top of your head and turn away from me," Tom explained while pressing the pistol firmly into Philip's teeth. This in turn helped the man turn around.

Philip slowly complied.

With his hands on top of his head, Philip began to think of how things were going to unfold.

Brian walked over and quickly searched Philip for any weapons. Satisfied that Philip was unarmed, Brian nodded at Tom, indicating he was safe.

"Philip, turn around. Take a seat on the ground and put your hands under your ass. Do as I say, now," Tom ordered as he backed away just a few feet.

Philip Bilkowski complied.

"Now, that we know you're not an immediate threat, Philip, please tell us your story. Tell us what the fuck you're doing in this God-forsaken land," Tom said as he lowered his pistol.

Philip's shoulders relaxed, and he took a few deep breaths. "The f-f-fact that you ha-ha-haven't killed me yet leads me to believe you two are not with the a-a-assholes who took me a f-f-f-few days ago."

Philip shook his head and let out a little stress-relieving laugh. "I'm a f-f-freaking janitor at Mecklenburg High School, I wa-wa-was going to get my jacket a f-f-few days ago and woke up here. In this world. I wasn't awake long be-be-before I was knocked out and taken captive. I woke up for the second time in a f-f-fucking Walmart, getting a water hose as if I was a f-f-four-alarm fire."

Tom and Brian listened intently to the man's story. He was wearing a pair of tattered sweatpants and a shirt with several rips and bloodstains. The man's feet were swollen, black, and bleeding. He had obviously been through hell.

Tom took the next thirty minutes and explained to Philip everything he knew. He told him about THEM, the SEEKERS, and SOLOS. He said to Philip that if he chose, he could come to join them at the hotel and wait for the SEEKERS to return with a possible way back home.

Philip looked at his beat-down body. Then at his clothing. He looked at his hands, swollen and hurting. With a tear rolling down his cheek, Philip looked up at Brian, then over at Tom, and replied, "I'd really like to go with you guys."

The flood gate of tears opened as Philip realized, for the first time in this parallel world, he had found hope and the stress melted out of his mind and body through the river of tears.

Chief Sanders walked through the balloons, listening to children giggling. His jaw clenched with stress as he moved toward that tall old oak tree.

"Keep moving, men," Chief said while hoping they were close to the end of this bizarre field.

Ziggler was upfront leading the group past the giant oak. "It opens to the forest a little way past this tree," he said with hope in his voice.

The men followed. As each man passed that tree, the ground became softer and softer. The earth under their feet turned to liquid, and Ziggler was sucked inside. Disappeared into the planet. Gone. No longer existent. Vanished.

The men stopped. They were in disbelief as Sanders yelled, "Get the fuck back!" Chief Sanders took off running at a ninety-degree angle from the oak tree, yelling, "Follow me!" The harder he pushed, the firmer the earth below him became. The men, while struggling, followed his lead.

The balloons were bouncing off his face, and the children's laughter became louder. He ran toward a wood line in the distance. Sanders and his men ran for their lives while the voices of children laughed.

Sanders reached the end of the balloons and jumped into the woods. He stopped, turned around, and waited for his men to join him. He could see the balloons moving toward him. One at a time, his men emerged from the balloon field, but not all of them made it.

Like an unforeseen car crash, every balloon in the field burst at one time. The sound was deafening, and blood filled the air. Each balloon had been full, and now the field was a river of red. Three of the men, including Ziggler, never made it out. They were all gone—vanished into the earth.

"Let's move. Nothing can be done for those men. We have to move, or we will join those poor bastards," Sanders ordered as he walked into the woods. The men looked at each other and quickly followed.

"At least the children stopped laughing," said one of the men.

Chief Sanders led his remaining men through the woods while his mind quantified what he had just witnessed: a field of balloons turned to a river of blood, killing three of his men. Sanders thought it wasn't much different from the book of Genesis. It preached about the story of Cain and Abel and how, at the end of that story, the earth was left cursed to drink Abel's blood. Sanders thought it was God's will, and his will be done. He walked, passing tree after tree and thinking about the books of the Bible, punishment, and death.

Philip picked himself up and wiped his face clean. "Thank you a-a-again," he stuttered.

"Philip, look around and see if you can find something new to wear. You look like shit." Brian chuckled. "I saw an aisle of work boots against the wall on the other side of the store. Tom and I will finish gathering food and supplies. We will head back to the hotel when you're ready."

Philip nodded his head and walked off, looking around. He headed toward the area Brian had seen the boots.

Tom continued to gather canned goods, packing his backpack to capacity and then packing a second one he would also carry—one on his front and one on his back. Brian did the same.

Philip stood in front of a wall of boots, eating peaches from a can. They were old but filled his belly, and the juice went down without him taking a breath. For the first time in forever, Philip had a smile on his face as he looked for a size twelve pair of boots.

"The last pair," Philip whispered with a grin.

Philip sat on the floor, pulled on a fresh pair of socks, and a pair of red-wing steel-toed boots. A perfect fit. Small victories, but in this world, those were the biggest victories.

Philip, Brian, and Tom scavenged Big Ben's for supplies. Altogether they packed four backpacks and two totes with much-needed canned foods, dried foods, rope, ammo, clothing, candles, flashlights, batteries, and more. This location had provided well for them and would give so much more in the future. Brian pulled out his map, marked the spot, and added a note of returning for multiple trips.

The men were happy and feeling accomplished.

"Now, to just get back to the hotel," Brian said with a smile as he pulled out an old six-pack of Pabst Blue Ribbon beer. He handed a can to each of the guys. "An old-ass beer is better than no beer at all!"

In unison, they cracked open a can and started chugging. Within a couple of seconds, the beer was drained.

"F-f-fuck me; that was horrible," said Philip.

"Yeah, but it's better than being dead," answered Tom.

The men took a minute, downing the remaining beer from the original six-pack, gathered their bags, and headed for the front door. The light was starting to drain from the sky, giving way to nightfall.

"It's time to get back to the hotel, boys," Brian said as he slid open the front door.

One at a time, Philip, Brian, and Tom walked out into the abyss of the parallel world.

Chief Sanders and his men took a knee. They stopped before the edge of the woods, as it gave way to a road and an open parking lot on the other side.

The air was motionless. Not a sound. The atmosphere was eerie as night began to blacken the sky.

The men knew not to move. They knew not to make a sound, but rather take a few minutes to look, listen, and feel for movement or signs of life. They were listening for any sounds that could confirm any kind of danger. But, just as important, they would close their eyes and feel their surroundings for anything out of the ordinary.

Ziggler was gone. Ate by the earth. Chief Sanders needed a new lieutenant. A new guy he could trust with orders. A new guy who would do what he asked without question. A "yes" man.

"Chet. Chet Wigman," Sanders whispered out to his men.

"Yes sir; here," Chet said as he slowly moved to Sanders.

Sanders pulled out a four-inch serrated blade Spyderco and flipped it open. The edge was razor-sharp and reflected the last bit of daylight, across Sanders' face.

"God just spoke to me, Chet. He told me that you must kill the weakest link in our team," Sanders explained as he handed Chet the knife.

Chet looked at the knife in his hand and looked up at Sanders. "I'm sorry. What do you want me to do?"

Sanders looked at Chet, thinking what a fucking shit bird he was to question him.

"Trashman, upfront," ordered Sanders with a low voice.

Trashman crawled over as quiet as he could. "Yes, sir."

"Trashman, God spoke to me. He asked that Chet take this knife and kill the weakest member of our team. But he hasn't done it," Sanders explained as Chet handed him back the knife.

"Sir, I just don't understand," Chet said as Trashman took the knife and opened Chet's throat with it. His voice cut short when his windpipe was severed, and blood poured down his throat and outside all over him.

"He was the weakest link," Trashman said as he wiped the knife on his pants, folded it, and handed it to Sanders. "God's will be done."

"I thought he was. I mean, he hasn't killed one person in front of me. That's absurd. but I also knew you wouldn't let God or me down," Sanders said as he looked into Trashman's eyes. "Ice runs in your veins. I fucking love it. God loves it, and that's what we need to stop people from leaving God's new world."

"Ziggler is gone. He was a fine lieutenant. Now that's your job. Do what I say without question and live to rule this world," said Sanders.

Trashman nodded, accepting the position.

Tom, Brian, and Philip made their way across Big Ben's parking lot, passing all of the vacant white vehicles. All three men were carrying at least their own bodyweight in supplies. The hotel would be happy to see these men, but more delighted to get the supplies.

Trashman took a knee, still hidden by the woods, and he looked out into the parking lot.

Movement.

Trashman's eye caught a dark movement between the white vehicles. An older model Ford pickup and a small Honda partially obscured a man walking. The man passed the Honda, giving way to the other men behind him. Men with packs. Men carrying supplies. Three of them in total. He quickly signaled Sanders, and the hunt was on.

"Tom, can you reach that pack of Camels you snagged?" Brian asked with a smile as he stopped and turned toward him.

Tom dug a pack out from the top of the backpack he was carrying on his chest. "Keep walking, and I'll light you one up."

Tom put two Camel filters in his mouth, took out a newly acquired zippo, and torched them both. He took a deep pull. The embers were fire red as the smoke burned into his lungs. It felt like forever ago he had enjoyed a good quality smoke.

"Here you go, dick," Tom said with a smile as he handed over one of the Camels.

Brian took a deep pull and held the smoke in for a brief second. For once in a really long time, Brian was relaxed. His body was loose, and his mind was mellow. The problems went away for a brief moment or two.

All three men continued to walk across the parking lot, heading southeast back toward the hotel. The night air was calm and beginning to crisp.

Brian took in another lung full of smoke, and as he exhaled, he noticed Philip fall to the ground as if his legs gave out. He fell face-first onto the pack he had strapped to his chest in slow motion. As Philip lay on the asphalt, he heard the gunshot echo through the night. His mind was no longer content at the moment.

Brian and Tom looked at Philip on the ground, rolling in a pile of his own blood, screaming.

In Brian's mind, the world slowed to a crawl. He turned his attention to the wood line, past the cars closest to the main road. He blinked his eyes, and within seconds, armed men were exiting the woods yelling at them to get on the ground.

Tom and Brian quickly complied.

Three men were on the ground, with Chief Sanders standing over them. Tom and Brian's hands were empty and raised in submission. Philip lay shot in the gut, pissed off.

"My name is Chief Sanders. As you can tell, you are all fucked. No one is coming to help you."

"F-f-f-fuck you. I'll cut your head off," screamed Philip as his blood leaked all over the dirty ground.

Sanders pulled out a "Dirty Harry" kind of revolver, pulled the hammer back, and with a quick trigger squeeze, shut Philip's defiantly stuttering mouth.

"As I was saying. My name is Chief Sanders, and I'm here to tell you one thing. You're never leaving God's new world!" He explained this with a smirk from ear to ear. "Your friend thought he could lift my skirt, and I'd drop my panties. He thought wrong."

Tom looked over at Brian, then at Philip as he lay motionless in blood. The look on Brian's face was absent of fear but instead persisted of annoyance and hatred. Tom felt like they were alone, but needed to buy their time before fight-or-flight could take place. Currently, they were vastly outnumbered.

Tom knew now was the time to play the game, or they would both die.

Chapter 21: Doll Island

The "human windchimes" finally stopped as the ridgeline dipped into a small valley. Luke, Charlotte and Bran, Kent, Andrew, Juan, and Jordon all were mentally exhausted and near-frozen in the almost blizzard-like conditions.

Luke looked around and noticed a large uprooted oak tree, creating a natural wall of dirt and would provide them protection from the direction of the wind. "There," Luke said as he pointed to the downed tree. "Everyone grab some wood, and we can build a fire while we use that oak to shelter from the wind."

The group complied and spread out looking for deadfall and anything dry that would burn while Luke used his hands to dig out the snow around the base of the tree. Within fifteen minutes, Luke had a lifesaving fire roaring, safe from the wind.

Luke and the others huddled around that warm, soothing fire and the life-extending yellow and orange dancing flames.

"Everyone stay close tonight. Keep warm. The fire will provide some protection. We will start again in the morning. We aren't far from Doll Island, but the closer we get, the more this world is proving how soured it is. The closer we get, the more I believe the Book of the Black is near and inside of it lays our salvation," Kent said with a stare of complete conviction.

Charlotte brought her dog close. He would keep her warm and alert them of any dangers while they slept. One at a time, the others followed her lead. Huddled together, they survived, and they slept.

The daylight broke, and Bran commenced to bark. Everyone woke up, like a bomb went off, shocking their eyes open. The group had slept for nearly twelve hours but had no concept of passed time.

Kent stood tall, glancing around at the forest. "Where the fuck did the snow go?"

The snow vanished without a trace. The fire was down to embers and ash. The air was cold and the sound of the ropes rubbing against the tree limbs could still be heard echoing through the valley. The sound was haunting.

"Let's get ready to move, guys and gal. This world never stops mind-fucking, does it?" laughed Kent as he crammed his gear back in his pack.

"Here, Bran," Charlotte called to her dog. Nothing. No response. Charlotte tried again, but still nothing. He absolutely would not leave the far side of the downed oak tree. He ignored her, ears standing tall and a snarl across his muzzle.

Charlotte grabbed her pack and hopped over the oak. "What's wrong, boy? You smell something?"

Charlotte looked up and scanned the forest. She caught a small glimpse of why Bran was laser focused. The wind was blowing in her face, and she knew Bran was smelling oncoming death. A few hundred yards away, a dark mass, similar to a man but much taller, walked toward the horizon.

Charlotte took her waist lead off and hooked it to Bran's collar. "Let's go, boy," she said. Bran was forced to follow.

The group picked up and began to walk farther into the woods. Step after step, they got closer to Doll Island. Luke, Charlotte and Bran, Kent, Andrew, Juan, and Jordon all walked.

And walked...

And walked...

And walked.

After a few hours, Kent stopped the group, circled everyone up, and pulled out his map. "Here. We are here." Kent pointed with a brown pine needle at a spot on the map. "We should be able to hear the river anytime now. About two hundred yards west, we will find it and in the middle is Doll Island."

"There is a natural bend in it, along the shoreline, at the head of the island. If we cross there, the river's current will likely push us to the far tip of the island. The part that looks like the jaw of a doll's head. Hence the name of the island."

"Sounds good. I just hope that fucking water isn't as cold as that snow was yesterday," Jordon said. "If that water is too cold, we won't make it to the other side."

"Let's go get a look at what we are dealing with," Juan said.

The group stood up and walked the last two hundred yards to the edge of the river. They could see the island. The group would have to swim close to a hundred yards across. The current could cause them to swim two or three times that distance. It all depended to the skill of the swimmer and the strength of the river.

Kent bent down and touched the water. Excruciatingly cold. His face said it all. "Fuck me. That bitch is freezing."

"We will have to build a fire as soon as we hit the island. Hypothermia will have already set in. That fire will be the only thing keeping us from freezing to death," Charlotte replied.

Juan tossed an empty plastic bottle toward the center of the river and timed how long it took to make it the length of the island. He did this three times over about an hour. Bottle after bottle, he watched and judged its movements, considering its path and time of travel.

"Kent, I have a plan," Juan said as he looked over the group and back at the river. "I'm the best swimmer you have, and after watching the bottles work in the current, I have an idea of how best to enter the water, to make it to the island. Let me be frank: I know the angle to get to the island in the shortest distance and time based on the current. I have a pack full of rope. I can swim one end of the rope across and tie it to that far side oak tree, then you guys pull it tight and tie your end off. After the rope is well secured on both sides, the rest of our crew can make small rafts and pull themselves across." He smirked from ear to ear.

"Anyone else have a better idea?" Kent asked of the group.

No one spoke up.

The silence was broken by a hawk screeching as it circled above them and then the sound of the thud as the bird impacted the ground after a suicidal dive.

"Are you sure you can do this?" asked Jordon.

With complete confidence and serenity on Juan's face, he turned to his brother Jordon, "If I die, I die. If I live, we all live to see one more day. We all live to possibly make it home. It's not the matter of dying that fears my soul, rather it's the act of failure that would torment me in hell."

Juan dropped his pack at the edge of the river, stripped down most of his clothing, minus his skivvies and a skin-tight t-shirt. He then pulled out a thick trash bag and stuffed it full of his cold-weather clothing and boots. He tied a knot at the top, sealing it the best he could to make it watertight. Juan took one end of the rope and tied it around his waist.

"Bro, once I'm across, I'll tie it off. Once you have your end secured, pull it tight, and the first person across must bring me my cold-weather clothes in that bag," Juan explained as he handed the black trash bag to Jordon. "I'll be near death from that water. If I don't warm up fucking fast, I'm done for."

"I'll get the clothes across myself. Now, stop being a bitch and get the fuck in the water," Jordon replied with a wink and a smirk.

Juan hugged his brother and took his first step toward hell. One foot in front of the other led him to the river. With one deep breath, he stepped into a cold that would change him forever. Juan stepped on a rock after smooth-edged rock under the cold clear river. The lower he went, the icy water crept up his legs. After a few feet, the water was up to Juan's waist, so he pushed off the bottom, and the clock started on the swim of his life.

Juan's upper body submerged in the water, sucking the air out of his lungs, like the vacuum of space. The water felt like a razor blades ripping at his skin.

The pain set in.

Then reality set in.

The pain was tormenting. Juan swam stroke after stroke, unable to take the pain, he simply could not put his face in the water, as it felt like putting his face directly into an open flame. His arms felt like a blowtorch was eating them alive with its flame.

The island was now ninety yards away, but his mind, much like his body, was beginning to fail him.

Right hand, left hand, Juan pulled at the water, making slow progress toward the island as the current pushed him along.

Numbing. He was losing control. Juan could no longer feel his arms or his legs. His body was pulling every ounce of blood from his extremities to keep his organs warm and functioning. Strangely, Juan got the urge to urinate, but couldn't feel his penis to give his bladder relief.

Seventy-five yards away.

Juan could no longer feel the rope around his waist. He stopped swimming and rolled on his back. Juan could see the rope around him but still couldn't feel it. He turned back over and kept swimming, still unable to put his face in the water.

Sixty yards away.

Juan no longer felt the pain of the glacial water. He felt tiny at this point. His mind was open, and the island was still in sight.

Thirty yards away.

Juan stopped swimming. He looked up at the island, and the color in his vision drained to black and grey. He was so tired. Every ounce of Juan's energy was gone. His eyes closed, and his face sank in the water.

Juan swam, so close to the island, yet so far. He noticed a female laying on the bottom of the river. She was under the water, as if it were normal. She was pale with a wrinkled face, grey hair flowing in the current, wearing a black dress down to her feet, and no shoes.

Juan got closer to the woman and noticed her hands move. He wasn't surprised, but instead caught his curiosity as he continued to get closer and closer to her.

Juan swam until he was right over top of the women. Just a few feet from her. He was hovering in the water, face to face with her.

Then she grabbed him, pulling his body to the bottom of the river. She held him tight.

Jordon watched as Juan stopped swimming, about thirty yards from the island. He was worried.

"I fucking hope his body didn't—" Jordon said but was interrupted when Juan's body disappeared under the water. Like a fishing bobber pulled under by a fish, he was gone.

Juan was at the bottom of the river, and the old lady pulled him close and whispered in his ear. Juan's eyes widened at what she was saying. His mind field with her words.

A few moments later, the old lady gently pushed him away, and Juan floated back to the surface.

Jordon stood at the river's edge with Juan's rope in his hands. He contemplated pulling Juan back to him but knew this would end their chances of finding the Book of the Black and killing their only lead back home. Jordon knew if he pulled his brother back, they would all be doomed to that parallel world, forever.

Jordon waited.

A few moments later, when Jordon could no longer wait, Juan's body popped to the surface. Lifeless. Drifting in the current.

Within a minute of surfacing, he drifted into the rocks on the shore of Doll Island. Juan's head banged off a large granite slab, shocking his body awake. He lifted his face from his icy death, and his lungs filled with air like they did for the first time at birth. He was alive.

Juan looked around. His body was numb. His head was throbbing, and blood dripped down his cheeks. His energy was low, but Juan knew he had to secure the rope to a tree or they would all die.

"I'm here," Juan tried to scream across the river but came out as a watered-down whisper. His mouth was frozen, and no matter how hard he tried, he couldn't speak.

Juan still couldn't feel his arms but mustered up all the strength he had and slowly pulled himself onto shore. His vision was still colorless as he laid on the sandy grass shore of Doll Island. He was hypothermic, near death, and vomiting river water.

The rope was gently tugging at his waist as the river's current continued to push against it. This gentle nudge reminded Juan that he wasn't finished. He still had a job to do. He had to secure the rope around the tree.

"Juan! Juan, can you hear me? Just tie the rope to that big oak tree in front of you, and I'll come over," Jordon screamed across the river. He pleaded with his brother.

"Juan, we will build a fire and warm you up!" cried Charlotte.

Juan laid on the ground with his eyes fluttering open as he heard voiced from a distance. He lifted his head and saw a mature oak tree not far in front of him. Just on the edge of the tree line.

Juan pulled himself a few inches at a time until he was at the base of the tree. He could still hear the voices, and also the water flowing over rocks behind him. His body was shaking as he got sick in the grass near the tree.

Juan pulled himself up on all fours. He was exhausted, mentally broken, and physically destroyed. His body was begging to shut down, but his heart made Juan crawl. He crawled around the base of the oak tree once, and then he did it again, causing the rope to bite on the tree as his body continued to be the anchor. Then he passed out.

Jordon pulled on the rope, realizing it was tight. "He fucking did it!" Jordon screamed. "Just hold on bro, I'll be over there shortly!"

Juan had secured his side of the rope. Jordon and Kent began to pull the slack out of their end, while walking it over to a maple tree and tied it off. The rope was now a few inches off the water. It was ridged and a straight line across the river onto the island.

Jordon took a small raft the others had made out of branches and logs. He grabbed the gear, climbed aboard the small log raft, and started to pull himself over to Doll Island.

It worked.

A few minutes of pulling and Jordon was on the island with little water damage to himself or his gear.

"Juan!" Jordon mouthed with a tear rolling down his face as he ran to him. "Brother, are you okay?"

Juan was a tinge of blue, not moving, but his chest was raspy and rising.

Jordon knew he had to act fact. He had to warm Juan up, or he would die. Jordon quickly dressed Juan in his winter clothing. He then began to gather dry driftwood and deadfall as the others in his group built rafts to ferry themselves over to the island.

Charlotte was the next one to cross with Bran. They made it with no problem. Bran jumped off and ran to Juan, licking his face and whimpering. Even Bran knew the heroism displayed by Juan and what it meant for everyone.

"Juan, hang in there," Charlotte whispered in his ear and kissed his cheek. Minutes later, Charlotte was taking the rope from around Juan's black and blue waist and secured for good to the tree. Then she joined Jordon with building a fire.

The fire was built and raging just before the day turned to night. The group was all on Doll Island, with their main focus on reviving Juan. He had taken a colossal setback both physically and mentally for the group's ultimate survival. For the last hour, they have been warming him up, but he was still unconscious.

Juan's head had stopped bleeding, and his body was no longer a blue hue. His breathing was steadily increasing, and his skin was warming up. But was he in the cold water too long? Did they get to him in time?

The night was depressing. It felt hollow. Not a cloud could be seen, or even the slight twinkle of a far-off star. Just a bland and dark manifested sky above them.

The fire was dancing all around in the pit, casting shadows of the group in every direction. The fire was safety, sanity, and life all at the same time, but the fire was also taunting.

"*The book is here!*" Juan screamed as he sat up like a corpse in a coffin.

Charlotte was holding Juan in her arms when he sat straight up. Her heart skipped a beat, but she held on tight.

"What did you say?" Kent asked as he choked on a mouthful of baked beans.

The fire was soothing to the group, flickering with shadows still dancing around them. Luke, Charlotte and Bran, Jordon, Andrew, and Kent were all ears.

"She's here. Abigail. She's on this island, and so is her family," Juan slurred as his pupils expanded. His shoulders slumped over toward the fire as Charlotte held him. "She told me this, and that the Book of the Black is here too." Juan pointed over toward the river. "She was in the water with me!"

The group was amazed. This, as irrational as it seemed, was the first glimpse of hope in this twisted parallel world. A seed of hope will drive a man to achieve anything. A grain of hope could conquer this world. Hope is all they had, and it's all they needed.

"Abigail told me the book was buried with her, but also warned whoever disturbed her family, would burn a thousand deaths in hell," Juan said.

"She knew why we are here?" Kent asked rhetorically.

The group looked at each other. Nothing more was said. No one knew what to say. They knew hope was in the air, but within that same hope, a nightmare was brewing.

Jordon and Charlotte kept Juan company by the fire. He was recovering but needed more time. The icy water took its toll on Juan's body, but what he experienced in the water, nearly bankrupted his mind.

As night gave way to daylight, Kent, Luke, and Andrew began packing their gear.

"Listen up, guys," Kent said as he opened his map. "Charlotte, can you and Jordon stay with Juan while the rest of us begin searching the island?"

Jordon and Charlotte both agreed and laid down next to Juan and the soothing fire.

Kent, Luke, and Andrew dawned their gear and set off in search of the Book of the Black.

The island was named Doll Head, centuries ago, but over time came to be known merely as Doll Island. It was now well overgrown, decaying, and thirty acres of the netherworld.

The shape of the island was unique, with human-like features that resembled a doll's head. A small forest on the northern side resembled hair, and open land and rocks at the farthest southern point resembled teeth within a jawline.

The forest was thick, full of old pines and mosey oaks. Kent orientated himself, Andrew, and Luke with his map and pushed inland from the fire. They were off to find the book. They were off to find their freedom.

The men walked.

They walked, and the island let them in.

A little way from the river's edge, the men found an old road. The road was overgrown and covered with a crunchy grey material that the men couldn't quite pinpoint.

Kent looked at his map. "Boy's, let's see where this thing goes." He said as he started to follow the road deeper into the woods. The map showed the road leading south across the island, from one side to the other, edge to edge.

One step at a time, the men got closer to the key. One step after the other would bring them home again. One foot, then the other, the road crunched underneath them as they walked.

Juan was startled awake again. It was high noon, and the others were gone. He was alone. Breathing hard, eyes wide open, ants were crawling on him, and he was sweating like it was the dead of summer. He was painfully sick.

"Charlotte," Juan yelled.

No answer. But his voice was back. While still nauseous, Juan felt his strength beginning to return. But his body was scorching. So hot, he stripped his winter clothes off and stood tall by the smoldering fire.

The trees were bending at the top, with a small breeze on the forest floor. Juan looked up at the trees and back at the river. He could hear something. He could hear someone. Someone talking. Whispering.

Juan turned toward the forest and strained his ears for the whispering voice. Again, he heard it, but couldn't make out what it was or who it was. Yet the wind still blew.

"Juan," Charlotte said as she walked up. "You feel better, buddy?"

"Can you hear that?" Juan asked. "That voice. Can you hear it?"

Charlotte looked at Jordon. "What the fuck is he talking about?"

Jordon shook his head. "No fucking clue."

Juan, wearing only a t-shirt and shorts, began to walk.

Kent, Luke, and Andrew followed the road. It turned naturally following the terrain surrounded by tall oaks. The further they walked into the forest, the more the tree canopy obscured the sky.

After an hour, they came to the remains of a small stone-built structure. No roof, no door, just the semblance of an old building and tattered dreams.

Kent stood in the doorway, wide-eyed, and touched the stone entryway. It was cold and rough with green moss. He stepped inside and could see all the way through it. The only thing left of the structure was the front and left main walls. The floor was dirt. Nothing grew within the building itself. Leaving a perfect outline, giving credence that the structure stood years ago.

"Is this it, Kent?" Luke asked with a crack in his voice.

"It's not on my map. Which is a good sign, and my gut is telling me we have found the cabin," Kent answered as he walked back out. "Now, we have to find the graves."

The men spread out searching all around the cabin, with no luck. No markers of any kind. No unusual rock mounds. No slate markings. No stone markings, no wood, no nothing.

They kept looking.

Kent walked back inside the remains of the old cabin. He looked around and began to think maybe the family had been buried in the river. He noticed again that the dirt floor on the inside of the cabin was bare. It grew nothing, even after being exposed for so many years. Nothing grew.

"Boys, where would you bury your family to keep them safe from a pissed off town?" Kent asked as he dropped to his knees in the middle of the dirt floor.

Kent began to brush the dirt from left to right with his hand. Anything loose, he pushed aside. His gut told him he was right. His heart told him Abigail buried her family under the floor of the cabin. And if her family was there, then she was there!

Kent, Luke, and Andrew all dropped their packs and took out small, folded, metal shovels. They unfolded them and began to dig. Each man took a small section of the floor and started working.

Juan could hear the voice clearly now. It carried in the wind, through the trees and all around. The voice was a female, both gentle and honest. Juan began to run. Step after step, he ran down the grey road.

"Where the fuck are you going?" yelled Jordon. But Juan didn't answer. He kept moving with purpose.

"We better follow him," Charlotte said as she took off running. Jordon trailed, and Bran brought up the rear.

Juan ran down the road ignoring the pain his feet were in and cold his body was enduring. His mind was traumatized, and he was on a mission.

They all ran as the forest around them became darker. They ran as the trees moaned. They ran non-stop, until Kent, Luke, and Andrew were found.

Juan stopped at the entrance to the old cabin. He was doubled over, trying to catch his breath as he looked inside at Kent and said, "A sacrifice. The only way she will let us off this island, with that book, is through sacrifice. A human sacrifice!"

Kent looked up from the hole he was now standing in. He looked at Juan and then down at the pine box he had found but had yet to open. "Is this the right grave, Juan?"

"No! That's the twins, Sarah and Martha Black. Whatever you do, whatever you fucking do, don't open that box!" Juan replied. "Luke has the right one. Luke, Abigail is in your box."

Luke became sick to his stomach and hurled out of his hole. He got out and walked over to Kent. "Switch with me; I'll fill the dirt back in over her grave."

Kent agreed and moved to Abigail's casket. Kent took his hand shovel and edged it under the pine board holding the coffin shut. His mind was racing. He wondered who buried the witch. Surely, she didn't bury herself.

Kent pushed down on the shovel, and the old wood pried off easily. The air ran out and was visible to them all. It was like a set of clouds. They flew inside the remains of the cabin with them. The air circled the group up and down and then escaped skyward.

Kent put his shovel down and lifted the wood off and out of the grave. There she was. Abigail Black, wearing a black dress from neck to ankles, black leather shoes with shiny square buckles across her feet. She looked like time had forgotten her; she was untouched. No decay, no rot, but appeared to be sleeping—ageless, as she held a thick, brown leather-bound book.

"Can you hear her?" asked Juan.

Kent looked up at him, confused, but not totally surprised. "I guess you can?"

"Her voice is in the wind. At the top of the trees and now in this place. Human sacrifice is the price of admission," said Juan. "Take the book, Kent."

Kent looked at the others and back at Juan as Juan joined him in the hole.

"*No!*" Charlotte screamed.

"Shut up, bitch!" Juan quipped.

Juan grabbed Kent's face and turned him so they were eye to eye. "Take the book and get everyone home. Do it now! Get off this fucking island!"

Kent looked deep inside of Juan and knew his soul was dying. He could see a creature in the back of his eyes. He could catch a glimpse of hell, of where Juan was headed. At that moment, Kent knew, this was the only way they all go home.

While still affixed to Juan's gaze, Kent took the book.

As the book left Abigail's grasp, time caught up. Like turning on a faucet, her body liquefied, draining in the old box until bones were all that remained. Like a cruel magic trick, the witch was reduced to a skeletal memory.

Juan pushed Kent out of the way and climbed into the coffin. "I am the price of salvation. Don't you see it? The salt of my body will pay the toll. Seal me up and drown me in the dirt," Juan said with a single tear rolling down his cheek. "Bury me now, before it's too late!"

Juan laid on top of Abigail's bones, crossed his arms, and closed his eyes. He took one more breath as the blackness took him.

Jordon stood in shock as he watched Kent use his shovel to nail the lid back on the coffin.

"We can't do this," sobbed Jordon. "That's my brother. That's my fucking brother!" But deep down, he knew this was the only way. He knew this was the only way off the island and out of this mind-fucked parallel world. Jordon tried to convince himself that this was all just a nightmare, but inside of his soul, he knew better.

Jordon, Charlotte, Andrew, Kent, and Luke all shared in the work. One shovel full of dirt after another, they buried Juan and Abigail Black. The group was calm as the last bit of earth was thrown on the grave. Slowly, and completely, they buried Juan alive.

Silence was in the air. No wind, no birds, no nothing. Just silence.

Kent sat down, back against the stone wall, and motioned for everyone to gather around. Then, he opened the book. A grey/green and black smoke poured out as the pages moved like a pair of bat wings. The smoke flew around his hands, circled Kent's head, and flew directly into his eyes.

Kent sat still as his watch stopped, and the world no longer turned.

Kent was inside the cabin, the cabin was whole again, with a flickering oil lamp hanging from the ceiling. He could see a female dressed all in black. She was alone, sitting at a desk, writing in the book. It was Abigail.

Kent was conscious, yet had no control over his body as he walked over and behind Abigail. She paid him no attention; he was no more than a fly on the wall to her. She continued to write with a quill, dipping it into an inkwell between sentences.

His eyes grew wide as he read:

For my loves, I break my heart into three pieces. Each piece represents you, and each piece will grow to become a doorway to the dark world. Each piece will get you into the world, but only a righteous Madonna can show you the right way out of the darkness. Only a Madonna can bring someone back into the light. But beware of the addle-plot, who I create to stop anyone and everyone at all cost.

The mine, the water, and the insane...
The mine, the water, and the crazy...
The MINE, the water, and the EVIL...
The MINE, the WATER, and the misguided...
The MINE, the WATER, and the HELL...

Abigail put her quill down, closed the book, and stood up. Kent looked at the dirt floor beneath him. Four graves were now open, containing four coffins.

Abigail walked to the only open coffin, climbed inside and with the book upon her breast, crossed her arms and closed her eyes. The lid sealed itself, and the ground shook until all of the graves were covered.

Kent looked around, bewildered. He was still inside of the cabin, but not for long, as the oil lamp fell on the desk, catching the place on fire.

Charlotte slapped Kent across his face turning his eyes brown again. He was back.

Kent looked up at Charlotte and around at the others, "I know how to get home! I know where we need to go! I know what will take us home!" He took a deep breath and looked into Charlotte's emerald eyes, pointed at her, and said, "You are the key!"

Chapter 22: Baptism

Stripped naked as the day they were born, Tom and Brian were bloody and bruised, their hands bound together in front of themselves and tied to each other resembling an old chain-gang. Their supplies rummaged through, plundered. Their morale no longer existed, but at least they were still alive. For now.

This world was cruel. This world was unfair. This world was the snot blown from the nose of a giant who gave no reason or care for what it held or what it was. This world was hell.

"You will soon learn that God's new world will be all that you need, all that you want, and all that will be!" Chief Sanders explained. "You will join us, or you will die a death you cannot fathom."

Trashman walked over to the men and looked them up and down. "You nasty little dick fucks." He took out a zippo and a small bottle of lighter fluid, opened it, smiled from ear to ear, and began to squirt the legs on each man.

Trashman sparked his zippo, staring into the flame. He lost himself in the beautiful, warm, orange, flickering magic. "You will dance when we say dance!" Trashman said, sneering as he dropped the flame, and the ground ignited.

Tom's leg caught fire first, and then Brian's. They danced, and Trashman laughed with pure satisfaction.

Chief Sanders snickered, "Trashman, you kill me. Get these clowns moving. Let's take them to the church!"

Trashman pulled a blanket out of his pack and threw it over the two men rolling on the ground and screaming for God's mercy. Giggling with childish pleasure, he stomped on their legs until the flames were out.

"Get up! And move!" Trashman yelled as he pulled on a rope attached to Tom's neck. As if he were a dog on a leash, Trashman pulled, leading him and Brian back toward the woods.

Trashman spat on Philip's forehead as he led his captives away. Philip never moved; he lay bleeding on the filthy cracked asphalt. The group of THEM and Philip's newfound friends walked off, into the blackness.

"Mr. Bilkowski, could you come to my room for a moment, please?" asked Amber Lane. Philip leaned his broom against the wall, smiled with a dirty grin, and made his way into the empty classroom.

Amber Lane was a bombshell. She was just a few years removed from college, five-foot-six, and 110 pounds of pleasing curves. She was rumored to be a sexual deviant and loved to seduce the male teachers of the school; she wasn't picky, she would sometimes set her eyes on female teachers too. When Amber was horny, rules and couth no longer applied.

"My wastebasket is full. Could you please empty it?" Amber said as she sat back in her chair.

"No problem, ma'am," replied Philip as he noticed her dress was pulled up, just enough to reveal she wasn't wearing panties. Her legs were smooth as glass, slightly tanned, just enough to catch his eye.

Philip bent down to pick up the wastebasket as Amber turned the chair toward him, spreading her legs apart. He was on a knee, hands on the can, and looked up, seeing her shaven flower. It was visibly wet. She had been touching herself before he walked in, and it showed.

It was beautiful, like a Californian summer peach, and Philip wanted it desperately.

Amber smiled, licked her lips, and leaned back in her chair. "Take your pants off, and get inside of me," she whispered as one of her hands began to caress her breast.

Philip was as erect as a hundred-year-old pine tree. He wanted her so bad.

Philip took his pants off and with his rigid member in his hand, his eyes opened. He was lying on the blood-soaked asphalt. Philip's head felt like a truck ran over it, and he was alone in the dark. He looked at his dick in his hands, still erect, and became confused. Philip released it, sat up, and looked around. He was in the parking lot of Big Ben's Groceries, covered in blood. Amber was nowhere to be seen, neither were his friends Tom and Brian.

Philip had been shot twice. He was battered and bruised, malnourished, and once again alone in this parallel world of hell, but moreover, Philip was pissed.

The church bell rang loud and clear, echoing down Main Street. Slowly, earsplitting, with distinctive rhythm, the bell tolled. The First Baptist Church of Mecklenburg was in session.

The church was a clean, white, tall, and skinny building. It was odd looking. Unlike a typical southern church in a Bible-belt state. The church had one main room and could hold fifty people, tops. It was taller than it was wide, with a bell on the steeple. As if the church itself was a reflection from a funhouse mirror at a Fourth of July carnival.

"Brothers and sisters, take a seat. We are here today because God himself has willed it. He has commanded it. God has made it so," preached Jim Ratchford while pointing skyward and standing at his pulpit, above the dirty people.

"Amen brother, *a-fucking-men*!" yelled a man in the group.

Ratchford made eye contact with that man, and the man's face turned green. The man looked into the black emptiness of Ratchford's eyes and became physically ill. The preacher had no eyes. Yet he could see better than anyone there, and he smiled as the man puked a bloody bile.

"Our God has chosen us and has chosen this world to begin his new plan. His new start is our new start. His experiment with man has reached a conclusion, brothers and sisters. It's time to start over. To start the new experiment! *God* has spoken, and we will listen!" Ratchford preached as he smiled at the people.

The crowd was chanting back and forth, cheering, yelling, and becoming orgasmic from the preacher's words.

"We have naysayers in the crowd, good sir!" Chief Sanders yelled from the newly opened front door.

The crowd froze. All noise was sucked out of the room like the vacuum of space. In unison, the everyone turned around and stared with intrigue.

Chief Sanders walked in, and the crowd parted. His men followed their captives between them.

Tom and Brian were beaten, emotionless, dragging their feet with each painful step, as they lost the last bit of sweat in their bodies.

"Preacher, we need your counsel. We captured two naysayers. Two SEEKERS who want out of this world. We ask that you 'educate' them, good sir, and give them both the chance to rectify their evil and ungodly ways," Chief Sanders spoke with hate in his voice.

The crowd began to sigh and hiss at Tom and Brian. Brian looked up and was met with a fist to his nose. It broke instantly. Gushing blood, his nose sat crooked on his grime-ridden face. Brian's morale was non-existent. His will to live was also beginning to wane.

Tom and Brian were starved, naked, beaten, mentally abused, and forced marched for two days back to town and straight to the church, as the bell sounded for service.

"Fuck you," Tom said under his breath as a man urinated on him while laughing in his face.

"Bring those animals up here, Chief," the preacher said.

Chief Sanders nodded to Trashman, and he pulled the rope attached to the men, dragging them up to the pulpit.

Ratchford looked at Tom and Brian up and down, grabbing their arms and squeezing them about their bodies. "Boys, whose world are you in?" he asked.

Neither men answered.

Ratchford moved from Tom to Brian and grabbed his testicles with force so hard, Brian passed out from the pain. He continued to squeeze while he turned toward Tom. Tom lifted his head and noticed the preacher was soulless. His eyes were not only missing, but blackness with no end, had replaced them. He knew this man was not human. Tom knew he was unworldly and shouldn't be fucked with.

"I'll ask you two again. Whose world are you in?"

Tom looked in the preacher's face as he asked the question. He knew the answer would give him and Brian life, or it would give them instant death.

"It's God's new world, sir," answered Tom as drool dripped from his mouth.

"Liar. You don't believe that. Do *you*?" Ratchford responded with a hard slap across Tom's face. "Make me fucking believe it. Make *God* himself believe it!"

"Separate them," Ratchford commanded of Trashman.

Trashman took out his knife and cut the rope that bound Tom and Brian's neck together. They were now separated, but both men still had their hands tied.

"Bring them," said Ratchford as he walked out the rear entrance of the church and toward the pond.

Trashman, Chief Sanders, and his men picked up Tom and Brian and collectively walked out to the pond.

The water was covered in a thick green algae with dragonflies skimming the top of it. The water was unseen but appeared black under the green mass.

Ratchford was waist-deep in the water. "Bring him," he said, pointing at Brian.

Trashman pushed Brian farther into the pond until Ratchford grabbed him by his hair.

Brian was scared for his life. He tried feverously to free his hands from the rope but was fruitless in all efforts. He was weak and sad. All hope was melting away. His pants became hot and wet from the urine running uncontrollably down his left leg.

Brian's mind began to drift off to his wife, to memories of his kids. To a specific memory of his six-year-old daughter asking him to tie her shoe. At that moment, she had looked at him as if he were a king. It was burned in his brain; she was his love, his angel, his little girl, his life. This would be hard on her.

"What is your name, sir?" Ratchford asked Tom as he held Brian by his hair.

"Tom Porter, my name is Tom Porter," he whimpered as his legs shook.

"Well, Tom Porter, I ask you again. Whose world is this?" Ratchford asked as he forced Brian face-first into the water. He held Brian's head under that nasty green algae-covered liquid. "Whose world?" he asked again.

"It's God's new world," answered Tom.

Brian flailed as the water churned and splashed with every second of the fight.

Brian's head was mere inches from life-sustaining air. His lungs gasped and contracted sucking dirty microbe-filled water down his throat as he thrashed under the water. His lungs turned into water catchments.

"It's his world. God's. It's his!" Tom screamed.

Ratchford held steady as Brian continued to fight for his life.

Tom was at a loss. He knew Brian was at his end. "It's my new world!" he screamed with tears. Tom dropped to his knees in the water, putting both hands together. "Please stop; he can't breathe. You're killing him!"

Ratchford continued to hold Brian's head under the water but looked down at Tom. "Now... Now you are starting to see what I see. What we all see. What *God* has created for you to see, to feel, and to smell. This world is for you, given to you by God himself. You must never leave it."

Brian smiled under the water. At that moment, he was having a vision of his daughter. She was beautiful. Brian reached out for his daughter's hand as his body went limp. The fight was done. Ratchford looked at Tom as he let Brian float face down, farther into the pond.

"And God needs sacrifices," Ratchford said as Brian's body was swallowed by the water.

Ratchford walked out from the pond and over to Tom. "Look into my eyes and see my soul," he said.

Tom looked into the void where his eyes should have been. The holes began to glow from a tinge of orange fire to bright green. It was like a movie. Tom was looking into the preacher's missing eyes, and the green light was taking him for a walk in hell.

Ratchford grabbed Tom's face as his eyes glimmered with the green light. "See your new world; see God's plan!" Ratchford said as Tom began to float off the ground.

Tom could see. He could see himself walking in a vacant world. No noise, no color, no love, just miles and miles of pure unadulterated hatred. He felt weak and cold as if it were snowing, but the sun was burning the sky red. His body was frail. He had aged to a feeble version of himself. His hands were wrinkled, and his hair was gone again. His body looked like a prisoner in Auschwitz.

A wind picked up, blowing in front of Tom. That's when he noticed. He was being watched. Something dark. Something large was in the distance watching him. He could not see this thing but could feel it. Tom could feel its presence. He could feel it in his bones, deep in his soul; he could feel this thing was real, and it was pure evil. Sweat poured off Tom as he started to shake. It was in the forest. Watching. Watching him. And the Watcher had green eyes.

Ratchford threw Tom to the ground and said, "Now you've seen a glimpse of his world; a glimpse of the pain that could visit you." Bubbles surfaced in the pond as Ratchford pointed in that direction, "Your friend will burn in hell for eternity. You have but one chance to join us or join him!"

Tom's body shook uncontrollably. His body was rejecting his mind, and his mind was leaving his body. Tom looked up at Ratchford and saw the devil. Flames burned in Ratchford's hollowed eyes. Flames—orange, dancing, translucent flames.

"All you have to do is take my hand, Tom," Ratchford said as he held it out. "Just take my hand, and you will be free."

Trashman stood at the water's edge, smiling. Laughing. He took his hand and dirtily slid it in his pants, grabbing himself. He began to stroke as he watched Tom reach up from the water, taking Ratchford's hand. He knew Tom's soul was no longer his own but now belonged to God's new world.

Chapter 23: The Journey Home Begins

Kent stood facing the others. "Let's get the fuck off this island," he said.

Luke, Charlotte, Andrew, and utterly depressed Jordon all grabbed their packs and followed Kent.

And it began to snow.

Minute after minute, the river grew closer as the group walked back the way they came, retracing their steps down the overgrown road.

As the group walked, Bran followed Charlotte but was uneasy with the "taste" of the moment. Bran's ears perked up and he pushed forward, taking the lead. They all followed. After all, Bran's nose was the best in the group.

Thick snow fell through the black, heavy, cloud-ridden sky. It was as dark as a raven. The winds pushed the darkness in circles over the top of the group as they walked, dropping inches of snow by the minute.

"The temperature is plummeting!" Kent yelled as he took a knee, pulling a thicker jacket from his pack.

Jordon began to cry. "He's gone. We're all going to die. We have to get out of here." Freaking out, his mind now shattered, Jordon dropped his pack and began to run for the river. It wasn't in sight, but his thoughts were miles past rational and took a giant turn to crazy town.

"Jordon, stop!" Charlotte yelled as she held Bran back from following him. "Where are you going?" Charlotte looked at the other guys, who were just as confused as to why Jordon was running and acting like his hair was on fire.

"Let him go. He needs to get his mind right. I'm sure Jordon will meet us at the river." Kent told the group as he zipped up his new jacket and dawned his backpack.

Jordon's heart was pounding through his chest. The arteries in his neck were swollen and beating like a drummer during a concert solo. His brother had sacrificed himself for him, for the group, for everyone fighting to get out of this fucked-up world.

Juan was dead.

Step after step, the white road crunched under Jordon's feet. His heart was broken and his mind was following suit. Jordon, psychologically, was plummeting down Alice's rabbit hole. He knew his brother had died for them all, but he couldn't accept it. Juan had practically raised him, as his mother was a common street whore, and he was clueless as to who his father could be.

Jordon ran and ran.

And the snow fell harder and harder.

"Kent, we can't make the river tonight. The snow is getting too deep. We will all freeze to death before we get off this island," said Luke as he pointed up at the storm.

The wind picked up and blew snow into the group as they were walking.

"Luke's right, guys. We have to stop," Kent replied.

The group stopped, and just as quick as the snow started, it turned to rain, while lightning began to jump in the sky. The wind shifted to their backs, and the lightning lit the forest in short bursts. Charlotte took a breath as the lightning danced above. When it flashed, she noticed the trees bordering the road. The oaks looked alive in the storm.

"There!" Charlotte screamed between lightning flashes, as she pointed to the left side of the road. A few hundred yards ahead of them, a silhouette appeared, just beyond the trees. "Look, there!" she said again.

The group looked to the far side of the road, in the area Charlotte was pointing. Lightning cracked again, and as the brightness flashed, they could see it. The outline of a small building. Maybe a tiny cabin. The group looked at each other and instinctively began to walk toward the silhouette.

Lightning jumped off the blackness above them and finally came crashing to earth. The group was facing in the direction of the building when the bolt came down. They all witnessed the horror. They all were wide-eyed as the bolt of lightning struck a man standing in the road near that distant cabin. Then their ears felt the electrically charged explosion. Bran immediately ran for his life. Charlotte fell to the ground as blood-soaked through her hands covering her ears. The ringing was unbearable; it was borderline maddening.

Bran was gone.

Kent was the only one in the group that was unfazed by the event. He stood tall, with the Book of the Black inside his jacket, held firm against his chest.

Luke was on his knees, shaking his head, trying to regain his bearings. "Did you see that? This island isn't going to let any of us leave. It's going to try and kill us one at a time," Luke yelled as his ears rang.

Kent unzipped his jacket, pulled out the book.

Charlotte crawled over to Luke, and Andrew followed suit.

Everyone that remained huddled tightly together as the wind swirled around like a tornado. The rain continued to pound the group as Kent opened the book and began to read.

Kent read page after page. No one in the group could understand the language he was speaking. It was trance-like. Robotic, alien...

Kent stopped. Silence fell as he shut the book.

Kent stood tall, holding the book skyward, yelling, "I am the holder of the Book of the Black. I command safe passage off this island!"

The earth began to shake as the sky turned blue. The winds calmed, and the rain subsided. The snow started to melt as fast as it fell. The melt drained down the center of the road, but the temperature continued to bite with razor-sharp teeth.

The group stood, dawning their gear.

"What the fuck just happened?" Charlotte asked.

Luke shrugged, looking at Kent. "Are you okay, man?"

Kent shook his head, closed the book and placed it back inside his jacket, again safely next to his chest. "I'm not sure, but this book keeps me warm. It feels good against my skin."

"Let's move. I have to find my fucking dog!" Charlotte said. "Bran, Bran, here boy. *Here!*"

"Follow Charlotte. If we don't get off this island, we will all die, and if we all die, no one will ever leave this world!" said Kent.

The group walked, spread out, abreast of each other but all within eyesight.

"Bran, here boy... *Bran!*" the group called for the dog as they closed the distance to the cabin just off the road. That's when they found him. Bran was whimpering, laying on the man hit by the lightning strike. It was Jordon. Smoke was rising from his clothing and hair. He was burned, charred to a crisp.

Luke, Kent, Andrew, and Charlotte stood glaring at the river. Before finding the book, the river was flowing and cold as ice. Now it was frozen over, black as space and bellowed a high-pitched crackling sound from beneath it.

Charlotte took a step off the shore onto the ice. It held her easily. She walked a few feet out from shore, tuned to the group, and with a frightening, bloodless pale face, said, "It's as hard as concrete and black as tar." Charlotte looked around her and called to her dog. Bran ran out to her on the ice.

"Let's go. Follow the girl!" Kent yelled as he started to run.

The group picked up the pace on that hard darkness. They all followed as Charlotte led them across the frozen Black River.

The air felt absent around them as the group ran effortlessly on the ice. It wasn't slick but rather course like sandpaper. The ice broke as they ran, echoing cracks with each footfall.

The far shoreline drew closer and closer.

Ronald Black stood in the woods, hidden by several mosey oaks, dead pines, and shadows. He held a single white latex balloon. Ronald stood watching and smiling while Luke, Kent, Charlotte, and Andrew ran across the frozen Black River.

Ronald was a statue, frozen less than eighty yards from the group as they climbed onto the shore. He stood motionless.

Then he let the balloon go.

Kent was the last to step off the Black River. His heart was rapid as he turned to look back across the water at Doll Island.

It was gone.

The island was lost in a ground fog that appeared as the frozen river turned liquid again right before Kent's eyes. The river turned back to the water. He stood with an amused face, then he noticed a white latex balloon skip across the water and swirl off into the mist.

The group was tired and mentally defeated, but they pressed on. Step by step, one foot after the other, they began the long walk back to the hotel. Symbolically, each step brought them closer to escape, closer to their families.

Hours passed, until one by one, they each fell from exhaustion. Kent had pushed them to their limits, and it was time to rest for the night.

The sun broke the horizon, shining a small light through the natural crack between the curtains of Charlotte's bedroom window. The light slowly increased, and after a few minutes, she began to wake. Charlotte yawned and rolled over, placing her hand on an empty cold spot in her bed. *Strange*, she thought. Her daughter fell asleep next to her last night.

"Diane," Charlotte said as she woke up.

No answer.

Charlotte stretched, slowly pulled herself from her comfy bed, and grabbed a sweatshirt and slippers. She pulled the warmth of the shirt on and walked down to make her morning coffee. She sipped the black java while thumbing through the morning paper. Charlotte enjoyed her early quiet and private time.

The lead story was of a shooting a few days earlier, not uncommon, and almost comical. Charlotte sipped her coffee, the nectar of life that woke her daily as the news continued to amuse her.

"Momma!" a voice screamed from Diane's room upstairs. It was gut-wrenching, fraught with fear and pain. "Momma, *help* me! You're not my dad! Let me go! *Help me!*"

Charlotte's coffee cup dropped to the tile floor, exploding as she instantaneously took off, running up the stairs.

Her legs felt heavy as she ran. One step at a time, she felt so far away. The closer to Diane's room she got, the further away her mind perceived she was. The closer she got, the more her stomach churned with sickness.

Four seconds of running slowed to minutes.

Charlotte reached the top of the stairs, turning to the hallway. The carpet ignited under her feet. Flames danced like tormented demons around her as she picked up the pace. Diane's room was at the end of the hall, with a blue light flooding through the door seam.

"Diane!" Charlotte screamed as she ran down the never-ending hallway.

Gasping for air, Charlotte stood tall in front of her daughter's bedroom door and opened it. The door opened to a vacant room as Charlotte stepped inside. A breeze from an open window spiraled like a tornado against the walls. There was no furniture. No sound. No Diane. Just four walls with a dim white light above.

Charlotte turned around, looking at the walls covered in old faded missing person flyers of a ten-year-old girl. Hundreds of them, from floor to ceiling, the walls were covered with flyers of her missing daughter.

Charlotte took a deep breath and fell to her knees. Her eyes opened again; she woke up. Kent was shaking her. This time she was back to reality. Back in the cold of that world she was trying so hard to escape.

"Charlotte, are you awake? You were on your knees talking in your sleep for a few minutes now," Kent explained as he held her.

Charlotte blinked her eyes, realizing she had been dreaming. She was still in the woods of this parallel world, and her daughter was still missing.

She was still in hell, fighting her way home.

Kent gathered what was left of his crew, Charlotte and Bran, Luke and Andrew, and with the Book of the Black nestled inside his shirt, took out his compass and plotted their route. "This way, guys. We can be back to the hotel before nightfall if we hustle," Kent said with confidence.

"Kent, I'll stay close and put Bran out front again. He has served us well so far. Why fuck up a good thing?" Charlotte said.

Chapter 24: The Rat

Ratchford smiled as he looked down on Tom. "Your life is now his and has new meaning. No longer will you be cold, scared, hungry, or poor. You will live his word. You will sacrifice for him. You will love him, and you will never leave this new world!" Ratchford stroked Tom's hair. "Do you understand me?"

Tom, while uncontrollably shaking, nodded in agreement.

"Good," Ratchford said as he took Tom's left hand into his. "To remind you of your commitment," he said as his jaw made a popping sound as it unhinged, opening his mouth wider than humanly possible.

Tom found his voice and screamed as three of his fingers were bit off. Blood ran down Ratchford's face, pouring into the nasty water below.

"This will be the first of many sacrifices, my son. It's all in his name. You will learn our ways. You will live our ways. You will, or you will burn. It's really as simple as that, Tom," Ratchford demanded after his jaw realigned.

Tom was in exceptional pain. He took a deep breath and then another. He swallowed his pride, his self-worth, and his self-identity but looked up at Ratchford, and with a quivering voice, said, "I will learn. I will obey. I will sacrifice and force others to see our new world."

Trashman smiled as he finished himself off inside his grungy pants. Human suffering was a fetish for him. Trashman always got off on it.

"I'll take him, preacher," Trashman said with a laugh as he pulled Tom to his feet.

Trashman and Tom walked out of the pond, leaving Brian and Tom's soul deep in the murky water. Trashman placed handcuffs back on Tom, tying a rope around the linked chain between Tom's wrist. "Let's go, fucktard," Trashman said as he began to walk.

Tom followed Trashman. He had no choice in the matter. Three of his fingers on his left hand were gone, leaving only his thumb and pinky. He was still bleeding. His wrists were cuffed together and tethered like a dog. Time was beginning to slow down for Tom, and his vision was losing all contrast and color. They walked back to the church.

The bell rang, and the church doors opened wide and he was pulled inside. The room was quiet as Trashman led Tom to Chief Sanders.

Sanders took the rope from Trashman and leaned over, whispering in his ear.

Trashman smiled and began to snicker as Sanders spoke softly to him.

"Yes, sir. Thank you. I'll get the men," Trashman replied to what Sanders had whispered in his ear.

Sanders led Tom into the center of the room, where there were two chairs. "Please, have a seat, Tom."

Tom sat on the cold, black metal chair. His wrists were still bound. Still naked. His rectum bled as he shook with fear. The pain in his hand was nearly gone, as the leftover meat of his hand was white from total blood loss.

Sanders looked at the church people. Those dirty church people. He grinned, made a circle motion with his hand around Tom, and the people began to move. They slowly and silently encircled Tom and Sanders.

"Now that you have met the preacher and understand what the true lamb of God commands of us, I will only ask you once: where did the others from the hotel go?" Sanders asked as he sat in the folding chair just inches in front of Tom. Sanders was uncomfortably close, between Tom's legs and well into his personal space.

Tom was bleeding, exhausted, and scared. He knew precisely what Sanders was asking. He knew his answer would either kill him or kill those searching for the book.

"You know the group, Tom. The one with the dog and sexy female," Sanders said with dirty lust in his voice.

Tom knew he had to play ball or he would die. He wondered how much THEY knew about the SEEKERS. How much THEY knew about the hotel.

The people began to chant, "Kill him!"

The churchgoers were no longer silent.

"Kill him if he doesn't tell us, Chief. He knows what we want. He knows where they are," screamed a man from the crowd.

The room temperature noticeably rose with the voices.

"Kill him!" said a female in the back.

The people closed in on Tom as they chanted. Sanders sat, staring intensely at Tom.

Tom knew his time in this world was ticking away, but he needed to buy a few brief moments. He needed time to think. Tom looked at Sanders as the crowd chanted. Sanders was waiting for the answer he wanted. Like fine china dropped on concrete, Tom broke. His body went limp, and eyes let loose a river. Like a freight train running free down a mountain, he quickly decided to play ball.

A baby began to cry as Tom opened his mouth, sealing his friends' fate. "They went to find the Book of the Black."

The crowd gasped all at once. Sanders's eyebrows raised as his pupils drew wide.

"The book," the crowd whispered. "Not possible. No... it's a myth. They can't find it. No."

"Where?!" Sanders shouted. "Where did they go?!" Sanders grabbed Tom by his throat with easy pressure and lifted his head up so he could look into his soul. "Where are they?!"

With a moment of hesitation and a soft voice, Tom said, "Doll Island. After that, they will head back to the hotel."

Sanders held Tom close to his face. Eye to eye, they were. "What hotel, boy?"

"The Mecklenburg Hotel off of Route 3," Tom answered as he gasped for air.

Sanders smiled. He knew what needed to be done.

Sanders helped Tom to his feet and removed the cuffs that bound his wrists. "Welcome to the flock, Tom," Sanders said as he held Tom to his chest.

At first, Tom was in shock and stood still as Sanders held him. A few moments later, Tom let his breath out and wrapped his arms around the evil man. He felt dirtier than a used condom. His mind was turning while his soul was burning.

"That's it, son. We will take care of you, and you will take care of us. God loves you," Sanders said.

Tom began to cry.

"Stop those tears, boy. No need for them. We will clothe you, feed you, and mend you," Sanders whispered in his ear.

"Thank you," Tom stammered.

Sanders let the embrace go and walked away. Tom stood in the center of the room, bleeding and still naked as the day he was born and again on today, the day he was reborn.

"Get him to the doc," Sanders told the crowd just before walking out of the church. "Trashman, gather the men. There is work to do. That group we were tracking is looking for the Book of the Black. We need to resupply and pick up more men," Sanders explained. "If they have that book, war will come and war it will be!"

Trashman smiled a devilish grin. He knew to resupply they would be forced back to the Costco, and once back at their "base," he knew of a short-haired whore he wanted to pay a visit.

"Roger that, Chief. When are we headed back?" asked Trashman.

"First light," replied Sanders. "Oh, and Trashy," Sanders turned back, smiling, "I got first dibs on that red-headed whore. You know the one. You can have her when I'm done."

Trashman laughed.

Chapter 25: Mecklenburg Hotel

The Mecklenburg Hotel occupants were running operations smoothly, with resupply operations becoming increasingly lucrative. This was happening while the main mission to find the way home was still afoot. Survival in this parallel world would ultimately lead them back home. Or so they hoped. They were sacrificing blood, sweat, and tears for hope. Hope was all they had, and hope is all they would need.

One meal at a time. Just taking it one meal at a time would breakdown this fuck show so simplistic that eventually, they would be one meal away from getting home again.

Daylight began to flee into its nightly hiding spot. The streetlights outside of The Mecklenburg Hotel turned on one at a time in a mechanical timing dance. In the distance, American flags shuttered in the wind, and a wild high-pitched whistling crept through the alleyways.

The hotel had the mandatory thirty percent security in place. Kids walked the perimeter of the building, acting as sentries, armed with walkie-talkies. The highspeed avenues of approach were blocked by abandoned cars, and 360 degrees around the hotel were covered by men acting as rooftop snipers.

Philip was a little over a mile away from the hotel, but he knew his best chance to survive was to get to the SEEKERS at the hotel. He had been in and out of consciousness for two days but finally started to gain some form of composure.

Philip found himself sitting with his back against the front passenger tire of a white Buick, laughing. Philip couldn't catch a break in this world of hell. But he still had his sense of humor.

After a few deep breaths, Philip rolled to his side. Inch by inch, Philip fought his strength and stood up. Leaning on the hood of that old Buick, he looked around and wondered where Tom and Brian went.

Philip looked down at the pieces of sweaty clothing and three empty Pabst Blue Ribbon beer cans that lay next to his own puddle of blood.

Philip's eyes widened, cracking the dried blood from around his temple. "Fuck. The beer," he whispered.

Those three open cans jolted his memory, bringing back the events after those beers were consumed.

"Tom and Brian," he said to himself as he shifted his focus to the far side of the parking lot. "They took Tom and Brian!" His head hurt. His legs had been shot and were not doing well. The noise they made as he shifted his weight led him to believe he had some bone issue. "At least my brains aren't laying on the ground right now," Philip giggled to himself.

Philip knew he needed help. He knew he had to get Tom and Brian some help. But, most importantly, he knew he had to take a chance on The Mecklenburg Hotel, to save his own life.

Philip stood on his broken, gunshot legs looking around the parking lot. He noticed a flatbed industrial shopping cart on the far side. It was away from the woods, and close to Route 3. Philip used to use this type of cart for large items at his favorite home improvement store, Lowe's. It held wood and drywall and lots of bricks for him in the past. It would indeed hold his body.

Philip started to ease his way back to the ground and slid right off the hood of that Buick. "Fuck!" he screamed as the pain engulfed him with the impact of the asphalt.

Philip lay still for a couple of minutes, breathing hard and sweating profusely. His eyes were closed as he tried to control the pain. His legs were swollen and severally discolored. He looked at them and thought they resembled Paul Sheldon's legs, from Stephen King's *Misery*. "I'm your biggest fan," Philip said jokingly.

Philip took a deep breath and began to crawl away from the Buick, toward the flatbed shopping cart. One arm pull at a time, inch by inch, and painful minute by painful minute, Philip made his way closer to that lifesaving transportation.

An hour later, Philip drug himself onto the cart. "I made it. Fuck yeah, I'm home free," he yelled. "Wait. Fuck, I said 'fuck' and didn't stutter. My stutter is gone. What a fucked-up world this is."

"The gunplay must have fixed my stutter," Philip said to himself, slyly. "At least I got that going for me."

Philip lay on his stomach, using his arms to pull the cart in the desired direction. It was working. The wind was even to his back. Philip smiled in thoughts that his luck was turning. He was still around a mile from his much-needed hotel, but regardless, he was making his way to it.

Thirty minutes into his journey, Philip's hands were stripped of skin. The rhythmic left-right-left, pulling his body on the cart through the street, had taken its toll, leaving his palms bloody and raw. The pain was excruciating and all over his body.

Philip stopped briefly to take a break on Route 3 near the Starbucks. He pulled the cart to the storm drain near the entrance and laid his head on his arms. He was a few blocks from the hotel, but his body was shutting down, again.

Philip was having the worst week imaginable, and his body shut the fuck down. His mind slipped away, and down the rabbit hole it went. Philip's mind was protecting itself from the reality of his pain, and from the validity of this fucked-up parallel world. He was chest down on that industrial cart, fast asleep.

As morning crept through the streets, the cart began to shake and shift. At first, it was a slight nudge. But after a few minutes, the shaking escalated violently. An emaciated black dog was chewing on Philip's leg.

Philip woke up slowly, turning his head toward the shaking as his eyes opened. He saw a skeletonized black dog gnawing on his leg.

"Get the fuck off me!" Philip yelled as he reached down and smacked the dog's mouth. The dog yelped but kept chewing. Philip pulled his arm back as far as he could and dropped a fist to the back of the dog's head, with a golfer-like follow-through. The dog flew back off the cart, hitting the concrete curb skull first. This time the black skin and bones didn't get up.

Philip's mind was coming back to him now. He had been dreaming about his senior prom. He had been holding hands and slow dancing with Amy Bolin. He could still hear Def Leppard playing as they danced. Philip smiled and inhaled deeply as he could still smell her hair. She was so beautiful, and he was deeply in love with her. Philip knew she was the one that got away.

Now that the dog was no longer a threat, Philip looked around and remembered he was still gravely injured and needed to get to the hotel. Philip's stomach started to turn. A crampy, bubbling pain. "I gotta crap," Philip said out loud as he began to push the cart off the curb.

One pull after the other, he inched his way down Route 3.

"One foot in front of the other will get you where you're going. *Swansong*. What a great book," Philip said to himself and laughed as he moved down Route 3. His mind was hurting and needed any kind of hope he could get. Philip thought maybe that mantra from *Swansong* could help him. One foot in front of the other—but in his case, one bloody hand pull after the other.

Barbra was a young teenager, fresh in from the new world. She was bold and scared. She came to The Mecklenburg Hotel by pure chance. Her father had crossed over with her but was killed by a skinny man with one eye. That nasty soulless man ate him in front of her. She didn't stick around to see a lot but knew her father's fate in the depths of her heart and soul.

Barbra was able to escape while her father was killed and was lucky enough to be close to the hotel when sentries noticed her. That's how she came to live at the hotel, ultimately becoming a sentry herself.

Barbra was walking the main building perimeter near Route 3. "Barbra to crow's nest, You there?" she asked on her walkie-talkie.

"Go ahead, Barbra."

"Movement coming down Route 3, near the old church on the corner, not far—" Barbra reported but cut herself short as she began to hear the movement yell out in obvious pain.

"We've got eyes on Barbra. Good job. It appears to be a man on a flat and blue cart. He is dragging himself. He's covered in blood," responded a voice from above her.

With Barbra's job done, she continued to follow the protocol. She retreated to the safety of the hotel, locking the door behind her.

Two people in the crow's nest were using binoculars and a rifle with a high-powered scope to observe the bloody mess of a man. The morning light was enough to illuminate the guy. With the viewing equipment, they were able to see the extent of his injuries.

Philip kept pulling and pulling. A foot or two at a time, he was creeping closer and closer to the main entrance of the hotel.

"Stop at the sidewalk in front of the hotel and state your business. We can see you're injured and can help you if that's what you need," a voice from the hotel said over a loudspeaker.

Philip stopped where they instructed and briefly thought to himself, *No shit, I'm hurt.* He took a few breaths and rolled off the cart, then sat himself up against a tree. "My name's Philip. I've been shot a few times. I need help badly. My friends were taken captive. I need water and—"

Philip stopped mid-sentence when he noticed a small team of people running toward him with medical supplies. "Thank you," he said as they approached.

"Philip, quickly answer me one question, and we will help you," one man said.

"Anything," Philip replied.

"It's simple. Do you want to go back home to the real world or not?"

Philip began to cry loudly, "With all my heart, I want to go home. Do you know how to get there?"

The man gave a smile and a quick nod to the group. Like a well-oiled machine, the group gently but efficiently picked Philip up with the litter. With a person on each corner, the group ran Philip into the hotel, straight to their medical room.

Philip now lay on a bed facing a flaking white ceiling. He could hear people talking and moving about in the room. Then a gunshot rang out. He didn't flinch.

"Don't worry, Tim; that shot was one of the snipers above us putting that nasty wild dog down. It's the same skin and bones that was gnawing on your leg," said a tall man wearing thin white surgical gloves.

"Philip, my name is Philip Bilkowski. I used to be a janitor, now I'm just lost in hell apparently," he replied. "Thank you for taking care of me."

"I'm sorry, Philip. I swore someone told me it was Tim."

"You can call me an asshole for all I care, doc," Philip smiled in pain.

"Well, you've been shot and lost a lot of blood. It's a miracle you made it to us," replied the doctor.

Philip smiled as he passed out from the pain. He was off into his mental rabbit hole again.

A bell rang out in four short dings. Everyone in the hotel stopped what they were doing. "Head to the kitchen. Everyone make their way to the kitchen," they whispered to each other. The bell rang out again in four short dings.

The sentries all entered the hotel, headed for the assembly area. The crow's nest did not change. The spotter and shooter teams stayed but became more vigilant, with all the doors locked and barred for their safety.

Most everyone was now in the kitchen. Somewhere around twenty-five or thirty people strong now.

"Everyone, cut the chatter and listen up." A voice yelled as he stood on top of a table near the kitchen door. "The injured man we took in a few hours ago is one of us. He has been seeking a way home, much like us." The crowd shuffled closer to the man on the table. Now he had their full attention. "He's in bad shape. We've worked throughout the night to save him, but only time will tell. Subsequently, and maybe the most important thing, well, while we were working on the man early this morning, he told us a story of a group of bandits that left him for dead as they took Tom and Brian. They were SEEKERS out scavenging food for us here at the hotel."

The man addressing the group was known as Doc. He was tall and muscular, a hard man in his own right. He looked like he hadn't eaten sugar in ten years. In the real world, he was an emergency room nurse, but here in this world, he was the only doctor around.

"Sanders. The preacher," the group whispered. "They took them."

"Listen up. We do believe Sanders and his crew took Tom and Brian. Which means at some point, they will break, and when they break, it will only be a matter of time before THEY find us," Doc said. "We must anticipate them coming here."

"We will be ready, Doc!" a voice from the crowd yelled.

"What about the others? The group Luke took in search of the book. Any word from them?"

Doc looked around, then the bell began to ring out.

"Incoming," a voice yelled out down the hallway. This person was repeating himself as the voice also became closer. Doc jumped from the table and walked into the hallway. The group followed.

"Incoming," the voice said. "We have a group approaching."

The man stopped, hunched over, catching his breath as Doc approached him. "Who's approaching, son?" Doc asked.

After a few breaths, the man replied, "Luke's group is approaching. They're back. The book seekers are back." The man handed Doc a small black two-way radio.

"Hotel to Luke. Do you copy?" Doc asked into the radio. His breathing became noticeably deeper and faster. His body even knew Luke's mission to find the Book of the Black was the key to surviving this fucking world.

"We copy. Coming in hot. Open the rear garage door for us," Luke replied with finality and relief in his voice.

Immediately the group disbanded, and work was quickly getting done. Doc and a few others handled the roll-up doors, only opening one when the group was on top of it.

"Open it," Luke said over the radio.

A sniper on the roof concurred, saying, "I have you guys covered; move straight in. No one's behind them. It's all clear."

For the first time in days, but what seemed like a few hellish weeks, Luke, Kent, Charlotte, Andrew, and Bran were all back in the hotel.

Luke grabbed Doc and held him tight. "I'm so damn glad to see you. We have it," he whispered in his ear. Doc pulled away enough to look Luke in the eyes. "Doc, we found it. Kent has it," Luke said.

Doc looked over at Kent. Then at Charlotte and Andrew. A single tear of sure emotional relief rolled down his face. "Where are the brothers? Juan? Jordon?" he asked.

Kent shook his head with sadness. His eyes were red and watery. Doc instantly knew they were gone. He'd never see them again. His heart knew they were both dead, but his mind, for the first time, wondered, if he died in the parallel world, would his soul be trapped there forever?

Chapter 26: Tom Porter's Decision

The wind pounded the window like a circus monkey clanging symbols during a show. Whether Tom had his eyes open or shut, made no difference. The pounding between his ears was loud and constant. Was it the brutal weather outside, or was it the stress of impending death? Tom had zero control over any outcome, as he was handcuffed to an old wall radiator in the attic of the old church—Ratchford's deep-rooted occult of a church.

Tom's left hand was swelling despite missing most of his fingers. Each hand was individually cuffed to the vintage radiator with a pair of old rusted handcuffs. His back was against the vertical metal, where the water would heat up the tubing when turned on, and his head was directly under the window. Tom had been in this position so long, his neck muscles threw the old towel in, causing his head to slump over to the left as he cried.

"God, please help me. I beg you," Tom said, just above a whisper. "I'm sorry for my sins, Lord. Please, please, please save me. Don't let me die like this. Not here. Not like this. I'm scared to die."

The night passed, and so did the following day. No food, no water. Much like the days leading up to this one, he was starving to death. Tom was cuffed to that vintage radiator. He assumed he would be sitting on his ass until sweet death carried him to the afterlife. His mind was lost. He was in a level of pain most people could not survive. Tom nodded off.

A buzzing began to slowly fill his ears. At first, it was slight, but over the course of the day, it became louder. *What the fuck is that?* Tom thought.

Minute after minute passed, the buzzing became louder and louder. It began to sound like more. Not one thing buzzing, but hundreds of things buzzing.

Tom looked around the best he could with his blown-out neck. One of them landed on his face. It was a fly. "Just a harmless house fly," he said to himself, but loud enough that anyone in the room could have heard it.

One at a time, the flies landed on Tom's face. One became ten, and ten became a hundred. With no rhyme or reason, hundreds of flies were landing on Tom's face, walking about like it was a dog park, and Tom's face was the dog shit laying in the grass.

Tom tried to move his head to shake the insects off but to no avail. Some would fall off and then buzz right back, while the majority stayed and crawled around.

As Tom opened his mouth and began to scream, the flies commenced entering his body. Like a sick and twisted child's game of follow the leader, the flies entered the closest hole they could find. Some went in Tom's eyes, some in his ears, and up his nose. But most of them walked, crawled, or flew into his mouth. They traveled down his throat, choking the life out of him.

Tom jerked himself awake. The flies were gone. No more buzzing, no more crawling, no more flies. He had been asleep or hallucinating; he could no longer tell the difference.

There was an antique clock on the wall. It was dirty, with dash lines for numbers, a black minute hand, and a red hour hand. Neither hand moved nor made a sound since Tom arrived.

Under the wall clock was a small bookshelf that appeared to be a walnut wood, with a crack running the length of the right-hand wall brace. On top of the shelf was a metal stamped rabbit. It looked to be off of an old weathervane. The rabbit was rusty and perched on the ledge facing an old embroidered cloth that read, "Home is where the heart is."

"Fuck you," Tom said, staring at that rabbit. "*Fuck you!*" He screamed as tears rolled down his face again.

Tom was mentally tormented. This parallel world, which THEY call the new world, was pure hell. Tom was beginning to believe he would not survive. Eventually, he would die. He had no choice in the matter. Tom was convinced he would die in that room. It was just a matter of time.

He slept again... until the door opened.

Tom shifted his eyes upward to see a beautiful woman walking in through a hazy background. She kneeled down, grabbed his face, and lifted his head up. They were now staring eye to eye with each other. It was his wife, Kate.

"Baby?" Tom whispered questionably as he drooled and whined. He was a broken man.

Kate smiled and spoke softly, "Ultimately, Tom, you must decide whether to accept that you are already dead and fight for what may be life at the end of this. Or simply roll over and die. Those are your only two options, and only you can decide."

Kate gently kissed his mouth and let him go. She stood up, turned to exit the room, and as she walked away, began singing, "Oh, won't you come home to me."

The door shut, and Tom was alone again.

Chapter 27: Sanders

Sanders slept twelve hours that first night back. He was tired but had also scored some old scotch while on the hunt a few days prior. His bed was comfy in his shitty stale trailer. It was soiled from the past, but then again, in this parallel world, one man's trash is another man's treasure. He had filled his gut, warmed his bones, fucked his red-headed whore, and was ready to get back to business.

Trashman enjoyed his night back home as well. He wasn't as fortunate as some of the other men. He slept in a handmade hammock, in the back of the Costco, near the old cereal aisle. But slept soundly, nonetheless. He even snickered in his sleep while dreaming about that field of balloons and blood.

In the real world, Chief Sanders and Trashman had been nothing. Just a couple of meth addicts who never held a real job. They broke into homes and sold what they could find. Typically, they would take jewelry, small electronics, and always targeted firearms. Anything easy to carry. It was all about the quick money. They were bred to be scum and would ultimately die scum.

While they never knew each other on the outside, inside of this parallel world, they were important. They were gods. Or at least they thought they were.

Sanders drank his coffee slowly that first morning back. He took a mental walk through the past few days. While he wasn't successful in finding the Book of the Black, he got the next best thing: a rat that let him know where the book would eventually be.

He looked out into the street from his trailer's rotten front porch. Sanders sipped that coffee, thinking of what the last few days brought them. He paused, realizing he had seen the white latex balloons before. Not like the ones growing in that hellish field of death, but where? Sanders took another sip, and the warmth reminded him of where he'd seen those balloons before. Near Harbor House. Before he came to this new world.

Sanders finished his coffee, grabbed his pistol, checked the barrel to ensure a round was in the chamber, and slid it into the back of his pants. He began to walk toward the Costco. He needed to find Trashman. It was time to do God's work.

Trashman lay in his hammock, drinking a warm leftover beer from the night before. He was rested but hungry. It was time to start his day. He tossed the beer aside and stood up, stretching tall. This world was a fucked-up place, but he loved it.

Trashman took his pants, shirt, and dirty boxers off. "These are done," he said to himself as he tossed them next to an overflowing trashcan outside of the employee locker room.

Trashman turned the bathroom light on. Smiling, he walked in and turned the shower on. The water would heat up quickly, but only last a few minutes, but he didn't care; he was going to scrub his nuts and wash the blood off of him "just like Jesus," he said as the blood flowed out of his hair and down the drain.

Trashman laughed and laughed. Then he heard a voice.

"Trashy. Where the fuck are you?" Sanders called out.

"In the shower, Chief," he replied while scrubbing his body with an old hairy bar of soap.

The steam was heavy and warm in the air as Sanders walked into the row of communal showers. "Washing your nasty ass for a change?" he asked Trashman while striking a wooden match. Sanders touched the flame to his stale Marlboro. He inhaled deeply, as Trashman replied, "Washing off the old blood, to make room for the new blood boss."

"Trashy, you're an animal. Wash all of the last few days off; we have some new death to cover us in. Open your ears; I have a plan," Sanders said.

Two of the worst humans ever conceived began to plot and plan while the shower turned ice cold. They planned for nearly thirty minutes. In the end, Sanders began to walk away and turned back to Trashman. "I'll tell the preacher. Ready your boys," he said, and walked off.

"Today, the Lord brings us all together as one. He has forsaken all the others and gave us this new world. The Lord wants us to start over with his vision," Ratchford preached from his pulpit. "Look around. You will not see your loved ones—your wife, your husband, nor your kids. The Lord chose you, as your family was full of sin, and he knew they could not be trusted to properly serve him in this new world."

"Amen!" The congregation of nearly forty strong echoed into the air of the church. "We will follow his word, preacher. Before God, we swear his word will trickle from our lips," a woman said.

Sanders walked into the church, took a seat, seizing the moment of the education from the sermon. He always enjoyed the rule of God rolling off the preacher's tongue. It was settling to him, soul-cleansing, as he wholeheartedly believed he was righteous in all of his actions.

An hour later, the sermon was over, and everyone had left the church. The preacher noticed Sanders walk in halfway through and took a seat in the back.

"Chief Sanders, come on up and talk with me," Ratchford said with a serpent-like hiss. The preacher knew Sanders was fresh in from the hunt and expected good news.

Sanders was used to Ratchford not having eyes. It wasn't like he was always blind, but rather, one day the preacher chose to take his own eyes out. Regardless, the fact that he always knew when Sanders was in the room reinforced that the preacher was chosen by God himself to lead this new world.

"I have news, preacher," Sanders began explaining as he walked upfront.

The preacher licked his lips.

"We did not find the group we sat out to hunt. We did, however, learn the group was searching for the Book of the Black," Sanders began.

The preacher jumped off his pulpit and appeared to "float" down to the ground. Sanders continued, "We did not find the book either, but we know where it is going!"

The preacher smiled with his dirty, shit brown, stained teeth and began to speak with Sanders. After a while, a plan had been formulated, and Sanders was sent off to execute it.

Tom Porter woke up to a rotting smell. He couldn't quite figure it out. Was it him, or was it the demonic church attic in which he was held captive? He was clueless, and his will to find an answer was fading faster than his resolve to live.

Tom was mentally torn; his mind was melted down like a candle fresh out of wax. He was physically exhausted and beaten to a shade of color not even his mom wouldn't recognize. He hurt so bad. The pain traveled all the way into his soul.

Tom had been shot, beaten, kidnapped, and maimed for life when Preacher Ratchford bit off three of his fingers, witnessed his friends being tortured to death, and left handcuffed to the radiator in the attic of an old demonic church.

Tom's body slouched as the minutes and hours ticked by. "Fuck you, rabbit," he slurred. "Fuck—"

He was cut off. Tom was staring at the embroidery next to that rabbit. It read, "Home is where the heart is," with a red heart stitched in the center. But now, that heart was beating.

The heart seemed to be in rhythm with Tom's. With each breath he took, the embroidered heart would beat. Tom's pulse began to race when he noticed what was happening. The walls started to creak. It sounded like air rushing through an old, unused, metal water pipe. It was spine-chilling. Then he noticed the heart stopped beating and started bleeding.

The blood started as a slow drip. One drop at a time, every second or two, it would pulse out of the heart and run down the cloth. Tom continued to stare at this sadistic anomaly.

Drops of blood quickly turned to a steady flowing stream. Out of the heart, down the wall, and on to the floor in front of Tom, the blood flowed.

Tom began to scream. The blood started to cover his legs. The room was flooding. Flooding with blood.

Tom thrashed about; his legs were slipping and sliding in the slippery, copper-smelling, life-sustaining liquid. "*What the fuck!*" Tom screamed while trying to pull his mangled left hand through the old, rusty stainless-steel cuff.

Tom was getting mad. His mind jumped off the "suicide bridge" and left his body behind. Tom fought as the room was flooding. He was covered up to his chest with an unstoppable blood bath.

It was now or never. This was the pivotal point for Tom. He had to accept the fact that he was already dead, and start to fight right now, or roll over and give up. Either fight or open his mouth and willingly drown to death in blood. It was time to start living or start dying.

"*Fuck you, rabbit!*" Tom yelled while using every ounce of strength he could muster. The blood was closing in on his chin. Tom ripped his mangled hand free from its binding.

Tom stood up, his right hand still cuffed to the radiator. He was in pain but shut it out. Tom was a new man. His anger fueled a hatred that could save him while the crimson copper-tasting blood continued to fill the room.

Tom surveyed the attic for anything that could help him. Offhand he didn't notice anything of value, but then his left foot stepped on something under that lake of blood. "Well, looky, looky," Tom said as he fished out that rusted metal rabbit.

Tom smiled, thinking the rabbit had been taunting him. But now he realized maybe that rabbit was there for him to use all along. Perhaps the rabbit was never taunting him, but instead staring at him as if to say, "I'm here. Use me, you fucking idiot."

The rabbit was a thin sheet metal, yet sturdy and sharp in his hand. Tom got to work while he was now knee-deep in thick sticky blood. His first thought was to use the jagged metal like a knife to skin his wrist enough to slip the cuff off. His second thought was to use the rabbit's ear to shimmy the cuff open. The blood was rising faster, and the noise of the old pipes in the wall was ear-piercing.

Tom was standing in the window with a metal rabbit in his hand, blood flowing up his legs, and his right wrist cuffed to the radiator. His left hand was missing three fingers, making it next to impossible to hold onto the blood-soaked metal rabbit. He attempted to slice around the palm of his hand, but his mangled hand wouldn't allow him to create enough force to cut into his own meat.

"*Fucking rabbit!*" Tom yelled. He was just about to throw that metal curse away when he noticed a little girl outside on the sidewalk, looking up at him. She was beautiful, dressed in a ruby-red dress. The girl was staring directly at him.

Tom paused briefly, while the little girl, maybe ten years old, shook her head slowly, with a stern face. Tom stared back, unconsciously shaking his head. The girl was telling him not to give up. He realized, again, this was his last chance as the blood consumed the room.

Tom now went with plan two. He shimmied the rabbit's thin metal ear into the cuff between the ratcheting metal teeth and, just like that, the cuff gave way. Tom was free. He looked out the window, lifting both hands up, signaling he was free. The little girl in the ruby-red dress continued to gaze upon him, waving her hand toward herself, as if telling Tom to come to her and leave that demonic church, so she could show him something.

Tom did not hesitate. He opened the door, allowing the river of blood to rush down the steps as he made his escape.

Chapter 28: The Book

Luke James was back at The Mecklenburg Hotel and back in charge. Doc gladly stepped away from the overall responsibilities, retreating to his medical duties. He had done a fine job in Luke's absence, but it was hard keeping the hotel together.

Luke wasted no time. He asked for a warm meal to be made for the newly returned men. They would eat and get right to business.

Kent's mind replayed the horrors of the past few days, as he sipped his black coffee. It felt like ages since he had such a sweet-tasting pick-me-up. He thought the food was above-average. Fresh smoked ham from a top-shelf Hormel can. Fresh carrots cooked in butter, fresh salad, and even some almost-stale Little Debbie's for dessert. Nothing but the best for the weary.

The group finished their meal and wanted to hit the water-bucket showers, then go to bed, but time was of the essence. They all knew the key to escaping their tormented parallel world was inside of the Book of the Black. They just had to read it, understand it, and interpret it.

Doc looked across the table at Kent. He was scared but asked anyway, "How do we get home? What's the book say?"

Luke started to speak, but Kent beat him to it. "I'm not sure what it says. I mean, I think I can read it. Well sort of. The script, I mean language—oh hell, I mean both, really. They are nothing I've ever seen before. But when push came to shove, I was able to read some of it. That's what got us off that fucking island."

Doc stared at Kent and Charlotte, who was next to him. They both looked dirty, beaten, aged. Luke and Andrew were in the same condition, yet Bran seemed as jovial as ever.

"What the fuck happened out there? What happened to Jordon? To Juan? What happened?" he asked with sheer shock in his eyes. He wanted to know the answers but also didn't what to know. He couldn't help himself. Over the next ten minutes, the answers came. Jordon was still dead, and Juan was left buried alive on the island. Doc regretted asking, as internally his heart waned.

Kent pulled the old book from inside of his shirt. "Strangely, it's always warm against my skin," he said as he laid it on that dining room table.

It was old. Cracked, faded grey leather, probably from aging. The book was hardbound with thin, uneven leather sewing holding the cover to the spine. The pages were glued in place, as most books were, but the glue's residue a dark maroon red and smelled of copper.

The Book of the Black was folklore, or so the people of this parallel world believed, until today. Now it was on the table before them. It was their key to going home, but it was also a piece of evil damned by the blackness of the very women that created it.

Kent opened the book as it lay on the metal table. The leather binding and spine cracked like an old person walking. The pages fluttered slightly as an unnatural breeze blew dust into the air, off of the pages.

"Do you feel that?" Charlotte asked. "Put your hands on the table. It's getting warmer."

The group touched the table and realized Charlotte was right. The cool touch of the metal was gone, and the longer they put their hands on the table, the warmer it became.

"The first time I opened the book, strange things happened," Kent explained. "But it also opened the door for us to escape the island."

Kent began to read. At first, it didn't make sense. The letters weren't right. Kent felt they were, well, out of order was the best way he could describe them.

The minutes began to tick off, and the dining room became more and more uncomfortable. The temperature was rising, like a fire had broken out and no one was trying to stop it. The air became thinner and warmer.

As Kent turned page after page, people got up from the table, sweating heavily and left the room. The temperature kept rising. Everyone left the room except for Kent and Luke.

"Are you okay?" asked Luke as he could no longer stand to touch the table. Kent did not reply. He kept reading to himself. Luke stood up and began to pace around the tables. He walked over to the snack area, grabbed a cup of water and a Nutter-Butter. Nervous eating, some people would call it.

Luke chugged down a glass of water, paused for a second, and downed another one. "You thirsty, man?" he asked Kent. Again, he received no response.

Kent stared intensely at the pages, moving his lips without the pause that naturally occurred while reading. His hands were tight around the old leather. The visible amount of sweat running down his face was uncanny. Luke was beginning to take note of everything about Kent and everything about the dining room. The changes were fast and without reason.

"Yo, Kent, are you okay? You want to take a break? Get some water?" Luke asked. Again, no response. Kent did not flinch. But instead, his face became pale.

The temperature in the room continue to rise, and Kent continued to read.

Luke's lungs began to burn with every breath. "Fucking hell, I feel like I'm breathing in fire over here," he said while Kent ignored him.

Luke unbuttoned his shirt, hoping for some reprieve from the heat. No luck, so he took it off. The air was stifling. Luke never had an issue with claustrophobia in the past, but he was beginning to get a little queasy and scared.

Kent's lips continued to move, absent of sound. The air was thick, humid, and hot.

The lights in the dining room began to dim and flicker. That was the final straw for Luke. He ran around Kent's table and grabbed the doorknob. "Fucking son of a bitch!" Luke yelled as his hand smoked. The knob was timeworn metal and burned into his palm, leaving a perfect MH, for Mecklenburg Hotel. He screamed. Kent's painful voice rang out as he fell to the floor next to the dining room exit doors.

On The Mecklenburg Hotel roof lay multiple snipers. Were they trained snipers? No. But it was the best the SEEKERS could do in this parallel world. They typically operated in pairs consisting of a shooter and spotter. The teams were always short on people and rifles that could shoot a longer distance, but when fully staffed, they would have at least three teams on the roof.

"Command, come back!" radioed a desperate-sounding sniper running the roofline. "We are headed in *now*!"

The weather had takin a turn for the worse; clouds above the hotel looked like a dirty avalanche in the sky, all black and rolling. Within a few short minutes, the snipers watched multiple dark grey and black funnels form on all sides of the hotel. The unpromising clouds brought wind gusts circling around the hotel.

"What the fuck is happening?" one of the spotters screamed as he ran with the others, headed for the door leading to the rooftop steps.

Lightning bounced around the black funnel above the hotel, constantly flashing every couple of seconds, with zero time between the thunder rolls.

"Get inside—"

Lightning hit the roof, burning one sniper, instantly charring him. The other three made it to the roof steps. They hit that doorway so fast, the first guy fell down the stairs, breaking his arm. The other two, a sniper and spotter team, picked him up and took him the rest of the way to safety.

What was left of the sniper teams made it to the hallway outside of the dining room. They were met by Doc and a handful of others.

"It's a tornado. On the roof," the man with the broken arm said. Bran was barking loudly, while Charlotte attempted to control him. The man stopped talking as he noticed the intense heat emitting from the doors next to him.

"Get out of the way!" a man said as he ordered a small group of men to use a flagpole dressed in an American flag as a ram. Blow after blow, the men tried to force their way into the dining room. The flag waved with each strike as a strange orange glow emitted from under the double doors.

"Is the kitchen on fire?" asked a surviving sniper.

Doc was yelling for Luke as the others were breaking the doors. Each strike brought them closer to what they needed, what they had to get: inside.

"It's the book!" Charlotte yelled in response to the sniper. "We have to shut the book, or we are all going to die."

After several minutes, both doors broke open, but the right door was blocked by Luke's body. The heat was close to overwhelming the group. But Doc was able to use the group as a temporary shield, long enough for him to drag Luke from the deadly heat.

The group pulled back away from the door, watching the mirage wave in the air. The heat was so incredible, paint was melting, turning to liquid and running down the walls. The mirage was dancing and rising off the floor, like hot asphalt on a summer day. From the hallway looking in, the room looked like an oven.

Charlotte stared into the dining room, and Kent was sitting facing them, motionless, eyes rolled back in his head. Kent held the book as his hands smoked and his lips moved, still void of any sound. She knew if she did not shut the book, the hotel was doomed.

Charlotte grabbed Bran, and with one command, sent him running at Kent. Bran jumped up on the table, launching himself at Kent. Bran clamped down on Kent's right forearm and his momentum separated Kent from the book. Success. A moment later, Charlotte ran in and held her breath while picking up the book.

The book shined orange as her hands burned, but only until she forced it shut. Like waking violently from a nightmare, the book was closed, and the heat was gone. The air temperature was lowered, and the table was cold again. They could no longer hear the storm above the hotel, and Luke was waking up.

Kent lay on the ground with Bran attached to his arm. Charlotte put the book on the table and called Bran off and back to her. He complied easily.

Luke sat up, breathing deeply and soaking wet, like he took a shower with clothes on. Luke held his hand to his chest. He was burned badly. "Could someone get me some ice, please?" he asked as he stood up, walking into the hallway. Even though "it" was over, he did not want to be near that dining room.

Blackness clouded Kent's mind as his eyes were shut. He was in the same room with his friends. The same room where he broke bread with them, before and after the hunt for the book. But he couldn't see them. The Book of the Black was holding him, imbedded in his brain.

Kent was finishing the story in his head. The story the book wanted him to know. The story his lips were soundlessly reading— the story of the book itself, of the town.

Kent could see a tall female dressed in black. She was old, pale, decrepit, and floating. He was staring at her, mesmerized as the old lady lifted her hand, pointing her boney finger at something behind him. She wanted him to see something. Kent turned his head—

"Wake the *fuck* up!" Andrew screamed as he drew blood with a slap across Kent's mouth. "*Wake up*, damn it! Open your eyes!"

Kent's skin color was turning ripe as blood flowed back into his face. His body cooled, and his eyes rolled open. He looked around, took a deep breath, and quickly sat up. His body was so wet, you would think he just got out of the pool.

"I know where the exit is," Kent spoke with a high-pitched crackling voice. "We all came here after touching a stone, and the way back is no different. I found the exit stone. She showed me. That old lady showed me. It's inside Harbor House. The psychiatric hospital. In the basement—"

Once Kent spoke those words, the Book of the Black ignited. A fire flashed tall, straight out of the pages, fast and violent. Everyone in the room ran for the exit. The fire spread quickly. It danced from the book onto the ceiling and spread like water inside of the *Titanic* as it sank. Brilliant orange and red flames spread across the dining room and into the kitchen.

Charlotte was the last one out of the dining room. She turned after she left and pulled the doors shut on the orange flames while they consumed the room.

The beginning of the end was upon them.

Chapter 29: Good versus Evil

The blackish hell above the hotel vanished quicker than when it first appeared. The flags out front were no longer ripping apart in the wind. The tattered remains lay motionless against the silver pole itself. The stars were barely noticeable, but the blue background was still intense. The storm departed quicker than God snatching souls at a car crash.

Debris littered the sidewalk out to Route 3 and across Central Avenue. The storm was quick and violent, but its destruction was mostly centered over the hotel.

Trees were broken over at their base, laying on the road and sidewalks. A power line fell across Route 3 in the distance near the Starbucks. And a white Border Collie sat like a statue in front of the police station.

William Close, a salty SEEKER, was on sentry duty out front when the storm hit. He was caught outside and had a choice to make. While standing at the flagpole, he had to chance running to the shelter of the hotel a couple hundred yards behind him or take cover in the sewer system ten yards in front of him—the same system Kent crawled out of last week. He chose the sewer.

William descended into the open manhole and waited the storm out. He was used to horrendous weather and strange things in this parallel world.

Once the storm passed, William stretched his legs and started to crawl out of the damp sewer. As he stood back on the road, movement down Central Avenue, near the police station, caught his eye. He continued to stretch his back out but focused his attention down the road.

"There," he whispered to himself, "right there."

William's eyes were last tested at twenty/ten vision, and not much got past him, if anything.

The police station had two lighted domes on the front steps that read "Police" and could be seen for blocks. They must have been solar because they were always brightly lit. William noticed from his angle, only one dome was readable. Then, a second later, they both were readable. *Movement*, he thought. *Someone just ran across the street and passed that dome*, he thought.

"Contact, Central Police Station, we have *contact*," William relayed into his two-way radio. He looked again with his radio still in his hand. William now saw a mass movement of bodies run across Central Avenue, from the far side of Bob's Barbershop, and in front of the police station.

William estimated thirty to forty people were running across the road. "Command, do you copy? Contact! We are being attacked!" he yelled into the radio. William could hear the people getting closer. He knew right away it was a group of either bandits or THEM, and he wasn't sticking around to find out their intent.

William ran for the hotel. Step after step, the doors got closer, as did the sound of the oncoming people. Just before entering the door, he looked over his shoulder and the real evil appeared. One man was on hot on his tail with a cleaver in one hand and joy in his eyes. This man was leading the onslaught of the masses thirty yards behind him.

William pulled the door open, entered, and in a series of fast, trained movements, shut the door and chained it secure. He stood in front of that metal door and heard the massive thuds from the other side, and right in the middle of the thuds, he heard a man start talking.

"Men, we will get inside of this hotel if it kills every last one of us. We will dine on their blood today. They will see our God, one way or another, they will see our God!" Trashman preached to the hoard of people as they bashed themselves against the door. The fight was on.

Charlotte stood outside the dining room; doors were shut with a fire raging behind them. Luke was awake, catching his breath and profoundly sweating. Doc was in awe at what was happening, and Kent was silent. They all knew what was transpiring inside of the dining room, but on the outside, where they were regrouping, what was more important, was one single word: hope.

Kent just gave them all hope. There was a way home. A way out of this fucked-up world and an end to this madness. Kent built hope in seeing his wife again. Charlotte was full of hope to get home, but sad that she had yet to find her daughter.

"Command, do you copy? Contact!" a two-way radio squelched in Doc's hand. It was a sentry, warning of something. "Command, go ahead? What did you say?" Doc replied over his radio. No answer.

"They said contact, goddamn it. Get your snipers back on the roof. We are about to be engaged," Luke yelled. He stood up and moved with a purpose. "Charlotte, you know where we need you. Do it!"

Charlotte grinned devilishly. "Bran, come," she commanded of her dog. She ran to her room, grabbing her scoped rifle, and a couple of boxes of ammo. She was about to deal some "death," and Bran followed with his tongue hanging out.

Luke ran to the command room with activity buzzing around him. He grabbed a spare radio and his rifle. "Get everyone ready. We have been found," he said.

Doc ran to the arms room and opened the door among several people impatiently awaiting to retrieve a firearm. It was a glorious gift, when one day, on a food scavenge, a group of SEEKERS came across a fully stocked gun store. Grant's gun shop was a hidden gem, untouched and full of ammo, rifles, pistols, and black powder. The SEEKERS stripped that place clean to the bone, and today all that effort was about to pay off.

Gunshots echoed from outside. "There is a massive amount of people at the front door," a sniper radioed from the rooftop. "We have our guys on the corners of the roof. Right now, the contact is all out front."

"Keep us posted. Do whatever you have to do to keep them out of the hotel," Luke answered as he was instructing people to gather fire extinguishers for the dining-room fire.

"Command, the doors to the kitchen are buckling from the fire. I've used my last extinguisher!" radioed a SEEKER.

For the first time in weeks, Charlotte stepped onto the roof with her rifle. She was quite a marksman. Better than anyone else at the hotel. Gunshots echoed in the air while she lowered her center of gravity. Charlotte crawled on her belly to a spot near the center of the roof, dragging her gear behind her. She stopped at a safe area that would give her a perfect view, lay on her side, set up her Remington 700 bolt action rifle, and rolled to her back. Charlotte was a few feet from the edge of the roof. She pulled a zippo out from her front pocket and lit the fuse attached to a small pipe bomb in her right hand.

"Go back to the hell where you came from!" she screamed as she tossed the pipe into the crowd of people below her. For a moment, the pipe smoked and sparked while the invaders were working hard, trying to get into the hotel.

The explosion rocked the side of the hotel. Flesh, blood, and burned clothing painted the hotel brick three stories high.

Charlotte rolled over to her rifle and calmly began scanning the area in front and below her for people to drop. This was her favorite thing to do. The power behind that scoped rifle was absolute. Charlotte and Charlotte alone decided who would die once they found themselves inside of her scope. This power was too much of a burden for some, but not Charlotte. She thrived on it. She craved it. She was a natural at separating a soul from its body.

After the explosion, a mist of blood cascaded the roof, spraying across Charlotte's back and left cheek. She found herself looking for bodies and wondering how many she had killed with that display of high ground dominance.

The commotion below her was silenced for the moment. She noticed a few people running toward the road. *Squirters, three hundred yards to the manhole cover*, she internalized in her mind. *Wind zero*. She let her breath out, gently squeezing the trigger as she trapped a thirty-year-old male running into her crosshairs, just before Route 3. He fell in stride right at the manhole, dead before he hit the ground.

Charlotte ejected the empty bullet casing from her rifle's chamber. It made such a sweet sound as the empty brass casing bounced on the rooftop. She loaded the next round smoothly, and quickly, as she acquired person after person. Man or woman made no difference to her. She was there to do a job, and by God, she was going to succeed. She was stacking bodies from a distance.

"The door had been breached, they're inside—" a voiced yelled on the radio.
Luke just sent a group off to fight the fire in the kitchen. He was becoming overwhelmed, so in an attempt to calm his mind, Luke began to breathe slowly and rhythmically. He did this to slow the events in his mind so he could make the best decisions possible for the SEELKERS. "All hands, we have a security breach, prepare to defend yourselves!" Luke replied on the radio.

The kitchen fire was raging. Flames engulfed the walls, the floors, and the ceiling, creating a type of tornado effect of dancing swirling fire. Like a whirlpool, it churned and devoured anything it came into contact with. The doors were buckling outwardly, about to explode, when the newly appointed "firefighters" arrived with their extinguishers.

"Spray the door and the base of it. If we can push the flames back enough, we can open it up and push the fire back until it's smothered," one of the SEEKERS said.

A man and a woman stepped up, spraying the doors. One extinguisher after the other were used. It appeared to be working. The doors were moving back to their standard shape, and it seemed the intensity of the heat was decreasing.

Another man showed up, dragging a hose and yelled, "Turn it on! Turn it on," as he stood firm in front of the doors ready to fight. He was holding an actual firehose.

"Where the hell did you get that thing?" asked a girl.

"I broke the glass out and pulled it out of the wall from around the corner," the man replied as the hose charged with water. He sprayed the door and yelled, "Open this bitch up and help me hold the hose."

The pressure hit high as the group stood holding the hose in front of the doors. The water stopped briefly enough for the doors to be kicked open. The water turned back on, and the group stood staring at a midnight-black charred room.

"Where'd the fire go?" the same inquisitive female asked from behind the group. No one replied.

The lead SEEKER continued to spray the room, turning the water into steam, which pushed back into their faces, leaving contact burns. They handled the hose and made their way into the kitchen.

"Command, the fire seems to be under control," another man in the group radioed.

"Command copies. Great job."

The men continued to spray water with a jovial banter believing they had won the battle. The smiles were short lived, as a metallic moaning was heard. It sounded like a whale inside of a pipe. The sound increased in volume, becoming creepier and creepier.

Super-heated air rushed through the kitchen, blowing a whale sound over them, across the dining room and out into the hallway. The airflow was so intense, the people in the hallway were knocked off their feet.

"What the fuck was that?" the questioning female asked while flat on her back.

The group set up, just in time to watch the flames follow that horrific whale sound in the air, over the men in the kitchen, out into the hallway, instantly burning them all alive. The fire ripped through them like a tornado, raging once again. But now it was no longer contained to the dining room and kitchen. The fire was loose, eating the hotel an inch at a time.

Charlotte's ill-placed pipe bomb killed numerous people, but ultimately the explosion also breached the door, allowing free passage inside for all. Trashman was now inside the hotel and was seemingly unfazed by the blast. The evil was about to commence, with a hatchet in one hand and a knife in the other. He was bleeding from the ears as he walked around inside with hate in his heart and murder on his mind.

Kent was in the command center with Luke when Doc staggered in, yelling, "They're inside, and the fire has made it down to the arms room." Doc collapsed with smoke rising from his clothing. The left side of his face was burned to a crisp.

"You okay?" Kent asked just before Doc fell into his arms. He laid Doc's motionless body on the cold tile floor. "I think he's dead," said Kent.

Snipers on the rooftop were dropping people every few minutes. Some close up, but most were using buildings across Route 3 for cover and periodically would poke their head out for a few moments too long. Trashman's group of Bible-loving believers were savvy. A lot were killed in the explosion, but not all of them.

Trashman and his surviving men walked through the breached hotel door, caused by Charlotte's misplaced pipe bomb.

"Command, we have a problem," radioed the rear-watching sniper. "I'm out of ammo, and a group of bandits just breached the rear service roll-up door! They've entered the hotel!" A shot rang out just before his radio fell silent forever.

"Luke, we now have two doors breached, and the fire is taking over the west wing. We have to get out of here! We have to get to Harbor House. It's our only chance!" Kent yelled.

The command room fell eerily quiet. The air was full of fear and hope for Luke to guide them to salvation.

"Give the evacuation order. Ring it out constantly. Loop it on the radios and head for the rally point!" Luke commanded with confidence.

"Where's the rally point?" Kent asked.

"There's an old vehicle maintenance building, on Duke Mining Road, near the dead-end of Route 3, just outside of town. It's about four miles from here. Straight up Route 3," Luke explained. "Ironically enough, it's not far from Harbor House." He laughed, shaking his head.

"I'll meet you there. Get the word out, save as many people as you can. I'll meet you. Then we will all head to Harbor House, and we *all* will go home," Kent said with a confidence Luke had never seen before. He knew Kent meant what he was saying and they were all going home.

"Don't be late," Luke jokingly replied as he embraced him.

Kent ran from the room, and the evacuation order was sent.

A siren started howling from the rooftop of The Mecklenburg Hotel. Charlotte looked through her scope, squeezed off another round, dropping a "looky-loo" from the side of Bob's Barbershop. It was a guy she recognized from the real world. Charlotte hated his guts back home, so she sure as fuck hated his guts in this parallel damnation. She smiled as he bled to death on the barber's floor.

Charlotte heard the bell tower ring, and it didn't stop. Gong after bellowing gong. She knew what it meant, and she could smell the blazing fire inside of the hotel. Black smoke was blowing up, rolling over the west wing roofline. She knew it was time to get off the top of the hotel and time to evacuate to the rally point. She knew all was lost, and the proverbial ship was being abandoned.

Charlotte collapsed her rifle's bipods. Bran was still by her side; the rest of the snipers and spotters were either gone or dead. She knew they were mostly dead.

Charlotte crawled to the center of the roof, looking for anything to scavenge from the dead. She moved over to Harlon. His head was split like a dropped melon. She knew he carried a rope on him. Harlon would use it to hoist his gear from the ground or for resupply operations. Charlotte snatched it up, took some food from his pack, and replenished her ammo with what Harlon had left. Charlotte bent down and kissed Harlon's now cold, pale cheek. "I'll tell your wife you loved her," she said with a tear in her eye.

"Bran, here boy," Charlotte commanded her dog. Bran came as ordered, leaning against her leg. She slipped the rope through the loop on the dog's body harness and pulled it halfway through. Now the rope went from 120 feet to sixty feet in length.

The fire was getting worse. Charlotte knew she was going to have a hard time escaping that hot shitty rooftop, and more than likely was about to die, just like the others.

"Bran, I may die, but I can't let you die with me. You'll at least have a fighting chance. I love you!" Bran licked Charlotte's face, while she kissed him back, rubbing his head.

Charlotte held both ends of the rope, gunshots echoed in the distance and rounds zinged by her head. She crawled to the edge of the roof. Looked over the edge surveying the ground, no one was there.

"I'll see you again," she told Bran in his ear, just before lowering him to his freedom below. Hand over hand she lowered him, ultimately pulling the rope all the way through the loop on his harness.

Bran was safely on the ground. He was free. No matter what happened from this point forward, Charlotte had given Bran a fighting chance. She gave him the command to "hunt," and off Bran went into the forest, looking for a fight.

Charlotte surveyed the rooftop, quickly looking for an anchor point for her newly acquired rope. She was going to try and escape in a way much like Bran. Charlotte couldn't find one that would hold her and her gear. So, she had to make do.

Charlotte crawled back to Harlon and moved his body lengthwise on one side of two drainage pipes. She wrapped the rope around Harlon's torso and tied a knot. Charlotte threw the other end of the rope off the edge. With a thick pair of gloves and gear strapped to her back, Charlotte grabbed the rope and began to slide with control to the ground.

Charlotte swung her rifle around her body and into her hands. "Here, boy. Bran, here," she called for her dog. But too much time had passed since she saved him. Bran never came. He was gone, and Charlotte was on her own.

The hotel was compromised. A fire stormed through the hotel, and two different factions were now inside, killing any SEEKER they could get their hands on. A group of THEY and a group of THEM. Who knows if they would fight each other or come together in a common bond of the destruction of the SEEKERS?

"Andrew, follow me!" Kent yelled while passing him in the hallway.

"I'm with ya!" Andrew replied.

Kent led the way down the hall, running for the stairwell while people ran past with Andrew screaming as they ran by, "To the rally point, everyone to the rally point!"

Kent pushed the door to the stairs open, heat and grey mechanical-tasting smoke rolled toward them. "We have to get to the basement," Kent said as they contemplated going down the stairs. Andrew had been a resident of the hotel for a while. He knew what was kept in the basement and knew precisely what Kent had in mind once they reached the bottom.

"Fuck it, man; hold your breath and let's run for it," Andrew said. Both men took a breath and ran into the blinding smoke. They hugged the walls and flew down five flights of stairs. They realized the door to the third floor was open, allowing the smoke to funnel up to the top floors. The men moved until they were three floors below the fire and could breathe again.

Kent took off his backpack and pulled out a hammer. He wasted no time breaking the multiple deadbolt locks off of the entrance door to the basement. The sign on the door read, "No One Enters," and both men hated they were going inside but had little choice at this point.

The basement door opened to a dark and damp airtight hallway with three other doors. Behind each door was a cell with multiple people inside. They called these people "crazies" because they survived solely from cannibalism.

"The plan is simple, Andrew. Our people need all the help they can get. We let the crazies out and start running. Hopefully, they will follow us to the assholes attaching our people upstairs. I know these fuckers hate THEM and THEY more than they hate us. Let's hope we can use them as weapons to even the score or at least buy us some time to get as many people out to the rally point as possible," Kent explained.

"I thought that's what you were gonna say," Andrew said as he patted Kent on his shoulder. "I'm with you. Let's make this quick," he retorted with sweat pouring from his face.

SEEKERS were running all around the hotel, trying to escape the fire and the horde of attackers. A small group of women and one man were running down the east wing second-floor hallway when they came across Trashman.

With blood oozing from a nasty cut on the side of his head, Trashman walked straight for them with a hatchet in his hand. The male of the group stepped up, attempting to shield the women by fighting this mad man, but was of no challenge for Trashman's biblical cleaning of souls.

Before the man could scream, the hatchet was soaring through the air and met its mark, dead center of the man's face. He was dead before he hit the ground, and the women continued to scream.

Luke James was running down the east wing stairwell with other survivors, trying to make their way to the rear roll-up doors, so they could make their escape to the rally point.

Luke led the way out off of the stairs and through the loading dock. The roll-up door was destroyed from the earlier assault. A nice man-sized hole was cut into the door. At least now it was making for an easy exit.

Once the outside light hit Luke, he noticed Charlotte was just off of the dock, fighting two people. Luke, while still in stride, pulled out his pistol and dispatched both of Charlotte's attackers.

"Charlotte!" Luke yelled.

"Thanks for that, my pistol jammed—"

Her words were cut short by a small group of THEM armed with hammers and sickles, advancing at them from the forest.

"Fuck, fuck, fuck," Luke said, while the group he just led outside stopped dead in their tracks. "Back inside, quick," he yelled as everyone turned around and ran back through that man-sized hole in the roll-up door.

Charlotte took Luke's advice and followed the group. "Quick, help me push this," Charlotte said as she began pushing a meat freezer from the kitchen to the loading dock. "We have to block that door. We need to barricade it, and then we can all run out the front entrance."

Everyone quickly pitched in. Within a few seconds, they were able to jam that man-made entrance to the door.

"That will buy a few minutes. At least from that group, it will," Luke said. "Follow Charlotte; she knows where to go." Without hesitation, Luke intuitively handed over command to Charlotte.

They fled the loading area as the outside group of THEM fought to get past the barricade.

Kent opened up all three doors exposing the metal containment cells within. The smell wasn't quite death, but it wasn't life either. He counted nearly ten crazies split among the rooms. They were pale people. Their eyes were a milky white, like what you would see in decrepitly old people with severe cataracts. Even the two kids had "those" eyes. Their clothing was torn, with bloody grime smeared all over, and all of them were missing shoes. They stood a few feet from the cell door with confrontational posture; clinched fists, slightly leaned forward with racing heart rates beating from their neck.

With the doors open, Kent stood in the center of the hallway. "I mean you no harm, but there are people in this hotel that do. They are vile people and easily recognized. We are going to let all of you out. Do what you will, but the hotel in on fire." The crazies didn't move. No acknowledgment of any kind. They were starved and so hungry they couldn't understand their only chance to survive, depended on whether or not Kent opened the cells.

"Kent, I'm starting to think this is a bad idea," Andrew said, shrugging, just as the crazies, in unison, turned their gaze at him.

"When we open the doors, follow us," Kent said.

Andrew gave the nod letting Kent know he was ready. He would open the first door, farthest down the hall. As Kent opened the second door, Andrew would leapfrog him and open the third door, and once the last cell was open, Andrew would follow Kent up the stairs to the second floor. The plan was perfect—dangerous, but perfect.

Kent opened the first cell, and the crazies stood still. Kent ran past Andrew, and Andrew popped the door on the second cell. Again, the crazies stood motionless. Like statues in a museum, they didn't move. Kent ran past Andrew, and Andrew did the same as Kent opened the last cell. With all three cell doors open, both Kent and Andrew ran out of the basement and up the stairs.

Trashman was running amok on the second floor. He was on a killing spree and reveling in it. His beliefs were so skewed and warped that he was preaching to people as he killed them. He wasn't trying to convert anyone on this day. He was bloodthirsty and had a never-ending "flask" to fill.

Trashman left an elderly man lifeless on the now blood-soaked hallway carpet. He walked down the hall, stepping in a wet raspberry slush of blood soaked deep into the carpet. Trashman made his way toward the center of the hotel. The second floor was unique in the fact that it was also the ground floor for the rear of the hotel, especially the loading dock area. A beautiful balcony area overlooked the first floor, which was the ground floor for the front of the hotel.

"'I will punish the world for its evil, and I will break the wicked for their iniquities!' Isaiah 13:11. 'I am his wrath and his sword. For whoever chooses life, chooses him, and whoever chooses him will forever live in this world!'" Trashman yelled while he walked.

Trashman was dragging a large bladed knife against the wall when a small child ran around a corner, near the center stairway. A little boy, with no parent around. He ran right into Trashman, falling to the ground.

Charlotte could hear a kid crying around the next corner. She was ahead of the group and signaled everyone to slow down, stop, and keep quiet.

Luke silently shuffled up to Charlotte, and she put her pointer finger against her lips. "*Shhhhhh,*" she whispered. Luke nodded.

Charlotte shuffled up to the edge of the wall and noticed a nasty man standing over a little boy. She knew this revolting man as Trashman. A member of the faction of THEY.

Charlotte pulled back and, with no verbal communication, told Luke to take the others and break for the exit down the hall. Luke knew that stairwell had an emergency ground level exit, and they could cross Route 3 from there. Luke knew Charlotte could handle herself and whispered in her ear, "See you at the rally point."

Charlotte's pistol was empty, and her rifle was damaged during the rooftop escape. She was left with a serrated blade—one she found the hard way when she killed the man who stabbed her with it.

Charlotte prepared to attack.

With a rusty bloodstained blade in his hand, Trashman said, "Then Abraham reached out and took the knife so he may slaughter his son—"

Charlotte sprung from the corner, slid in low on Trashman's right side, and drove her knife into his kidney. The movement was fast and accurate. She rolled to the front, scooping the young boy up and moving him away from the demonic man.

"You'll spill no more blood, you fucking psycho!" Charlotte yelled while shielding the boy and moving to create distance. The boy cried as he hid behind her, holding on tight to her waist.

Trashman bend over in pain, but laughed and moved around, matching Charlotte's movements. He held his side as blood gushed out. "The Lord will get you, whore. I'll kill you both before I leave this place." He pointed the knife directly at her while still moving around. Trashman was hurt but didn't care. He laughed and drooled. Though the wound was fatal, it would take time to kill him.

Kent and Andrew ran up the stairs. They knew to avoid the third floor, as it was engulfed in fire.

"The second floor," Kent yelled. He knew it was the closest one that would allow them to reach an exit.

They passed the first floor, made the turn going up to the second when they heard the rage coming from below them. "The crazies are coming," Andrew said. "Run faster!" They kept moving.

Kent was the first to reach the second-floor door. He pulled it inward, allowing Andrew to leave the stairwell first.

Andrew felt a hand grab his wrist as he left the stairwell. The pressure hit him before the pain did. Reflexes caused him to pull away, from the man who just sliced into his forearm from his wrist to his elbow. He consciously grabbed his arm, but the damage was done. The amount of blood flowing from his artery looked like a car wash bucket tipped over on the floor. Andrew was spraying blood everywhere, like a burst water main.

Trashman smiled. He knew he snatched a soul from yet another man. Andrew was now on borrowed time.

Kent could hear the crazies picking up speed. The sound reminded him of his grandpa's old sheepdog, pushing cattle into a corral. The crazies were almost on top of him, so he purposely froze. He knew Andrew was about to die and knew hell was running up the steps at him with deathly intentions. Much like the crazies during his speech, Kent became a statue, while holding the door with a sadistic smile. If that smile had a voice, it would say "happy hunting." He did this in those brief seconds while Andrew's life was spraying everywhere in the hallway.

Charlotte pushed free from the boy. Trashman was bleeding heavily in the center of the hallway with his back to her. With that shitty knife in his hand, Trashman was laughing at just having cut the life away from Andrew.

Charlotte took a step back and, with her size seven, black, vintage Air Jordans, with every ounce of muscle she owned, kicked Trashman center of his spine. The momentum drove him away from everyone and forward in front of the stairwell door that Kent was holding open.

The crazies hit the second floor, turned, and ran through Kent's open door. They paid him no attention. They simply turned, because, right in their face, was that coppery smell of blood that they craved, flowing from Trashman and Andrew. The crazies jumped on both men and began to feast for the first time in weeks. Five crazies on each man. They never fought each other over the meat; subconsciously, they knew there was enough to go around.

Andrew was already dead when the crazies got to him, but Trashman was eaten alive. Trashman screamed and cried as he was torn apart.

Charlotte paused briefly as the screaming intensified. "That's the death you deserve for the lives you've ruined. That's the death I hope you get over and over again in hell, motherfucker!"

Trashman screamed a high pitch nasally whine that would haunt this group for life, like a small pig before the slaughter.

During the bloody chaos, the little boy Charlotte had protected, ran off with some passing people. She screamed for him to come back, but she never saw him again.

"Charlotte, let's get the fuck out of here," Kent yelled with his hand extended to her. She grabbed it, and they ran down the hall. They were headed for the same east wing stairwell Luke and his group used to escape before Trashman's violent interruption. Tired, bloody, and hungry, they ran for their lives. They ran for their freedom. The closer they got to Harbor House Hospital, the closer they were to getting home.

Chapter 30: Rally Point

Luke ran down the center of Route 3, and people followed. In his former life, he ran marathons for fun, and today, that stamina, that heart, was paying off.

His followers were mostly women and children. They tried with all their might to keep up. But one at a time, they dropped off. Luke ran and ran. His heart rate never broke 150 beats. He ran with comfort and commitment.

Luke knew he had to get everyone to the rally point. He thought most people were keeping up but quickly realized the youngest were dropping off and dangerously being left behind and by themselves.

Luke had to make a decision. Slow down and risk no one making it to the rally point, or forge ahead and get the majority there quickly and safely.

Kent and Charlotte hit the exit door of the hotel. "Either we take the open road or the forest," Kent said to Charlotte while holding her hand.

Charlotte noticed Kent was still holding her hand, and she didn't mind. Actually, it made her feel safe and wanted, but shook it free anyways. "In the forest. All damn day!" she answered. "I'll follow you, and keep your eyes peeled for Bran. I—I kinda let him go—I mean, fuck, just keep an eye out for him."

Kent shimmied his way to the edge of the hotel, looked around the corner and to the safety of the trees. "It's all clear," he said.

Charlotte grabbed his arm, turning him back toward her. She reached up, kissing his mouth gently, pausing, and then again before finishing with a smile. "Thank you!" she said.

Kent blushed and kissed her back. This time firm, with a sense of passion and a hint of a possible future. "Let's get the hell out of here," he said as he grabbed her hand for the second time. After another quick peek around the corner, together, they ran for the trees, disappearing into the wild.

William was a survivor. He lasted multiple years in the parallel world for one simple reason: he was resourceful. William could hide awfully well by using his surroundings to facilitate safety. When Trashman's hoard of people attacked, he ran inside, chained the door, and simply hid behind a false wall he had constructed in that specific hallway, in case of a rainy day. The false wall gave him three feet of width and ran the length of the hallway, about ten feet, enough room for William to lay down, with or without his gear. The best part was, he told no one of its existence. The hidden wall was his little secret.

Once the explosion breached the door, it rocked William, rendering him unconscious for a few moments. When he awoke, a small fist-sized hole was now in his secret wall. His eyes adjusted to the incoming light just in time to witness Trashman and about twelve of THEM enter the hotel. He held his breath while they walked right past him without notice.

With no further sign of any faction fighters entering the breached hotel door, William emerged from his secret place and ran for his life. William noticed the light in the sky was a strange tangerine, quickly fading to a wavy black.

Peculiar was the first word to enter his mind while running with his eyes focusing skyward. The next phrase that washed over him was from an old horror movie of his childhood: "Something wicked this way comes!"

William put his head down and ran directly to Route 3, stopped,and snaked his way into a storm drain, back into that thoroughly used sewer system.

Luke slowed his pace. "You guys get the majority of the group to the rally point. I'm turning around to pick up the slower ones," he said, knowing this could cost him his life. Internally Luke was torn about this decision. He wanted to go home desperately. But Luke knew if he didn't do something meaningful in this fucked-up world, he'd never be able to look any family members in the eye when he got home and explain what happened.

The lead man acknowledged Luke and continued running down Route 3. Luke fully turned around and started running back to gather the young, old, and the slow.

Kent and Charlotte ran through the woods, but only as fast as being unseen and unheard, would allow them to go. Tree after tree, they passed with Route 3 now about a half-mile to their left, they turned and paralleled it.

Both Kent and Charlotte could hear constant gunfire echoing in the distance. They slowed to a walk, becoming more aware of their wooded surroundings.

"I know this land, Charlotte. If we stay deep in the woods, we will have a couple of roads to cross, once we get closer to the rally point," Kent said while stepping over a dead oak tree.

"I trust you. I know that there is a twenty-four-hour window for everyone to make it to the rally point. After that window closes, the group will move on," she replied as they walked.

"Do you know anything about the rally point? That maintenance building for the mine. Have you ever been there?" Kent asked.

"Months ago, a small group of us made two trips with supplies to stash there. In the garage, we hid food, a few guns, and some ammo. Both were a quick drop-and-go kind of trip. I did not get to spend a lot of time there, and it was always at night," she explained. "Have you been there before?

"I have," Kent said. "I spent some time mapping that area. It's closer to Harbor House Psychiatric Hospital than it is to the mine. It should hide at least twenty of us. Maybe." He paused, placed his hand over Charlotte's mouth, and quickly rolled her under a cluster of knee-high trees growing between two large mosey oak trees.

Charlotte did, in fact, trust Kent. She went willingly with him, keeping quiet and motionless. A few seconds later, they could hear footsteps approaching them on the deer trail they had been walking on. The footsteps were getting closer and closer. Then they stopped, inches from their hiding spot.

Kent slid his hand away from Charlotte's mouth. Through the foliage she could see a man standing facing in their direction. Blood drooled down his face, covering his dirty white t-shirt. She instantly knew this man was not a SEEKER or a SOLO, but he was crazy. He was unarmed and had the trademark milky white eyes.

The man was sniffing the air and looking over the top of the underbrush they were hiding under. Kent and Charlotte were motionless, hoping the meat-eater would leave. But Charlotte knew the man's actions indicated he was smelling their odor and looking for them. At this point, Charlotte and Kent were faced with "do or die."

The crazed man turned his back to them, continually sniffing the air deeply. This was the opportunity Charlotte was waiting for. In one fluid movement, she drew her knife and sliced the man's Achilles-tendon of the leg bearing the most weight. The dirty blood-soaked crazy fell to the ground with his chest to the sky. The last thing he saw with those ghostly eyes was the six-inch steel blade Charlotte drove into his skull.

"Nice job," Kent whispered. "Let's get moving."

As she stood up to leave, Charlotte tried to pull the knife from the man's head. It wouldn't budge. The wound was airtight, refusing to give back the knife. The man was dead, but his skull was keeping her knife.

Kent took a quick glimpse at the man as he began to walk off. "That guy wasn't in the hotel basement. I don't remember seeing him there. Hopefully, there's no more of those things."

They kept walking and after a couple of hours, came across the first road.

Luke ran down Route 3, toward The Mecklenburg Hotel, gathering up the weak, old, and young kids as he went.

"Guys, I have one question. Do you want to go home?" he asked a couple of young kids between the ages of five and six, crying and asking for their mommies. They became separated from their parents during the fire and had no one to take care of them.

"Yes, please. We want to go home," an older lady with bleeding hands said. She looked to be in her seventies, short, skinny, and weak.

The rest of the group nodded while tears dropped to the ground.

"I'll slow it down, but you must stay with me. If you don't keep up, you will be risking everyone's life. I'll get you home if you just give everything you've got. You're going to have to push your body to its very limit. If you can't, don't try and follow. If you do, you will have signed the group's death warrant," Luke explained.

A metal can was intentionally kicked out onto the road, right into the center of the group. The label read "mustard sardines." It came from an obscured dark alley behind Stephen's Vintage Books. Luke thought it was weirdly fitting, seeing how, in the real world, that vintage bookstore was full of dark arts, unique first editions, and ancient books. Their catchphrase was, "We specialized in the darkest horror stories ever published."

The old lady, without warning, left the group. She walked into the horror of where that sardine can originated. She took Luke's speech to heart and walked into the darkness, looking for her death.

The group ran. Luke led the way off of Route 3, cut behind the mom-and-pop-run hardware store, and began using a less-traveled route to the rally point. They were a couple miles away, and the night was fast approaching.

A metallic click resonated in the sewer line when William turned on his pink pocket light that read "Murder Mile" on the handle. William found it during a food run months ago, used to advertise Mecklenburg's annual Halloween fundraiser, which was a one-mile costume run. Over the year, the event was nicknamed "Murder Mile." *Oh, the irony*, thought William. He knew the path to the rally point could be a real murder mile—or more.

With his flashlight focused down the dark and damp concrete tube, he began to walk. The sewer was a tall typical concrete pipe, with a small bit of greywater running down the center. He stepped on either side of the water as he moved, each foot on a slightly curved angle. William moved with aggression. He knew only one thing: get to the rally point before tomorrow's morning sky.

Tom Porter, covered in blood, opened the church doors to the light of day, taking his first steps toward freedom. His eyes ached from the light in the sky as they struggled to adjust. A few seconds later, his pupils corrected, and he saw her again. The pale little girl in the ruby-red dress. She was across the street; still on the sidewalk he had seen her standing on, while he was in the attic of hell's church.

The girl waved at Tom. He smiled. She was emotionless, almost robotic as she waved her hand toward her body. He knew she wanted him to follow her. But to where?

Without hesitation, Tom Porter walked across the street. Time appeared to be slowing down for everyone and everything around Tom, except Tom. His perception of himself was in real-time, but his perception of the world around him was slower. It was just behind reality, but was it, in fact, reality? Tom felt familiar, but what he was seeing—and how he saw it—was psychedelic. He saw white wavy lines in the wind, and the concrete had vapor trails.

The pretty little girl in the ruby-red dress was waving, still gesturing to follow her. This time her mouth was moving. "Find my mommy," she said. Her hair was waving in the air but was like she was underwater.

Tom tried yelling out to the girl but fell silent. He didn't understand it, but his voice was gone. Was Tom in a dream? Was he hallucinating? Or just delusional? He questioned himself. Tom felt like he was dreaming. But had to follow that ruby-red dress. He knew deep down in his soul, he had to follow her. He had to help her.

The girl walked, and Tom followed.

Charlotte held her fist in the air, indicating Kent to freeze. Kent stopped in his tracks and held still. The forest was beginning to thin out, and she could see the first of two roads they would need to cross.

"Let's sit here for a little bit and watch," Charlotte said. Her feeling was to stop look and listen for any activity that may get them caught or killed.

"I'll push a little right and watch the buildings across the street," Kent replied. They were lucky no buildings were in their immediate path, and their field of view was quite wide from where they lay and watch.

A few minutes of watching revealed nothing. They didn't hear any movement, see any activity, or could smell anything faintly suspicious in the air. Kent and Charlotte believed the coast was clear.

"Charlotte, look across the street to the right of the pizza joint. Do you see that hand pump next to the water well?" Kent asked.

"Yes. It's in that tall grass."

"That's it. We need to get some water as we cross. I'll pump, and you drink. Then I'll drink for a minute. But do it quickly. We have to stay out of sight," Kent explained, severely dehydrated. They have been fighting and moving for hours, without food, water, or rest.

"I'll run across and wave you over when it's clear," Charlotte said. Kent gave a smile and nodded in agreement.

Charlotte slowly crept her way to the edge of the trees, took a knee, glanced back at Kent, smiled, and gave one last look left and right. The coast was still clear. She ran across the road and laid in the tall grass next to the well.

Charlotte slowed her breathing, calming herself while she kept her ears open and eyes surveying the area. There was no one in sight. She pushed her body up to a knee and waved Kent over. He looked left and right one final time then ran to join her at the water well.

She pumped the handle, and glorious spring water commenced to flow.

The rally point was an old vintage building used by Duke Mining for vehicle maintenance. It was a dirty-white, single-story building. The paint was so incredibly old, it was peeling and flaked off in the brisk evening winds. The facility was also fenced in, with a modest concrete parking area in front of the roll-up door bays.

Behind the maintenance building, the mining company also owned an archaic, derelict of a two-story house with a robust steeple-pitched roof above the front porch and rotted steps leading to the missing front door, which was sealed with plywood. At first glance, the steeple led the SEEKERS to believe it was an old church, but ultimately realized it was used as a family home.

The rally point was somewhat secluded, with only farmhouses in sight and Harbor House Hospital at the end of the road. Duke Mining was at the other end of the road, with a national forest surrounding a lot of it.

Luke and his small group of kids and the elderly were the first to make it to the rally point. Luke was visiting for his third time. The two previous stopovers were to drop off supplies just in case a day like today ever came.

Luke unlocked the front gate and, with his pistol in hand, made his way directly inside the maintenance building. The inside was dark and smelled of oil and antifreeze. He walked around, looking for any squatters. The vehicle area was spacious, with three openly connected garage bays, all with typical hydraulic lifts, but one also had a pit area below the concrete. The center lift was in use. It had a white work truck, a Chevy 1500, a few feet off the floor.

Luke peered around with a pistol in one hand and flashlight in the other. The work bays appeared to have been used, but not recently. His light bounced off the walls and ceiling. He was reasonably sure he was alone in the room.

Luke walked back into the lobby area, looked around, seeing nothing of interest. He walked into the two offices next to the lobby. Finally, he checked both customer bathrooms and the customer waiting room. Nothing. Just eerie silence and unlike the work bays, these rooms smelled of old stale air, with a touch of a retirement home's mildew smell.

Satisfied the building was safe for the group to enter, Luke walked back into the bays, in order to open the rear door, so everyone could have an effortless and shorter run from the forest.

Luke placed his hand on the rear door lock, when he heard a noise behind him. Off in the distance of the work bay, he heard the distinctive sound of a metal object dropping to the concrete floor. His head, on impulse, turned as he raised his pistol in the area of the sound. "Who's there? Make yourself known now, or so help me God—I'll kill you!"

He knew that sound well. As a small child, Luke would help his father work on vehicles at home. Every time a tool was dropped on that concrete garage floor, he would pick it up and give back to his dad. Luke always associated that sound with joy and reward because it was associated with helping his father. But the smile from that sound today drained away to dread, turning on his "fight" switch.

"But God loved the world. Didn't he?" a whimpering voice drifted out from the shadow near a stack of used Goodyear tires. "He gave his only begotten Son," said the voice. The man stood up, showing himself to Luke. He was tall, bald, pale, and naked.

Luke stared the man up and down the best he could, his pistol still pointing at him with caution, and finger on the trigger. "Show me your hands."

One hand at a time, the man complied.

"Drop the knife!" Luke yelled. The man was out from behind the tires, crying, slobbering, and holding a pearl-handled steak knife. "Drop the fucking knife," he said calmly as he slowed his breathing, ready to shoot the man.

"I woke up in hell," the man said. "Where am I? Was I in a car wreck? What is going on? Am I in hell?"

The man was confused and stepped forward with the knife still prominent in his right hand. The muzzle flash was blinding, and the sound was earsplitting inside the bay area. Luke squeezed the trigger twice in quick, accurate succession. The man was dead before he hit the ground. Luke stepped forward, towering over his body, and noticed an upside-down cross tattooed on his back. Luke checked the man's pulse. He was lifeless.

Light quickly drained from the sky. The night was upon Charlotte and Kent as they made it to the second road they were forced to get across. They were less than a mile from the rally point.

Just as they did at the last road, Charlotte crept up to the wooded edge, looked both ways, and ran across. This time there was no water on the other side. Rather, just a couple of broken-down cars.

Kent followed suit and soon was on the far side with Charlotte. They scampered for the woods, toward the rally point. Then the rain began.

William walked the sewer lines for the last three miles, right under Routed 3, out of the chaos, alone. Just like he enjoyed it, by himself. He was an introvert and didn't care about socializing with anyone, except for an occasional female that caught his eye.

William smiled as he walked in that sewer. His flashlight was dimming but should last the trip, or so he thought. It had been a long time since William was with a woman. The last one being a dark-haired girl—he couldn't remember her name but could remember she actually picked him up at that bar. She bought him a couple of beers, and the conversation was decent too. *Damn, what was her name?* he thought to himself. *She was so pretty, big tits and perfect teeth. What was her name?*

William walked and thought about that girl. "It was something like Sarah. Samantha, Sam! That's it. Sam was her name!" he smiled, remembering how good she was sexually. *Sam. Damn, I liked that girl. I wonder what ever happened to her*, William thought. And as soon as the realization of her name popped into his mind, the wind began to flush the sewer tube.

William stood in the sewer, flashlight pointing into the wind, as a roaring sound commenced. "What the fuck is that," he said out loud. It sounded like a building was collapsing. The earth started to shake as the water hit him. As if a dam broke, rushing water engulfed William, filling his lungs rapidly as he desperately fought for air. He died underground in that sewer. He died, just as he lived, all alone. William died in that avalanche of greywater.

The rain came swiftly, hateful, and was callous in every aspect of its occupation. Kent and Charlotte, for the most part, aside from one crazy in the woods, were able to successfully avoid trouble during their journey to the rally point. But the relentless rain was making the final mile a soul-snatching hell.

Within minutes, several inches of rain fell on Mecklenburg, focusing the length of Route 3, causing flash flooding south of Harbor House and Duke Mining, but north of The Mecklenburg Hotel. Strangely, the rain focused around those two boundaries and would not stop.

The SEEKERS escaping this world were rats trapped on a sinking ship.

Luke opened the back door connected to the maintenance-bay as rain belted the old metal rooftop. His heart rate was back to normal. He was getting used to violence in this world. No rapid breathing or nervous sweating. The killing had become a customary business for survival. The things his eyes have seen, would his mouth do the tale's justice at the end?

"Three, two, one," Luke said as he took off, running to the woods. He covered the distance quickly, taking cover behind a deep-rooted maple tree.

"What happened? Are you okay? We heard gunfire," said an older man. Luke made it back to that group of kids and slow elderly. They were soaked. Some were pale, and some were turning a tinge of blue.

"It's okay. The building is good. We can all go in—" Luke said but stopped when he noticed the oldest man of the group was lifeless, face down in the mud. "Hey, man, are you okay?" he asked the man. The man was no longer with them.

The man died in front of the group's eyes, and no one knew.

"Mr. James, if I die here, will my soul find heaven?" asked a small little boy with shock in his eyes.

Luke didn't know how to answer that question. The boy was just a kid. All of maybe seven years old. Luke thought to himself, and started to lie, but stopped. "God knows your true heart, son. He will find you wherever you are, and he will take you home." That was the best answer he could muster. Luke wanted to be honest and tell him that they were walking through hell but decided to give the kid as much hope as he could. He believed false hope was better than no hope at all.

The rain was pounding, and Luke needed to get everyone to shelter, but still had to keep the group positive. "We are almost home. Our first step is now—follow me!" Luke yelled and waved his hand back over his shoulder as he started to run around to the building's open door.

The group followed, and lightning struck nearby, shaking the earth.

"Charlotte, stay close; the mud is getting thicker," Kent said while they continued in the woods toward the rally point. She followed his instructions as lightning bounded in the clouds above them.

They walked the woods for nearly an hour as the earth below them turned to soup. The movements were becoming more and more labored. The incredible amount of water saturation was stripping the soil from around the trees. As the two moved, they could hear trees falling with the wind. One after another, trees fell over as the ground could no longer hold their massive weight.

Kent walked down the ridge line and found himself in a valley of fast-flowing water. He looked at it, knowing it wasn't there hours ago, but rather the flash flooding swelled the brook they needed to cross. They were so close, literally a few hundred yards from the rally point. They just needed to cross the impromptu river and climb the hill. The rally point would be so close at that point.

Kent was getting pissed. Rage was starting to build inside of him. He had walked through hell on multiple occasions in this fucked-up world and now this. A fucking rainstorm and flash flood. He stood on the edge of the flowing water and thought about swimming. "You think we have a choice, Charlotte? What are the odds of us making it across?" he asked.

She laughed. "I'll go where you go, but that water is an open casket waiting to be filled." She was fed up but wasn't about to give in. Now she was starting to get mad. Kent sighed.

Charlotte leaned against a tree, and it moved. She caught herself from falling while noticing the pine tree was exceptionally tall but skinny. She sized it up, realizing she had indeed moved that tree. It was now at a noticeable angle, favoring the side where the water was flowing.

"Kent, take a step back this way." Charlotte said. The rain continued to pour as Kent moved behind her. Charlotte dug her feet in the soft ground, bent over, and with all her strength, began to push the pine tree toward the water.

Kent, realizing why Charlotte was trying to do, leaned forward and began to help her. If they could push the tree over, it would give them a safe way of crossing the now raging river. With two sets of hands, they pushed.

The tree at the base was as big as a man. The pine towered nearly five stories high and swayed in the storm. The river was eating away the ground around the base of the tree. The more the river swelled and raged, the more dirt caved in.

The green pine roots were bowing and folding, finally giving way to the massive weight of the tree as Kent and Charlotte forced it toward the rising water.

"Almost there! Keep pushing!" Kent screamed as rain belted them.

Charlotte locked her arms out, with her feet dug in deep to the earth, the tree was moving past the point of no return. Both Charlotte and Kent let the weight of the tree take it the rest of the way down. The massive pine crashed into the hill on the far side of the water, burying itself in the earth. The tree was held solid on both sides as the force of over a million gallons of water hit it.

"The tree won't last long! Move!" Kent screamed as he jumped up on the log, turned, and helped Charlotte climb. They both ran across as the water rose and, in moments, began cresting over the tree.

The rain was coming down in buckets as they made it to the other side, each jumping off of the log back onto the rain-soaked ground. Soaked and elated, both sat on the hillside laughing, believing they were starting to win. Hope. They were beginning to again build up hope. Then, in the middle of the joy and rain, they heard Charlotte's missing dog, Bran, barking.

"Kent. Do you hear that? It's my dog! Where is he? Do you see Bran?" Charlotte said in a panic as the river's fury began to rock the tree up and down from the earth's solid grip.

"B-r-a-n! Here boy! Bran, come here!" Charlotte commanded as loud as she could while standing up, looking for any sign of her beloved hero dog.

"There! On the far side. He's over there!" Kent screamed and pointed back to where they just came from.

The tree was rocking up and down with water surging over it.

"He must have been tracking us," Charlotte said. "Bran! Come now!" she screamed and pleaded for her dog.

Bran walked back and forth in front of the downed pine tree spanning the raging water. Whimpering and whining, he put one paw on the tree and took it off when the water surged moving the tree up and down, quick and hard.

"He's trying to figure out how to get up on the tree." Charlotte said as she stood up and yelled, "Up!" ordering Bran to jump up on the tree. The dog's ears stood tall and he jumped up on the big fat base of the tree.

"Bran, here!" Charlotte screamed, trying to get Bran to walk the tree and join them on the safer side of the river.

Bran walked, and the tree moved like a bucking bull in a rodeo. *Bran! Come here!* Charlotte yelled one final time with a dreadful, do or die urgency in her voice.

Bran's ears perked up, and he knew by Charlotte's voice he had to hurry. He picked up his pace and started to move.

The water was churning violent white caps, with what appeared to be a rush of water that looked like the dirty grey of an avalanche. Charlotte eyeballed the incoming wall of watery death. She knew Bran no longer had a chance. Deep in her soul, Charlotte knew Bran was about to die. She took a deep breath and, for the last time, yelled, "Bran!" as the massive five-story pine tree was swept away in the dirty water.

Charlotte last saw Bran, on top of that pine tree, in the middle of the river with his ears pinned back with fright. For the second time, Charlotte lost her dog.

The girl looked to be at least ten years old. Her feet were bare, but the ruby-red dress was brilliantly shining. She was pale. Even in the rain, she was pale, but that dress continued to shine. She walked, and Tom Porter followed.

The girl moved in a way that looked polished and slow. As she moved, wavy vapors danced off and around her. Like asphalt on a hot summer day, the air looked cooked and mystic around her. She made no noise, but walked just as anyone else could, robotically and beautiful. Tom walked to catch up to her.

The girl led Tom off the street and onto the sidewalk. They walked past the pond with the dirty water that still contained Brian's body. But this time around, it wasn't hurtful to Tom's tender mind. He was carefree now. Tom walked.

Tom felt strange. He had a sense of power for the first time in his life. A sense of purpose. Tom was now in charge of Tom. He had hope and hope was all there was.

Step after step, Tom Porter followed this little girl in the ruby-red dress. No matter how fast he went, no matter how long he followed her, the distance between the two of them stayed the same. He never fell back, nor did he ever get within thirty yards of her.

The little girl's face was so pale. Tom tried to get a look at her eyes, but never could. He just followed her blindly. Tom tried to talk to her a few times, but no words would come out of his mouth. He began believing he was dead and this beautiful little girl was walking him to heaven. Or was she really God? Tom didn't know. All he knew was, he had to follow her. Step after step, no matter where she went, Tom had to follow. Even in the pouring rain, Tom followed as if a rope joined the two of them for eternity.

Luke led his small group into the building and shut the door. The group was unique, made up of a handful of kids ranging in ages and one lone surviving old man.

Lightning bounded above the maintenance building. The metal roof took multiple strikes of that skyward white death. The weathervane adorning the peak of the steeple was also a lightning rod, with a copper wire channeling down the facade of the building, stopping deep within the ground.

The kids were chatty, bouncing around with scared, nervous energy. They all wanted to get home, some more than others.

"Where are all the others?" asked an older kid. His name was John Day. He was thirteen years old, skinny, with a big mouth. He loved to talk and talk he did.

"Son, I don't know," replied Luke.

"What the heck is going on? I just started running with the others because the damn hotel was on fire, and some man was getting eaten by crazy people on the second floor," John explained with his hands in the air and a confused look on his face.

Luke realized they never got the chance to tell everyone in the hotel that they possibly found a way home. The fire started so quick, and the invasion of THEM was exceedingly lousy timing. He knew the "evacuate and head to the rally point" signal was successfully sent out, so more people should be headed this way.

"Everyone, gather around. Kids, you have all been in this crazy place different amounts of time, but I'm here to tell you, the time has come to go back home," Luke said.

The room fell silent. Not a sound. Even the heavy rain on the metal roof was unnoticeable by the group. "Did you say go home?" John asked.

Luke smiled. "Yes, I did. We have found the way home. You have got to believe and trust that we have."

The old man stood towering over the kids. His face was cold and stern. "I don't trust the government nor my ex-wife, but I'll take a chance on you, sonny," he said.

The rain continued dropping buckets of water.

"*No!*" Charlotte screamed as she stood on the hillside, staring at the grey hell that carried her dog away.

Kent grabbed Charlotte's hand and started dragging her up the muddy hill. "Let him go. He's gone! There's nothing you could have done! We have to get up this hill, now! Let him go!" he said as she finally turned and started walking. The hillside was becoming so dreadfully soft. They were having to dig their feet in and pull themselves up the hill using the trees. Kent and Charlotte stepped and pulled until they were at the top.

Finally, they sat down for a second, taking a quick breath. Kent and Charlotte had made it to the top of the hill and could see into the open field. The rain was still falling with force, so they were having a hard time seeing the rally point, but it was there. They were about one hundred yards from the roll-up bays of the maintenance building and about fifty yards from the two-story building behind it.

"Which one is the rally point, Charlotte?" Kent asked, pointing to the building in the field.

"They both are, but the maintenance building is the main resupply point. We should head for the bay doors. If anyone has beat us here, that's where they would be."

"Let's hit it, then. I'm fucking tired of being wet," Kent said.

They stood up, and with no hesitation, ran for the roll-up doors.

Halfway into the field, the visibility improved, and Kent noticed a chain-linked fence surrounded the building they were running to. When they reached the fence, Kent started to climb but saw the front gate was open.

"Gate's open. Someone must be inside. Hope to God it's one of our guys," Kent yelled as the rain continued to pound the area. Kent jumped from the fence and together they ducked low, crouching and following the fence to the open gate and ran into the lot.

Kent and Charlotte went to the main door next to the roll-up doors. It was open. Kent didn't hesitate. "Sometimes, you have to take a chance," he said as he opened the door, and both of them entered the bay area.

Luke's chat with the group was interrupted when the bay door opened, and Kent and Charlotte ran in, soaked to the bone.

"Well, at least you're not going to kill us," laughed Luke as Kent stood in the bay, dripping water everywhere, with a knife in his hand. "You two look like a couple of puppies taken from a sack that had been thrown in a pond," Luke said as he walked over and wrapped his arms around both Kent and Charlotte.

Charlotte laughed, then began to cry. She walked over to the white Chevy 1500, leaned into the bed of the truck, and broke down sobbing. Her adrenaline dumped, and she lost all emotional control.

Kent left her alone. He knew she was hurting from the loss of Bran, among other things, Bran was like a kid to her. He took a few breaths and then grabbed Luke again, for a second hug.

"It's great to see you. I'm glad you're not dead. How the hell did you—" Kent was interrupted by Luke.

"I was just telling these kids that we found a way home."

"We really did, and tomorrow we are going to go find it," Kent replied.

Kent spent the next few minutes explaining to the group about the Book of the Black and all the trepidation they went through to get it. How they figured out how to get home and why they believe the basement area inside Harbor House was the exit point. Even the old man smiled when the story stopped.

Chapter 31: The End is Near

Luke James, Kent Prather, Charlotte Kane, and a small contingent of SEEKERS were the lone survivors. They were held up at a Duke Mining vehicle maintenance building, just over a mile from Harbor House Psychiatric Hospital. On a clear day, you could see the tall stone perimeter walls of the hospital, from where they were.

Luke was the first to wake up. The night was long and loud from the storm. He stretched, walked to the front door, and stepped onto the entrance steps. His shirt was whipping in the wind, as rain battered against the door, he was holding open. Luke shook his head in disgust with the weather.

Kent saw Luke standing in the entrance, and knew he was sizing up the day. He walked over and out into the rain. "Well, fuck me," Kent jested while his feet sank in the overly saturated soil. "We can't stay here much longer, man, or we will have to highjack Noah's ark."

"I know. We have about an hour before the window closes to arrive at this rally point. It doesn't feel like anyone else is coming. What happened to the others?" Luke replied.

Kent shrugged his shoulders. "Listen, man, Charlotte and I barely made it here. This parallel world is imploding. It's like the world itself is trying to stop us from leaving."

"I'm having a hard time wrapping my mind around it, but I feel doomed. I've done everything in my power to give those kids hope and hide my inner gut feelings, but I have a bad feeling about Harbor House," Kent explained with a sour face.

Kent walked up into Luke's personal space and stared at him dead in his eyes. "No matter what, no matter what happens or what the fuck you see, or what the fuck happens to me, promise me you will get Charlotte to the exit," he said while shaking his hand with a death grip.

Luke realized he was serious, and now wasn't the time to show any sign of weakness. "I promise, Kent," he replied with the purest heart. Luke knew he had to keep this promise, even if it cost him everything.

Charlotte, having been to the rally point in the past, knew where the supplies were hidden. In turn, she dug out some coffee, powdered eggs, canned pineapple spears, and some dried potatoes. The kids were still sleeping while Kent and Luke were outside chatting as it continued to storm.

The work bay was a convenient place to cook. It just so happened there was an old, iron flat top, wood-burning stove near the center bay, with black pipes running straight up and disappearing in the ceiling.

She loved her coffee and fixed that first. She used the top of the stove as a skillet, cooking up eggs, hash browns she made from the powdered potatoes, and room-temperature pineapple chunks for dessert.

Breakfast was ready, and the quaint home-away-from-home, freshly cooked food odor, began waking up everyone.

"Boys, coffee. You guys want to get out of the rain and grab a cup of joe?" Charlotte asked Luke and Kent. For the first time in ages, she felt happy and content. She knew she was close to home, but moreover, knew she found something special with Kent.

Duke Mining Road was in front of the Maintenance buildings. It was paved with a slightly angled asphalt, leaving proper drainage ditches on both sides. Once the road crossed over Route 3, the name changed to Harbor House Road, and the maintenance of that section belonged to the state. The state believed in gravel instead of asphalt and the drainage ditches were overgrown and inadequate.

The employees of the hospital complained about the road conditions quite often. Still, the state of Colorado never took it seriously. Not until the mayor's son was killed in a car crash out front of the hospital one night during a summer storm. The day after, a work order was submitted and approved to pave Harbor House Road. Unfortunately, in this parallel world, gravel with horrible drainage, is what faced the SEEKERS on this rain-soaked day.

The children filled their bellies first. Then the old man. "Rub-a-dub-dub, thanks for the grub," little John Day sang.

"You're welcome, son," Charlotte said. She kneeled down and, in his ear, whispered, "Here's a Hershey's bar for later," while slipping it in his jacket pocket.

John day smiled and ran off. Charlotte knew he would have talked her to death unless she gave him a little something to take to hide and eat.

Luke and Kent finished their coffee and walked over to the Chevy 1500. Charlotte followed. They were the three eldest of the group, minus the old man who had just filled his belly and fallen back to sleep over by the stack of tires.

"We have been at the rally point for twenty-six hours. Our agreement with everyone in the hotel was to wait here twenty-four and then leave with the survivors. That was the standard procedure if we ever evacuated to the rally point," Luke explained. He dropped his head, pausing with sadness. "We had more than forty at the hotel. I think it's safe to say we are the survivors. The few of us—six kids and four adults. That's it."

"Ten is better than none," Kent proudly said. "Let's get our people and get the fuck out of this world."

Charlotte thought of Bran and the look on his face as he stood, scared, on top of that giant pine tree. He was there one second and gone the next. Bran was Charlotte's guy. He had protected her and so many others. A tear rolled down her cheek. Charlotte closed her eyes and forced that unbearable pain deep down into her mind's little black box. "Kent's right. What's the plan?" she asked.

The old man woke to the sound of adults chatting close by. He knew it was time to contribute. He sat up and yelled across the open work bay, "The name's Maxwell Cole. My friends call me Cole or a handful of other derogatory names."

Kent, Charlotte, and Luke paused their conversation, turning their attention to the old man. "Cole, is it?" Charlotte asked.

"Yes, ma'am. But I'll answer to 'the old man' if you'd like," Cole replied jovially.

"I like the name Cole," she said. "My best friend back home is named Cole."

"Look, I know you guys are trying to get us the hell out of here. I know I'm old, but I still have some life left in me. You see that old Chevy 1500 over there?" Cole asked rhetorically as he pointed at the truck. "I can get it running. No shit, I was a NASCAR mechanic back before NASCAR was a thing."

A switch struck hot in Luke's mind. They were just beginning to brainstorm a game plan, and transportation—other than by foot— had yet to come up. But what a novel idea. "That's a bloody good idea, old man," Kent said.

"Please get that thing running. That's a great idea; it looks like it will hold us all," Luke added.

Cole agreed and walked off to gather tools for the job at hand. He had seen lots of Chevy parts laying around and knew he could get that old maintenance beater of a truck operational.

"While the old man is working on the truck, we need to gather a small number of rations. I'd say one day's worth should do it," said Luke. "Plus, we should go to the main house and double-check for anyone else who possibly made it here in the storm."

"I guess now's a good time to do that—while the old man is working on our transportation and the kids are asleep. The rain's never going to stop, so let's beat feet and get it done," Kent added.

Kent, Charlotte, and Luke all quickly filled up their backpacks with food and water provisions. They were good for at least the next twenty-four hours.

While packing his supplies, Kent noticed a small wooden box, bound in leather, laying in the bed of the white truck. It was dirty, sticking out from under a piece of moldy cardboard. The box was no bigger than a traditional paperback book and opened with a hinge on one side of it. Kent smiled at the contents.

"Charlotte, here's a replacement for that knife you lost earlier," Kent yelled and tossed her the wooden box.

She opened it.

The hinges creaked like a vintage cellar door, revealing a custom knife, about six inches long, with an elk horn handle. There were no stampings or writings inside the box or on the blade itself. Who knows how old the knife was? But Charlotte knew instantly, she would use it to get them all back home. Or die trying.

Charlotte tied the knife to her hip, elk handle bending forward, and stashed the rest of her day's supplies in the back of the pickup. Kent and Luke followed suit.

"Let's go check the house," Luke said as he led Charlotte and Kent outside and running toward the house.

The back stained-glass door was unlocked. Luke pushed it open, and the three of them entered without hesitation. Luke shut the door behind them. The door caught his eye as he took a second glance at it. Luke noticed the stained-glass was a black upside-down cross. Much like the tattoo on the man's back, whom he killed earlier in the maintenance building. *Strange*, he thought. Was that a sign or just a coincidence? Luke wasn't sure, but he was confident that now he was uncomfortable. So much so, his bladder was quivering to release the urine stored inside.

The trio stepped into the kitchen. The air was stale, and wooden floors groaned with age and rot. There was nothing unusual about the kitchen, just a musty, moldy smell.

Charlotte took a deep breath and the musty air took her back to a moment of her childhood, when she found her grandfather dead in his basement. "That smell," she said. Her hair stood on end, from her arms to the base of her skull.

"*Shhhhh*. Listen," Kent replied as he used his hand to cup his ear.

Kent internally was on edge the moment they walked in that house. This was out of character for him. Still, the body language displayed by the others indicated they, too, were feeling the same way.

They all stopped, looked, listened, and felt for anything out of place. An odd smell or noise. A couch, laugh, or any other sounds of movement. The group strained their senses. Other than the initial smell, nothing was out of place or out of sorts. Nothing but their gut instincts telling them to run.

Kent was the first one to see the wooden stairs with dirt leading up to the second floor. He grabbed the wall railing and started to move up the dirt path. The rail gave way with rot and mold from wet, plastered, wood-slated walls. It came off in Kent's hand and he let it go. The railing fell to the steps and slid in pieces from the top of stairs down to their feet.

Charlotte stood at the bottom of the stairs behind the others. When out of her eye, she thought she saw something. Movement down the hall and into the living area, where the fireplace was. She thought she saw someone in a dress. "Diane?" she questioned under her breath. Her brow was moist, and her teeth clenched. She was afraid, but the thought of finding her daughter was pulling on her heart strings.

Charlotte left Kent and Luke. She walked down the hall toward the movement. Her throat dried with each step, as her heart rate rose noticeably. "Baby, is that you?" Charlotte asked with hope and fear of the answer.

Charlotte turned the corner from the hallway into the living area. The fireplace was clean with a glistening orange flame dancing across a small stack of logs. The walls were a brilliant shade of Carolina blue. The floor was a beautiful maple hardwood with a white shag carpet center of the room. "Diane?" Charlotte asked the small statue of a female standing with her back to her.

She wore a dazzling white and yellow dress with her arms waving slightly by her side. The girl did not reply. She stood, waving her arms naturally by her side.

Charlotte walked to the female. Her heart was pounding, lungs rapidly breathing. The sweat above on her forehead was now dripping to her chin and running down her neck. "Diane," she whispered as she placed a hand on the female's shoulder.

Laughter rang out, echoing off the walls. Charlotte's hand became cold, and the touch of the female's skinned now felt of chilled plastic. Forcefully, Charlotte turned the female around to face her. The girl was now a headless mannequin wearing the same dazzling dress.

Charlotte turned around to the laughter's source. Chief Sanders stood in the doorway, dirty and naked, minus his old red-wing work boots. He was leaned forward in an aggressive position as his body dripped a black filth to the floor. His lewdness made it almost impossible to see the old deer-skinning knife in his hand.

The room's beauty faded to an aged wasteland, with a single cockroach scampering down Sanders' hairy leg. It swiftly became lost in the garbage below him.

The stairs went straight up. No turns. Just up, with a door at the top on the second floor. Kent couldn't take his eyes off the door. It was staring at him as he put one foot in front of the other. Kent and Luke traveled up that dirty wood, and together they pushed the door open.

Nothing. They stood staring into a black hallway.

Kent and Luke walked through the door, into the second-floor hallway. A slight breeze pushed at their backs until the door slammed behind them. The air was rank with a rotting meat stench.

The floor creaked under their weight as they walked. At the end of the hallway was another paint peeling, grime-covered closed door. Luke pointed out a shadow of movement he could see in the crack at the bottom of the door, as they got closer.

Together they paused before the door. Neither Luke nor Kent could speak. But with one stern but straightforward look, both men knew they had to open it.

"Come play with me," crept from under the door. It was a child's voice. Luke reached for the doorknob, turned it, and pushed the door open.

"Hello," Luke stammered as if his mouth was frozen. The room was jet black. Even the light from the hallway behind them didn't dare enter the room, ss if the light itself was afraid to enter. It stopped at the door, like a rational person should, like Luke and Kent.

"Can you play with me?" rang out from the darkness, followed by a small orange ball, with a Christmas bell inside of it, jingling as it rolled to a stop. Luke picked up the ball, and the door shut behind the two men. They were now inside the room, even though they never stepped inside. They were in the blackness and again heard the child's voice speak.

"I'm glad you're here to play. Daddy and his friends never wanted to play with me."

The darkness sucked out of the room, leaving behind an orange light illuminating the four walls. The walls were moving. Kent and Luke stood back to back, crippled with fear. The walls were moving in a wave of people covered in plastic. Each person rotting, wrapped in their own clear plastic from head to toe. Each person in their own pattern moved like a dolphin on the wall, bucking at their hips in a wave of bloody, dirty, putrid death.

Tom followed the girl in the ruby-red dress. She led him through the woods. Under trees and over trees, they walked in the woods not far off of Route 3 while the rain and wind purged the area.

Tom could see the wavy vapors emitting from the girl as she disappeared over a ridgeline. He kept moving. He was still bleeding from multiple parts of his body, yet his body was no longer in pain. His head and his hand were the worst of the two. Was he following an angel to heaven? He thought so. He thought that's exactly what he was doing: being guided to heaven.

Tom's hand was like a crab claw. Three of his fingers were missing, bit off by a demon. *So, why couldn't this pretty little girl be an angel taking him to heaven?* or so he thought as he reached the top of the ridge.

The ruby-red dress flashed in the light, fifty yards below Tom at the bottom of the ridge. She stopped and waved Tom down into the woods to keep following her. He did. Tom followed.

At the bottom of the hill, Tom came to a swollen creek. It was now a raging river. The girl was on the other side, staring at him. Again, she waved him to follow, but this time she stopped after one wave and pointed over to a large, broken pine tree. It was in several pieces spanning the raging water but also caught on other trees.

Tom understood he could use this tree as a bridge if he hurried. So, he ran. Once on top of the pine, he used his crab claw of a hand to help pull himself over the water, one branch at a time, until he made it across.

Tom was at the base of yet another hill, and the girl stood motionless, pointing at a dark clump of something a few yards upslope, under a tree. He walked up the hill to the dark mass. It was a dog.

Tom bent down and pulled the dog from under the broken oak tree. It was Charlotte's dog, Bran. He wiped the blood away from his mouth. The dog felt lifeless in his hands, so he breathed into his snout. Bran's chest rose and fell with each breath. The dog was cold to the touch, soaked and limp. Tom continued to breathe precious air into him.

The dog's eyes opened and once more, began to breathe on his own. Tom held the dog in his arms and realized the girl led him to Bran.

The little girl, in the ruby-red dress, was again walking up the hill. She was still waving at Tom to follow. He wondered what else the girl would lead him to. The rain was so intense, it felt like a needle repeatedly stabbing Tom's skin. But he pressed on.

Charlotte's eyes adjusted to the psychotic change of the room. Sanders stood just a few feet from her, smiling with a knife in one hand and rubbing his flaccid penis with the other. She was not only appalled, but the rage was building inside of her. Charlotte so desperately wanted to find her daughter. She wanted nothing more than to take Diane home, and Sanders was using this "weakness" against her.

"You have one chance to save yourself, lady. One chance is all you get—" Sanders was interrupted when a six-inch blade was shoved deep into his thigh.

Charlotte was first to strike. She gave no warning, nor did she hesitate. She pulled that elk-horned-handled blade and let it fly. The fight was on!

"*Do you see now*?!" a man's voice yelled from the corner. "I have so many things to show you. Beautiful things. You just have to take my hand and concede to this new world."

The walls continued to move. The bodies... the room was substantial, underneath their feet, but the walls were fluid with constant motion. Some bodies weren't just rotting flesh, but living people, trapped under the plastic. Some of the people were tearing the plastic from their faces while screaming.

"*Do you see now*?!" the voice yelled.

Kent was stricken with one particular female's body. She was wrapped tightly but her long red hair was sticking out in pigtails. He was mesmerized by this. Kent took two steps forward, then a few more, until he was inches from her. He reached up and tore the plastic away from her face. Her eyes were gone.

"*Do you see now*?!" the voice echoed again, but this time it was coming from the female Kent was staring at, except it was no longer the female. The female was gone, vanished and replaced by Preacher Ratchford.

The preacher grabbed his face and gazed into his eyes. Kent was now seeing the horror that the preacher intended him to see. The visions...

The girl in the ruby-red dress walked the wooded hillside, guiding Tom Porter through a stormy haze. He followed her to the top of the hill, as he cradled Bran in his arms.

For the first time since he began to follow the girl, he caught up to her. Standing side by side at the top of the hill, on the edge of the woods, they stood looking out into a field covered with a thin fog laying on top of the ground all the way to their feet.

The pretty girl in her shining ruby red dress was no longer waving at Tom to follow. He intuitively understood she had brought him where she intended to take him.

The girl simply stood, pointing with conviction at the two-story house beyond the ground fog. "Help them," she whispered as Bran sat up from Tom's arms. He sniffed the air and whined at the home.

Tom put the dog down on all four feet, and together, they stepped toward the rear door, leaving the little girl behind. Tom was badly hurt but had a reason for living, and his purpose in life had yet to end.

The door was cracked, and Bran's head was cocked back, sniffing deeply. He opened the stained-glass door with his nose and bolted inside. Tom could hear screaming, both male and female voices. Bran was out of sight as Tom entered the house.

"You filthy whore. You will take what I have for you. You will be my slave and never leave this world," Chief Sanders said while he straddled Charlotte. He was choking the life from her with both hands, while her knife stuck out of his leg. The only weapon Charlotte had left was inches out of her reach.

Charlotte was lying on a pile of dirty garbage in a shitty dilapidated house. She had fought a good fight. Yet, her mind drifted to her daughter Diane. She knew she would see her again, and that time was near. Her eyes turned to her side as time slowed in her mind. Sanders was squeezing the life out of her, as the blood vessels popped in the white of her eyes. Then, a sliver of hope entered the room.

Charlotte's vision faded to black as Bran entered the room and attacked Sanders. The ninety-five-pound dog grabbed the first piece of flesh that he could: the back of Sanders' knee and hamstring. Bran bit down hard and began tearing the bare skin, while also thrashing his head. Bran was so strong, he forced Sanders off of Charlotte, pinning him against the moldy wall.

Oxygen—life-preserving, lifesaving, precious oxygen—rushed into Charlotte's lungs. She took deep breaths as Bran was tearing and ripping meat from Sanders' leg. Every time Bran thrashed, he tore more flesh, more muscle, more yellow fatty tissue, and more tendons.

Charlotte rolled to her knees and stood tall. Her heart raced. "Get him, Bran! Hold that man!" she said with an emotional tornado flowing through her veins. Her hatred for Sanders was fueled by the joy of her dog being alive.

"Hold that motherfucker!" Charlotte yelled.

Sanders was moving back and forth, rolling around in the garbage just like the trash-rat he was. Bran continued to work. Charlotte noticed blood spraying and covering the area, that was unsuitable to sustain life. The floor looked like a slaughterhouse floor.

Charlotte knew Bran had severed an artery behind Sanders' knee, and it was only a matter of time before the pure evil man was dead. She just needed to decide if she would watch him die or help Bran kill him.

"Good boy! *Get him!*" Charlotte commanded. She was relishing in the idea Bran was killing this man, this epitome of evil. She watched as Sanders grew weaker and weaker.

Sanders looked up at Charlotte. Their eyes locked. "Your grave will not exist. No marker. No nothing. You will be left here to rot with the rest of the garbage. Food for the rats. Burn in hell asshole, burn in hell!" Charlotte said as she watched Bran thrash and rip his flesh down to the bone. She smiled as Sanders' skin turned pasty white and fell over limp. She bent down to him. "I'll take my knife back now," she said while retrieving that elk bone blade.

The life in Sanders' eyes slipped away and into the void. He lay dead on top of trash, bled to death, and left for the rats to eat.

"Bran, leave him," Charlotte commanded. She grabbed her dog and held him tight. With his blood-covered snout, he whined while licking Charlotte's face. "Let's go help the others," she said.

Tom ran up the stairs in the direction of the screams. He followed the dirty footprints, and at the top, pushed open the door and ran down the hallway. Tom's eyes widened, and breath was sucked out of his body. His eyes were not lying to him. There was the preacher, holding Kent off the ground, by his face.

Tom took one step, and at that moment, got busy living. The thoughts of dying melted away. They no longer weighed his mind or body down. He no longer cared about what happened. He leaned forward and picked up speed. Within a few steps, he hit Preacher Ratchford with a shoulder an NFL linebacker would be proud of.

Kent fell to the floor as Tom's violence separated Kent's body from Ratchford's grasp. Luke took the opportunity to attack. Ratchford hit the wall, and Luke began kicking him. Kent collected himself and joined in. It was an old-fashioned boot stomping.

The room turned black again. No more noise. No motion, no nothing, just total darkness. Outside the room, the men heard someone racing up the stairs, then a window crashing and loud thud. The door opened, and the light swept in.

The walls were back to the regular dirty off-white and shit smears. The only window in the room was broken outward, and the preacher was gone. The three men stood motionless and looked at each other as Charlotte and Bran ran into the room.

Kent walked over to the broken window, leaned out as rain battered his head, and saw nothing below. No preacher. No nothing.

"Luke, we have to get the fuck out of here," Kent said.

With a ten-millimeter socket-wrench, the old man Cole was finishing up with the old white Chevy 1500 work truck. He smiled, knowing he was about to see his efforts pay off.

The kids gathered around as Cole jumped into the driver's seat, jammed a large flathead screwdriver into the broken steering column, and lit the fire. The engine turned over with no hesitation. The old man pumped the gas a few times and let it idle. That work truck still had a lot of life left in her. But not a lot of gas.

Cole put together a small toolset and put it behind the driver's seat.

Kent, Charlotte, Bran, Tom, and Luke ran into the bays, out of breath and looking aged.

"Oh, you found your dog," Cole said. "The truck's running."

"Thank God. Get everyone. We are leaving now! *Now!*" Luke screamed.

Kent jumped into the driver's seat. Everyone grabbed their gear and jumped into the back. "I'll get this thing turned around," he said. "Charlotte, grab my bag!"

Charlotte grabbed her and Kent's gear, while Bran was glued to her side. She opened the passenger door, and she and Bran jumped in. Luke, the old man Cole, Tom Porter, and the kids all jumped in the back.

"What happened in that house?" Little John Day asked with a frightful stammer. No one answered. With everyone accounted for, Kent put the truck in drive and mashed the gas. The truck spun for a moment in the parking lot, then skipped off the chain-link gate and fishtailed onto Duke Mining Road.

Chapter 32: Exit

The old white Chevy 1500 work truck rolled past the intersection of Duke Mining Road and Route 3, continuing onto the gravel of Harbor House Road.

The rain relentlessly fell. The road was a combination of washboard-gravel, mud, and potholes with washed-out shoulders. Tom opened the rear sliding window and reached inside. He placed his hand on Kent's shoulder. "Ease it back, brother. Ease it on back," Tom said.

Kent's emotions were calming down and he was returning to reality. His heart rate began to slow, and knuckles were turning a nice cream color as his death grip on the steering wheel loosened. His eyes readjusted as he shook the horror from his head. This parallel world weighed heavy on Kent. Even the strongest of people, fall down at some point.

"What did he show you? The preacher—I know he showed you something. What was it?" Tom asked.

A single tear rolled down Kent's cheek. "He showed me the real world. He showed me this parallel world's true soul! We have to get the fuck out of here!" Kent said. "We are in hell! There's no other explanation for it! He showed me the pain, the horror, the never-ending sorrow!" Kent's breathing labored. "He knew about the rally point, and he knows about the exit. The preacher knows we are headed to Harbor House."

The washboards and potholes were bouncing the truck everywhere, as water overran the ditches, covering the road. The kids were starting to vomit off the side like they were on a deep-sea boat in a storm.

Luke reached his hand through the window, rubbing Bran's head. "Where the hell did he come from?" he asked.

Charlotte smiled and kissed Bran's head as the truck bounded left to avoid a washout. "He found me," she said. "He killed for me. He saved me."

The truck passed the well-known, tall, stone walls of the Harbor House Psychiatric Hospital. It splashed water onto the dirty stones, as the truck was closing in on the east gate's tower.

The wall was paralleled by a train track and forest on the opposite side of the road. The tracks were underwater, as the flooding pushed to the tree line.

"The gate's closed!" Charlotte yelled.

Kent pumped the brakes and slid the old Chevy to a stop. Tom jumped out and ran to the gate. "It's locked!" Tom said, as he looked through the fence for an alternate entrance.

"Tom, get the hell out of the way. I'm going to ram it!" Kent yelled. Tom ran to the side and gave Kent a thumbs up. The old man, Charlotte, and the kids jumped from the back of the truck and stood with Tom.

"They're all clear," Luke said while putting on his seatbelt. "Let's do this!"

Kent revved the engine and dropped the transmission into drive. The tires spun, flinging mud and gravel high into the air. The tires hooked up, launching the truck toward the gate. The white Chevy broke through the east entrance of Harbor House, like a baseball through glass.

And standing on top of Harbor House watching the show, was Preacher Ratchford.

Tom Porter led the others inside the gate. Still, his attention was caught by a white balloon floating on the ground; unnaturally, it hovered a few feet from him. The balloon seemed to move as he moved. Then he stopped, and the balloon drifted skyward. He followed it with his eyes. That's when he saw the preacher standing on top of the hospital roof. He was on the edge, dangling his toes off the building.

"What the fuck is that?" Tom asked as the others caught a glimpse of the preacher.

"*That motherfucker has no eyes!*" Kent screamed.

"But he's standing there staring at us," Luke added. "He's not going to let us leave. If we want to get home, we're going to have to kill him."

Bran began barking as the wind shifted, pushing the heavy rain toward the hospital. Thunderheads bounced in the clouds above Harbor House and lightning struck the roof adjacent to Preacher Ratchford. A second white flash of lightning struck the ground in front of SEEKERS as they tried to enter the hospital. A third bolt struck the tower next to the gate, and a fourth hit the roof of Harbor House, near the west end.

The preacher stood firm on the edge of the building overlooking the SEEKERS below. He lifted his arms and limped his body as if he were Jesus nailed to the cross and said, "Blessed indeed, are the dead who die in the Lord! So he says in the book of Revelation," he said, as lightning flashed in the clouds, and the preacher disappeared.

Charlotte looked up in the storm and noticed a steady stream of blood flowing over the edge, where the preacher had been standing.

"Get inside!" Luke yelled and pushed Charlotte from behind as she continued to stare.

The inside of Harbor House was dark, damp, and smelled of death. Most older buildings that were unoccupied in this world smelled of mold, spoiled food, and old people. But this one smelled of fresh bloated bodies.

"The smell," Charlotte said. "It smells like the staff vanished, leaving the patients to die in their rooms."

The floor was painted with a yellow line, providing people a safe distance from the patients' rooms. Puzzling, the closest section of the yellow line to the room was sparkling clean. But on the other side of that same line, the floor was aged and filthy.

The SEEKERS moved together, heading for the center of the building.

"Do we search for the preacher or search for the exit?" Charlotte asked the men.

"The preacher is mine," Tom said with a fire in his eyes. "I'll see you on the other side."

Tom Porter was a man on a mission. Before anyone could react, he took off running down the main floor hallway. Like a ghost, he vanished into the darkness.

Tom's disappeared so fast that no one had the chance to accompany him. He was all alone now. Kent, Luke, and Charlotte all looked at each other, realizing the implications of Tom's actions. Tom was finally free. Free of self-doubt, free of fear, free of worry, and free from death. He'd had but one chance, and that's all he felt he needed. Tom ran without care for himself or any care in the world. He knew only one thing: he was going to find the preacher and he was going to kill him.

"Get your lights out, and let's find a way to the basement," Kent said. "The exit is there. I can feel it." The group took a few minutes and retrieved their lights. The storm exploded with massive hail and water started creeping inside the hospital.

Kent turned on his light and began to walk on the dirty side of the yellow line. "Follow me. Look around and tell me if you see any stairs," he said.

The group walked in a single file, looking on both sides of the hallway. A sign on the wall indicated the nursing station was ahead on the right and the stairs would be on the left.

"There. To the left, near the wheelchair," Charlotte said. "The sign is pointing at that door for the stairs."

"Good eye. It's dark as Halloween in here," the old man said.

Luke walked around to the wheelchair and pushed it out of the way. The chair was old, rusted, and rolled with a mouthy squeak.

The group stared at Luke as the noise worsened with each step he took.

"Sorry," Luke said as he turned and pulled the stairwell door open.

"Bats!" Kent yelled as he ducked down and covered his face.

With flashlights focused on the newly opened door, a rush of air and sound of flapping wings rushed up the stairwell, as hundreds of black bats flew right through the line of people. They escaped, circling the group a few times, ultimately moving down the dirty hallway and outside.

"Well, that scared the shit out of me," a kid's voice from the group said. "This place is horrible. Can we please leave? I want my mommy!"

The oldest kid, John Day, put his arm around the scared kid and whispered something in his ear. Charlotte took notice and smiled.

The stairs were drafting that familiar smell of death. Kent knew the closer they got to that smell, the closer they got to going home. He looked at the dirty walls inside the stairwell and led the way.

One step at a time, the group walked down into the void. The stairs wrapped in a constant circle until they were gone. The group made it to the basement, under the east wing. They stood as one in front of the stairwell door, leading into the unknown. Kent knew they were close and hope of a quick exit was on his mind.

Tom headed to the west wing. His stomach churned with pain, knowing Preacher Ratchford would be on the fifth floor. His heart was pure, and his intentions were vengeful.

Tom found the stairwell well-lit with rain pouring inside. There was a jagged hole in the roof, allowing the daylight and rain in, causing the steps to flood. The rain pelted his face, and his feet were covered in water. Tom's mind turned to Brian and how the preacher held him under that nasty pond water till he died.

The water on Tom's feet felt like he was back in that pond with his dead friend. What were his words? Ratchford. What did he say as he held Brian's head under that green water? "Who's world is it?" Tom spoke out to himself. "You asked me, who's world is it? *It's my world*, you piece of shit!" Tom said, looking skyward, and running up the steps.

Tom ran to the fifth floor, yelling, "Where are you, preacher?!" He exited the stairwell, stood in the corridor, and panted like a dog.

Tom crossed over to the clean side of the yellow line in front of the nurses' station. Like walking in model home, the room was vibrant and clean. It looked like a real hospital. The fluorescent lights were shining bright. The floors were mopped and fresh. Tom could hear his shoes clacking with each step on the linoleum. No trash, no blood, nothing other than sparkling floors. He looked around at the orderlies working behind the counter. They were dressed in a brilliant white, walking past him, paying Tom no attention. They spoke with each other, but he couldn't make out anything they were saying.

Tom looked down at the yellow line. The left side was still dirty with blackness, dirt, and grime. The right side smelled of fresh air and was bright and clean. He stepped back across to the nasty side. The air still smelled of rotting bodies. He walked again across the yellow line to the clean side. The smell of death was gone again.

Tom stayed on the clean side this time and walked past the orderlies chatting and showing each other patient charts. He passed the fully staffed nurses' station. They were all wearing white dresses, with white knee-high stockings, white shoes and caps penned in their hair. It was like he stepped back in time and was invisible, as no one paid him any attention.

Kent opened the door, and Charlotte put Bran through it. The dog led the way into the basement hallway. No one was there. Bran came back to Charlotte, and the group entered.

The hallway was short, with several doors on each side and one at the end. They were all closed, and the yellow line on the floor was not present in the basement.

"Which door to we take?" John day asked.

"Kent, what did the book tell you? Do you know where we need to go?" Luke asked. "Whatever we do, I don't like hanging out in this catacomb-like hallway." The group's flashlights had been working overtime and wouldn't last much longer.

Kent's eyes widened as the hallway mentally raced at him from the door at the end. He knew that's where they needed to go. Kent pointed to the end of the hallway and shined his light on the door. "There. We need to go there," he explained with no hesitation. "Our ticket home is behind that door."

Bran started to grow excited, and Charlotte calmed him down.

Tom Porter walked past the nurses toward the east wing. At the beginning of the hallway, just beyond the hustle and bustle of the nurses' station was a security checkpoint with a metal door spanning the width of the hallway.

As Tom approached the checkpoint, he felt something strange drag over his right shoulder. It was a ribbon streamer attached to a child's balloon. For a moment, he thought he heard children laughing as the white balloon passed by his ear.

The white latex balloon floated down the hallway, just a few feet in front of him, toward the checkpoint. It was just like the balloon Tom noticed in the hospital courtyard, floating up toward the preacher. Or was it the same balloon?

The checkpoint buzzed, and the metal door opened wide. The balloon floated through the checkpoint and Tom followed. The balloon floated a few feet off the floor, down the hallway, and entered an open room at the end.

Tom hesitated outside of the room. The placard on the wall next to the door read, "Ronald Black, Patient 0227." Tom turned and entered the room.

The room was full of white latex balloons. Every one of them had a white streamer attached, and they were in a uniformed line reminiscent of a military formation.

Kent led the way to the end of the hall, right where the stench of death was the strongest. The kids were between Charlotte, Bran, Luke, and the old man pulling up the rear. They were the last of the SEEKERS.

The door opened without effort.

They all walked in.

The room was naturally lit with an orange haze. The ceiling was several stories tall, and in the center of the room was a stone that looked like a sphere. It was as tall as a man, and about three feet wide. It was hovering with an unusual humming sound surrounding it. This stone was like the one inside the Duke mine.

Tom stood at the doorway. The balloons were hovering at eye level. He stared at them like a kid staring at a clown, bewildered yet mesmerized by the show. His heart knew better than to walk into that room, but his mind was focus on retribution. His mind wanted payback and to kill Preacher Ratchford.

Tom took a step inside. The door shut behind him, and in unison, the balloons drifted high into the ceiling, revealing Preacher Ratchford, just a few feet in front of Tom, standing in the center of the room.

"You will never escape this world, boy. I told you once, and I'll tell you again. This is God's new vision. I thought you understood that as I killed your friend?" Ratchford said. "He died a coward's death. Oh yes, he did, my son. Just before his last breath, I read his mind. He told me about the rally point. Your friend told me everything as he begged for his life."

"Fuck you," Tom replied as his body tightened up, ready to attack.

"It's true," the preacher said as Tom's mind thought those very words.

Both Brian and Kent's minds wilted like a flower in the desert, when Preacher Ratchford forced them. They gave the preacher everything he needed. Kent read the Book of the Black and unknowingly gave the info to the devil himself, back at the rally point, during the fight.

Ratchford opened his mouth, and his tongue forked out like a serpent. He hissed and said, "You will never win, for I have already won. God has shown me his plan, and you will all die."

Children's laughter filled the air. It bounced off the walls as the sound assaulted Tom's ears and mind. It was loud and coming at him from all angles. It was madness, brought on by the balloons, horrifying in a white room of visual calm.

The group stood in awe of the floating stone. They could feel its power. The stone was black and tan, with a blue pulsing hue in the center, like it was alive.

"Who's touching it first?" John day asked, inching forward. "Can I try it? I mean, let me touch it and see what happens. I can be the guinea pig."

The old man grabbed little John Day's hand as he reached for the stone. "Hold on, just a second. Don't rush to your death, little one," he said.

"We don't have much of a choice; we have no other option. Someone just touch the thing," Luke said.

The old man let go of the kid's hand. Little John Day touched the rock in front of everyone. The kid with a million questions vanished. Like he never existed. Gone.

Tom stepped forward, and with every ounce of strength he could muster, spun and hit the preacher with the back of his fist. The fight was on.

Tom threw punch after punch, closing the distance between him and Ratchford. He was hurting him, but Ratchford was also hurting Tom. The two went back and forth, exchanging blows. The incredibly white room became speckled in a bloody castoff, as the shiny white linoleum floors became slick with blood, while the fight grew more violent.

"*Mmmm*, smell that copper, Tom? It's your blood," the preacher whispered in his ear as he climbed on Tom's back. "I love that smell. It reminds me of death."

Tom was hurt, but so was Ratchford. Blood poured from both men as they rolled on the ground. The preacher, while laying on Tom's back, wrapped his arm around his throat.

Slowly Preacher Ratchford squeezed Tom's neck like a boa constrictor.

"I told you God has shown me his plan, and you will all die," the preacher said, just before his jaw unhinged and his throat convulsed, opening wide like an animal giving birth. The preacher's tongue and teeth gave way to a shiny black spider. It had a small head, legs as long as a man's fingers, and body the size of a baseball. It crawled out from deep inside of him.

The spider moved over the preacher's arm, around Tom's face, and drove his fangs into Tom's neck, just behind his ear. The spider held tight with his fangs, transfusing its poison into Tom's blood stream.

When it finished, the spider turned around, retracing its steps back to where it came from. Just as quick as it appeared, the spider was gone.

Ratchford kissed Tom's forehead. "God's plan will be done. I'll see you again," he said, leaving Tom on the floor.

The preacher stood up, as the balloons fell to the ground, popping in unison. Ratchford was gone, vanished, leaving Tom alone on the floor.

The group smiled. "Send the rest of the kids and the old man after," Kent said with hope building in his heart.

One at a time, the kids touched the stone and vanished. The old man looked at Kent and Luke, gave Charlotte a hug, and with a stream of tears, placed his hand on the rock. Poof, he was gone. Like alcohol in thin air, vanished.

Kent looked at Charlotte and Luke. "What about Tom? We can't just leave Tom."

Tom flipped to his back, looking up at the ceiling where the balloons had been. He rubbed his ear where the spider bit him. He was alone, in the calm of the white room. Even the blood on the floor was gone.

Tom gathered himself. He was beaten and bloody. His hand hurt from his missing fingers, and his head was starting to burn, which he assumed was from the gunshot wound days ago. He picked himself up and ran.

Tom ran from Ronald Black's room down the fifth floor of the east wing. He came to the checkpoint and stepped on to the dirty dark side of the yellow line. Like a fly in a hurricane, the room turned to tormented hell and a damnation of darkness.

Tom ran for the basement. He knew he had gone toe to toe with the preacher and lost but didn't die. He thought maybe Ratchford thought he had hurt Tom enough and left him there to die.

Tom ran in the darkness, falling over an empty bed before making it to the stairwell that led to the basement. His chest pounded. His breathing was rapid and wheezy. Tom opened the door to the stairs and ran into the black hole. He used his hands to feel his way down each flight of stairs until he reached the bottom.

"We can't just leave Tom," Kent said, with a fiery tongue.

Charlotte agreed. She stepped up, kissed Kent on the mouth, and said, "Luke, you and Kent leave. I'll use Bran to find Tom."

"No," Kent replied. "I'll go find him."

"Listen, I know you don't want to leave me, but I'm the only one who can use Bran to quickly and safely locate Tom," Charlotte said. She was calm as she caressed his cheek and whispered in Kent's ear, "I'll see you on the other side, love."

Charlotte stood back, and Luke pulled Kent closer to the stone. Poof, they both vanished. Charlotte and Bran were now on their own.

Tom opened the door to the basement and walked into the hallway. He stood, shining a small flashlight down the corridor at a variety of doors.

The door at the end of the hallway opened. Tom's heart jumped when he saw Charlotte and Bran running toward him. They were a sight for sore eyes.

"It smells so fucking bad down here," said Tom as Charlotte hugged him. "The preacher is gone—" He tried to explain, but she stopped him.

"Thank God we found you. The exit is behind us through that door. Let's get the hell out of here," Charlotte said while ignoring what Tom was attempting to say.

Tom's legs turned to jelly, and he fell to his knees. Charlotte helped him up, and they trotted to the end of the hallway. They stood in front of the brown and tan man-sized stone. Tom was weak and pale. His body was giving out. With one arm around Tom's waist, his arm around her neck, Charlotte positioned Bran in front of them and just before she pushed the three of them into the stone, children's laughter could be heard echoing throughout the room.

A moment later, Charlotte, Tom, and Bran vanished into the rock.

Chapter 33: Home

Charlotte opened her eyes, instinctively holding her breath. She was underwater. She blew out some air and bubbles began floating above her. She was still holding onto Tom and started kicking her feet while using her free arm to propel herself upward, following the bubbles. She knew if she followed them, they would lead her to the surface.

The water was green, but she could see a moss-covered cinderblock with an old, dirty, frayed rope attached to it. The nasty timeworn rope was extended upward in the direction she was swimming. The visibility was limited, but she followed the rope and her bubbles, hoping she would reach the surface before her air ran out.

Charlotte pulled and floated and pulled, bringing Tom with her. A few feet later, she noticed a skeletonized body, attached by the neck to the other end of that old rope. The body had been picked apart by the fish and was still clothed.

Charlotte swam past the man, a few feet from the surface, and she realized that was old man Joe Hodges. He was last seen by a kid playing baseball on the other side of Darby's Pond. She was in the filthy waters of Darby's Pond.

Charlotte broke the surface of the water, sucking in precious air. She pulled Tom's head above water, and he gasped for air. "I got ya, Tom. Just relax your body and float on your back," she said as she noticed flashing red and blue lights on the shoreline.

She could see people waving at her from the bank of the pond. Charlotte continued to tread water, holding Tom's head in her arms above the water. "Bran, here boy!" she called for her dog.

Charlotte looked around and couldn't see him. Panic began to set in. "*Bran!*" she yelled as her hands frantically splashed, turning her body so she could look for her dog.

A small rubber boat with red lights made its way over to Charlotte.

"Charlotte, is that you? Give us your hand," a voice called out from inside the boat.

"My dog—" she yelled.

"Charlotte, we have him. He's okay. Just give us your hand," the voice replied.

Bran whimpered and shoved his head over the side of the boat and barked at Charlotte. His tail was wagging, and Charlotte was smiling. She pulled Tom closer to the boat, and the men pulled him from the water. Then it was her turn.

Charlotte sat in the boat, surveying everyone and everything around her. She let a breath out as tears began flowing like a broken faucet. Charlotte knew she was home. She knew she was back in the real world. She knew she had escaped hell, and she knew her daughter was still missing.

Tom Porter was taken immediately to an awaiting ambulance. His injuries were severe. Charlotte held his hand as he was loaded up. He was pale, sickly skinny, but amazingly conscious.

Tom squeezed her hand. "Thank you for saving me. I would have died there, in hell, or even drowned, if it weren't for you. Thank you!" he said with tears.

Charlotte smiled and gave him a kiss on his cheek. She let go of his hand and stepped away.

Tom turned his head and could see a man running toward him. He looked familiar. It was his friend, Walter Pauls. He was truly back in the real world, and seeing Walter solidified it.

"Hold on. Tom, holy crap," Walter yelled as he ran up to the ambulance.

The paramedic folded the wheels on Tom's gurney, loading him up. Walter jumped inside with Tom and grabbed his hand. Tom was happy to see his friend. The smile on his face was ear to ear.

They embraced as tears dripped down Walter's face. "I've been looking for you. I've had the law looking for you and I... I... I... I'm just speechless. Where did you go? How? What? I mean, gosh damn it, I can't believe you're home!" Walter said.

While crying uncontrollably, Tom hugged his friend the best he could. He was in so much pain, yet so happy to be home.

"I'll call your wife. She's been so worried. We all have. Hell, the damn feds are getting involved," Walter said, holding back snot and more tears.

Kent sat on the bank of the pond as the ambulance took Tom away. Charlotte leaned against him, with Bran by her side. Kent was exhausted. His body hurt as much as his mind.

"How'd you find Tom?" he asked Charlotte as he held her.

"We didn't. Tom found us," she said. "Thank God, he found us." Charlotte and Kent both laughed for a moment.

Kent looked into Charlotte's eyes. "I'm sorry I left you—"

She put her finger on his lips. He stopped talking. She smiled and laid against Kent, relaxing, catching her breath and processing the madness.

John Day could be heard in the background, chatting with Detective McKinney. Reunions were being had between the other kids and their parents, but the old man sat by himself.

Luke walked over to the old man and sat down. All the hoopla had interrupted a little league game across the pond. Firetrucks and police cars engulfed the area around the pond.

"Hey, old man, you did a great job down there," Luke said while pointing to the pond. "Where are you headed now?"

"I'm not real sure. I've been gone for a long time, Luke. I look at the firetrucks and police cars. They don't look like firetrucks and police cars I've ever seen. They didn't look that way before I ended up down there. The last time I saw this pond, there was no ball field. It seems time is a commodity that I don't have the luxury of. When I left, my wife was sick, real sick." Old man Cole's face turned red and he began to cry. He put his hand on Luke's shoulder. "I've been gone a long time. I'm afraid to go home. I know she won't be there. I'm afraid, Luke. She was my life, my love, and my reason for so many things. I look around and know too much time has passed, and I know she's gone."

Luke hugged Cole and held him tight. "You come home with me, and from today until the end, my family is your family. I'll take care of you till you're walking hand and hand with your wife again."

"Headquarters, let's get two more medics down to Darby's pond to evaluate a few people," McKinney radioed to command. He shut his patrol car door and walked to the edge of the pond where Kent and Charlotte were sitting.

"Folks, I have a couple of medics coming out to give you a look over. If there's anything I can do for you. Please let me know. We have been looking for you all for quite some time," McKinney explained.

Charlotte wanted to thank him, but movement in the center of the pond caught her eye. She sat up from Kent, thinking she heard a child's voice.

A ripple at the water's edge led Charlotte's eyes to the center of the pond. "There. Do you see that?" Charlotte asked as she stood up. Both Kent and McKinney turned their attention to the pond.

"Mommy," a young female voice cried out from the center of the pond.

Charlotte knew it was true. She dove into the water, swimming as hard as she could.

"Get a boat out there!" McKinney yelled to the firemen.

Charlotte pulled and pulled. One stroke at a time, she pulled the water back toward her, propelling her body toward the splashing.

"Help, Mommy, help me," the voice cried out as Charlotte swam closer and closer to her.

Charlotte swam to the point she saw the girl, but she was gone. The girl went under. Charlotte took a deep breath and dove down beneath the filthy green liquid.

A little girl in a ruby-red dress was just a few feet below the water, staring up at her. Charlotte grabbed the girl and fought to bring her to the surface.

For the second time, Charlotte broke the water into the crisp, lifesaving air. The girl was with her. They held each other tight as they tread water, waiting on the fire department's boat.

"Diane, my love," Charlotte said as she held her daughter.

"Mommy! Mommy, I've missed you so bad!" Diane, the girl in the ruby-red dress, replied.

Moments later, firemen pulled Charlotte and her daughter from the water.

"WITO 1100 am radio, where Mecklenburg's news comes first. This is your best and brightest, most dominant, and hated DJ Howard. Folks, we have breaking news," the DJ said. "If you have a missing loved one, get your ass down to Darby's pond. It appears they are... popping up, resurfacing from the pond itself. *It's crazy*! But true. Mecklenburg residents who have been missing are now coming home!"

The End

Coming Soon!

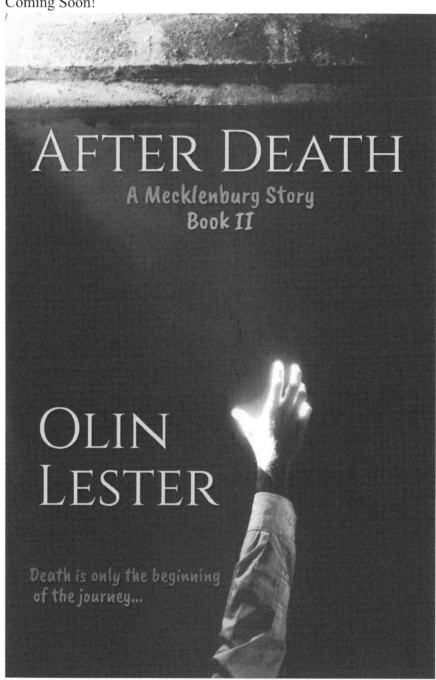

AFTER DEATH
A Mecklenburg Story
Book II

OLIN LESTER

Death is only the beginning
of the journey...

Acknowledgment and Thanks...

Thank you for reading my debut novel. I hope you enjoyed it, as much as I enjoyed building it. I use the word "building" because that's exactly what I did. I took a simple idea, spit on it and molded it into a place for my readers to escape reality. I built this world for fun, for you, and for me.

The town itself is evil, and just like a feral child, it will grow crazy as I feed it.

This is book one of many to come. The characters and places of Mecklenburg will suffer for a long time and I think you'll love it.

Take a moment to follow me on Facebook: Olin Lester-Writer
And follow me on Instagram, olin_lester_writer
And follow my blog: Charlottehorror.com

Also, I want to thank Ian Espinosa for his amazing photography, which I used for the covers of books one and two of the Mecklenburg stories. His work is amazing and you can find more of it at unsplash.com/@greystorm or email him for custom photos at ian3spinosa@hotmail.com.

Lastly, I'd like to thank John Day and Zane Worf for their contributions to this book. Both are talented beyond imagination and a master of their craft.

Made in the USA
Columbia, SC
23 July 2020